MATHIAS

MATHIAS

And The Battle for Britain

Matthew Robinson

Print information available on the last page.

Rev. date: 07/19/2016

To order additional copies of this book, contact:
Xlibris
800-056-3182
www.Xlibrispublishing.co.uk
Orders@Xlibrispublishing.co.uk
522118

J.C.Okoro
Jokoro
14.08.2001

PROLOGUE

The unforeseen events of the recent past have rattled humanity's belief in the impossible, as the astonishing resurrection of a race of giants from deep within the earth called the Neflium silenced the entire nation. This long-forgotten race became the first to disarm and immobilise America, but now they will keep her citizens grounded and for as long as their existence allows it.

This resurrected race of giants were carefully chosen and summoned by the Phoenix; they have stood proud for months in honour of defending that which matters most. These great beings have awoken to a new destiny, and the sole purpose of their reborn existence is one they cannot reject or dispute as the sheer power of the Phoenix is so phenomenal that even the gods of the great seven bow in its presence.

Unfortunately, their rebirth has caused far more damage than intended as their monstrous and shocking size unexpectedly disturbed the oceans' current, causing unstoppable waves of ice cold and destructive salt water hundreds of miles in land and obliterated everything in its path.

Having become the one person responsible for such chaos, the queen has endured many sleepless nights in guilt-ridden silence, and although she believes she has done the right thing, the shame is still too much for her to bear.

It didn't take long for word to spread of Britain's victory, but when it did, the world began to fight back by forcing the American troops beyond their borders, which allowed the nation's leaders to gradually redeem control of their god-given birthright.

In light of Britain's unexpected but remarkable response to war, the US president was left with no other choice but to stand down, as the result of his final fight gave birth to a far more costly outcome. He foolishly underestimated his opponent at every turn, but he has learned from his mistakes and learned well, for now he has discovered an unlikely challenger who knows how to have a little fun.

In America, there are thousands of people constantly patrolling the streets in nonstop support for the freedom fighters as the battle to enforce the ways of their homeland upon the world has resulted in this great country becoming a dangerous and lawless prison from which they cannot escape.

America's latest technology from the most secretive and classified departments of operation have created a daring response to the greatest instrument that the world has ever known, the one they call Mathias. He assisted in the rescue of weapon one, which gave the queen of England chance to reclaim possession and take back her true power, only this weapon has no trigger and no one knows the limit of her true strength.

At long last, she was born, a stunning woman with perfect features and a flawless body. She has been named as Nassa's Insidious Cyber Kinetic Intelligence, aka, Nicki. She has been solidly trained, physically and emotionally, from the very moment of her creation, she has been programmed with a single purpose that can only lead to one possible outcome.

Unfortunately, for the president, he has brewed some problems of his own by claiming rights to Peter for his gaming force but the arrival of this high-ranking driver has created a feud that is quickly and unknowingly growing beyond his control. This disagreement has spread throughout his army like a virus and has unexpectedly created a divide amongst his own gamers, but now the time has come to pick a side and pray that they have made the right choice, as the consequence will be catastrophic.

Life for Mathias, however, has been far more interesting; with sleepless nights in solitude, he has spent much of his time honing his gifts. He has perfected his skills with daring challenges that no human could possibly survive and has tested his limits at every given opportunity. Although his capabilities have already been pushed beyond what was expected of him, there are many ways to skin a rabbit, and now that his enemies have discovered his weakness, it is merely a matter of leverage.

The disappearance of Tom, however, was an unexpected turn of events, but he has wrongfully blamed himself for months. He has searched high and low, yet even with his formidable powers, he is unable to unravel a single trace, which in turn makes locating him seem all the more unlikely. To his confusion, every door has closed in his face and every possibility has been carelessly brushed aside, but the heavy thump in his achy heart is only telling one thing: the boy needs him and needs him now more than ever.

And so continues the greatest battle the world has ever known. . .

CHAPTER 1

The night is dark and cold with a clear and empty sky above, displaying thousands of sparkling stars, each with its own unique mesmerising glow. Small waves of ocean water repeatedly glide across the wet sand of an empty and quiet beach. The sound of rushing water pushing forward over the small retracting waves is calming and peaceful. A thick, dense fog sits low over the steady horizon, covering the ocean surface as far as the eye can see and dimming out the bright glare of the moon that shimmers off the ocean's mirror-like surface.

This peaceful view and relaxing sound of Mother Nature at her best is almost constantly disturbed, as massive and monstrous feet, made purely of decaying bone and patches of rotten flesh barely attached, smash in the steady sea just offshore.

In passing, the small waves are forced further inland and wetting the dry sand as though the tides have instantly changed. This giant beast is one of thousands that are forced to live with their bodies this way, but at night time alone. Half alive and half deceased, these functioning corpses patrol the shallow waters that surround one of the largest countries on Earth, that has been labelled by man as the United States of America.

Ordered by the queen of England, this ancient race of giant beings, better known as the Neflium, contain the terror within the land, to defend innocent lives all around the world and do their part in bringing peace back to humanity. They do not eat and do not sleep, for the power of the Phoenix has summoned them to this day, as the protection of their ship, known by them as the head of the world and once again labelled by man as England is Vital, and for that reason, they are sworn to obey.

Six months has passed since the day of the Neflium resurrection and all has remained quiet for the entire duration, until now. They will continue to fulfil their orders until the unlikely day of their defeat and fight to the death for the greater good, however severe or painful the punishment may be.

At the US headquarters, the president is sat at the head of a large black and shiny rectangular table, with young gamers sat in all the other seats; William sat at the opposite end. 'So,' said the president, breaking the silence that every child in there would have given anything to escape, 'a plan has been completed and the method requires one final test. . . Are the new drones ready for battle?'

'They are not just ready, Mr President,' said William confidently, 'they are fully prepared to take action at your command, sir.'

'And the drivers,' he asked.

'Our young drivers have been trained to operate the drones and push the new mechanics to their full potential.'

'Does that include the new recruits?'

'Of course, Mr President . . . they have all been trained at the same level . . . we are an army that acts as one.'

'That all sounds great, young man.'

William leans back in his seat so that he is almost slouching and releases a short sigh 'It's been a hard six months, sir, but your army is stronger than ever.'

The president stares him in the eye, trying to decide if he likes his confidence or not. 'What's your name?' he finally asks.

'William, sir.'

'Ahh, William,' he said, right before flicking through a small dark grey note book in front of him and stopping at a page that has clearly caught his attention. 'It says here that you're the commanding gamer in our force.'

William slowly leans forward and rests his elbows on the table; he looks around, catching eyes with his fellow gamers who are all staring at him and waiting to hear his response.

He drops his head in shame, catching his reflection looking back at him, struggling to accept the bitter truth that constantly taunts him. 'I *was* the best, sir.'

'Oh' said the president. 'So you were beaten then . . . How did it happen?'

'Well . . . Basically sir, I . . . err . . . I got a bit too big for my boots and truly believed that I was untouchable in the gaming world until. . .'

'Until what?' he asked, beginning to feel impatient.

William places his palms flat against his forehead, struggling to find the words that he can no longer hide. He rubs his hands down his face, stretches his skin, and forces his eyes wide open.

'I can't believe I'm going to say this,' he muttered under his breath. 'Until Peter was introduced to the game, sir.'

'Peter?' he asked curiously. 'So I take he's good then.'

'He's not just good, sir, he's the best gamer that I have ever faced. . . He um . . . he reminded me that I had lost respect for the game, and for that . . . I am glad to know him.'

'So is this Peter still gaming with us?'

'Yes Mr President, only . . . I don't think he is what you are looking for.'

The president instantly frowns from the boy's pure lack of respect and immediately replies with growl in his tone, 'I'll be the judge of that.'

'Forgive me, Mr President, I . . . should have known better.'

The president stares deep in his eyes, satisfied that he has successfully inflicted fear in the young boy and doesn't break contact until he nervously gulps. 'Now . . . like I said . . . is Peter still gaming?'

'Yes, Mr President,' said William, with a shake in his voice that he cannot control.

'Good . . . Have him sent to me . . . I want a private meeting with just the two of us.'

'Of course, sir, but . . . I feel you should know. . .'

The president glares at him and merely out of curiosity he remains silent, giving the boy chance to continue. Every other child sat at the table locks eyes with one and other, hoping to God that William is not about to say something they are all sure he will regret.

William ignores the subtle beg from his fellow gamers to keep quiet. He sits up straight in a proud fashion and carelessly blurts it out. 'He was the reason that weapon one was obtained by the English, sir.'

The president feels his heart begin beating faster than usual as a sudden rush of unsuspected anger spreads through his veins and the tone in his voice makes him sound more furious than ever before. 'So why is this traitorous little bastard still breathing.'

'Because,' said William, with a suppressed grin of satisfaction that he is hiding well, 'apparently, he is irreplaceable, sir . . . So his betrayal was overlooked.'

'And who made that decision?' he barked.

'Well, actually, sir . . . it was an in-house vote.'

'Amongst whom?' he snarled.

'The entire gaming force, sir.'

To all of their surprise, the president smashes the balls of his fists on the shiny surface of the table, making everyone present jump out of their skin. 'So you're saying that this boy betrayed us, betrayed his country, and for reasons that are beyond me, he is labelled as a hero . . . Did I miss anything?' he asked, with a very expressive frown.

William glances around at all the other gamers, trying harder than ever to ignore his nerves that are beginning to get the better of him. 'Would anyone else care to elaborate,' William calmly asked.

They all remain uncomfortably silent and too afraid to continue the conversation, given the topic of discussion. William looks at each of them individually, with a please-help-me expression, desperate to remove the president's attention from him.

'Jack,' he asked but receiving no response at all. 'Dion . . . Jake?'

The uncomfortable silence is almost unbearable, now that his once loyal and respected gamers that would have at one time not too long ago, gone to hell and back for him, are no longer prepared to put themselves on the line for his sheer ignorance, now that they . . . due to Peter's undeniable gaming abilities, see William as no more than a bog-standard regular driver.

'Anyone?' he begged, in one last hope that someone would speak.

'Right,' said the president out of frustration. 'I've heard enough. The reason I asked you all here today is because I thought it wise to go straight to the source of our strength . . . but this has regrettably turned out to be a waste of my time.'

He rises from his seat and leans forward, placing his palms flat on the table and does so while glaring at all of them looking extremely disappointed. 'So unless anyone has anything else to say, this meeting is over.'

No one says a word for a short intense moment until Jack finally breaks the silence. 'Actually, sir . . . I have something to say.'

'Good,' he replied, hoping to hear something constructive. He slowly and patiently sits back down, carefully watching the boy, who nervously gulps and takes a deep breath as he prepares himself to speak. 'The truth is sir, that William. . .' he said while pointing at him 'was the only person amongst all of us that voted for Peter's termination; however, because of his unique gaming ability, that is beyond anything we have ever seen, we simply could not destroy such a weapon.'

The president frowns and drops his head forward, purely out of disappointment, glaring at his own reflection in silence for a second or two, before locking eyes with him once again. 'So you are saying that you made this decision through the method of vote.'

Jack stands up almost fearlessly and turns to the president face on, resting the weight of his arm on his fingertips that are gently pressed against the shiny surface of the gleaming black table. 'Forgive me, Mr President . . . I say this with the upmost respect but . . . rulers of entire countries are awarded this position through a majority vote!'

The president's eyes remain fixed on him, surprised by the sheer cheek of the boy. 'That used to be,' he snarled.

'Nevertheless,' he agreed, 'that's all we did, sir . . . and the majority won,' he nervously stated.

The president continues staring at him with no emotion at all and patiently waits for him to display his fear.

After a short and extremely intense moment, he involuntarily gulps, making the president grin with pleasure.

'That's very clever, boy, you have quite the mouth on you, don't you. It could end up getting you in a lot of trouble.'

'I agree with you, sir . . . but fortunately, it has also saved my skin more times than I can count.'

The president displays a subtle grin before his reply, feeling happy that his young gamer has more guts than most of the grown men that serve him. 'I like you,' he said with admiration and rubs his hands together, releasing a long sigh of relief, happy that this meeting has almost come to a swift end. 'Have my gamers ready to take England . . . That pathetic little country has caused me nothing but hassle, and I want it gone . . . or at least under control . . . I'll be in touch soon. Be prepared to move forward, gamers, because things are about to get ugly.'

The president rises from his seat and proudly points at Jack and William. 'You and you . . . we will talk more about the strike on England, so be here at the same time tomorrow, and forget the personal meeting with that traitorous little shit . . . Just bring him with you tomorrow . . . I'll give him a chance to explain his actions.'

He shuffles some loose papers in to a neat pile and taps them on the table before placing them and his notepad into a clear folder and puts it under his arm. 'Now if you'll excuse me, I have a busy schedule.'

Without saying another word, he walks towards the door and exits the room, leaving silence amongst the children sat around the large table, only it doesn't stay that way for long.

William suddenly and aggressively bangs his hands on the shiny surface and shouts at everyone while displaying his teeth, purely out of anger, 'What the fuck was that . . . Why did no one speak . . . You all made me look like a fool.'

'No one had to,' said Jack, 'you made yourself look like a fool, all on your own.'

William puts both hands flat against his face and aggressively glides them downwards, stretching his eyes and mouth out of frustration. 'I fucking hate that Peter,' he snarled.

'Then why did you even mention him,' asked Jack.

'Because I thought. . .'

'We all knew what you thought,' he interrupted. 'You thought that if you told the president that Peter was at fault for letting weapon one go, he would have him terminated.'

William instantly argues in his defence. 'That is not true.'

'Yes it is, Will. . . You have a problem with him because you proudly challenged him, in front of everyone . . . and he destroyed you . . . destroyed your career . . . and . . . destroyed your prized possession . . . because of him, you lost the RCR 3000.'

William remains completely silent and frowning harder than ever before, mainly because it's the truth but also because he has nothing more to say on the subject.

'He took your life, Will, we all understand how you feel but this isn't about you anymore, this is bigger than all of us . . . look, you're a brilliant driver and at one time, you were the best, but you said it yourself, he's the best you've ever known.'

'I know what I said,' he snapped.

'Look,' said Jack, in a calm tone, 'this is going to be the battle of our lives so if this plan works then I want to be a part of it and if you do as well, then you need to get Peter to agree to come tomorrow.'

William replies slowly and aggressively with a growl in his tone, 'We don't need Peter.'

Jack stands up and looks down at him with an unforgiving expression. 'Maybe we don't,' he impatiently replied, 'but thanks to you, the president wants him . . . we have kept this quiet for so long and you just selfishly blurt it out. . . The president would kill him, just like that' he growled while clicking his fingers. 'He is our best and the army will follow him, with honour and you have jeopardised everything we have worked for . . . I hope you're happy.'

Jacob, having said nothing at all throughout the entire meeting, finally builds up the nerve to speak, now that he too is feeling frustrated by the actions of William. 'If I was you I would make sure you get Peter to come tomorrow, cause this is all on you.'

'But you know he won't come,' he whined.

'We all know that,' said Jack, 'but this is your doing . . . so good luck . . . Captain,' he sarcastically added while saluting.

William shamefully sits back in his seat and takes a deep breath, as the realisation of what he has done sinks in.

Jack walks away from the table, displaying his disappointment, not being subtle about it at all, and stops after taking only three steps, he turns to face him one final time, maintaining his expression. 'If you value your health . . . you will make this happen.'

He finally leaves the room in the hope that he will do the right thing and at least try to get Peter to come to the next meeting.

The rest of the children leave as well, following Jack to wherever he is going, really just to get away from William and his selfish ego, leaving him in silence with his own thoughts that are beginning to really wind him up.

He sits steady with his head shamefully hung forward while frowning and breathing slowly, he feels his heart rate increase dramatically as he leans his head back and shouts out of frustration and anger.

He glides his arm across the edge of the table, knocking some important papers to the floor, followed by a glass of water that smashes on impact. He quickly stands up, pushing his chair over with the back of his knees and hastily exits before someone notices what he has done.

CHAPTER 2

Queen Margaret is sat in a quiet room deep in the vast corridors of Buckingham Palace, swaying back and forth on a large cushioned and old-fashioned wooden rocking chair.

She is playing a spelling game with the beautiful 1-year-old baby girl who is lying in a wooden cot that looks typically Georgian and she is winning the game with minimal effort, making the queen look as though she has an extreme lack of intelligence.

'Okay,' said the queen. 'Try this one on for size.' She pauses for a short moment, thinking hard to find a particularly difficult word to really test the tiny genius. 'Aha,' she said proudly, having decided on one. 'Antidisestablishmentarianism.'

'Wow,' said the baby, in her high-pitched, heart-melting voice. 'That's a difficult one.'

The queen sits back and crosses her arms, happy that she may actually have a challenge for her, at which point she begins spelling it out one letter at a time.

The queen smiles at her, feeling more proud of her then ever. 'That's amazing, Gracie. . . You're so clever.'

'I wouldn't say clever' she replied, 'just fortunate . . . I think.'

'And modest,' said the queen as she shuffles forward preparing to continue the game. 'Okay then smarty pants, this one will test you for sure.' Before she has chance to speak, a loud knock on the door grabs both of their attention. She rolls her eyes in a playful manner; purely for the benefit of Gracie. 'Come in,' she called.

The door slowly pushes open and the largest, muscle-bound black man steps through, ducking his large head to avoid banging it on the door frame. He stands up straight, looking proud and fearless, completely covering the doorway from her view.

She breaks eye contact with Gracie while gently caressing her soft rosy cheek with the side of her index finger. 'Ah Abdul . . . come in darling, and close the door . . . that is if you haven't already.'

'Your Majesty,' he said while bowing his head, politely to announce his presence. 'Matthias is here and he is refusing to leave until he has spoken to you.' She fills her lungs followed by releasing a long sigh. 'Okay, send him in and leave us in peace.'

'As you wish, Your Majesty.' He respectfully leaves, gently pulling the door shut behind him and being careful not to damage the handle with his huge hand.

She locks eyes with Gracie for a short moment and once again melts inside. 'You're so beautiful,' she lovingly stated after watching her innocently blink. 'I'm going to leave you in there for short while.' She leans in the cot and pulls a soft quilt over her shoulders and tucks her in to keep her warm. 'Just pretend to be asleep or something.'

The door slowly pushes open and Mathias walks in. The first thing he notices is Gracie asleep in her cot, watching her tiny ribs rise up and down beneath the soft quilt as she fills her lungs over and over.

Queen Margaret stands and welcomes him in. 'Please sit.'

'Thank you, ma'am,' he replied, placing himself gently on a small white chair.

She sits back in her rocking chair and has one last glance at Gracie before continuing, 'So . . . how can I help you?'

Matthias, having no time for small talk and very little patience, immediately comes out with the reason for his intrusion. 'I have spent the last six months tracking down Tom and I am telling you . . . they have him but the only person that knows for sure is still in a coma.'

'You mean Paul,' she replied.

'Yes, ma'am, and as I'm sure you are aware, the poor man was virtually beaten to death so anything could have happened to Tom.' He closes his eyes and heavily exhales. 'But again no one seems to care and I don't understand why.'

'It's not that no one cares, Mathias. . . it's simply because further invasion is out of the question. . . If we push forward with this, more innocent lives will be lost, and I refuse to be responsible for further bloodshed.'

Mathias frowns at her and quickly rises from his seat, he glares down at her getting more irritated by the second, at the fact that she appears unfazed, with no concern for his safety. 'If it wasn't for that boy I probably wouldn't be here. . . It was purely the goodness of his heart that gave me the courage to continue. If it wasn't for him, Mathias would never have been born.'

She refuses to break eye contact yet remains calm and unnerved. 'Mathias please sit, we need to talk.' He doesn't move and simply continues to glare at her with a deep frown.

She stretches her arm out, pointing her delicate fingertips at the seat behind him and raises her eyebrows, silently advising him to be seated. He reluctantly sits and makes himself comfortable, keeping his eyes locked on hers. She elegantly lifts her right leg over the top of her left and places her hands on her knee. Silence descends upon the room while she tries to decide where to begin. 'I know where he is,' she finally admits.

'What?' he barked, seconds from seriously losing his temper.

'Please, Mathias. . . let me speak,' she begged, 'and whatever you choose to do is entirely your decision.'

He rolls his eyes and remains quiet but does so with great difficulty.

'I know where he is,' she repeated 'and he is safe . . . I promise you that.'

He replies with a threatening growl in his tone. 'You have known this whole time and kept it from me?'

'Yes . . . but for good reason.'

'And what is that exactly?' he sarcastically asked, doing his best to contain his anger. His heart begins beating faster and faster as his body fills with emotion. A drop of sweat runs down his cheek as his mind sinks deep in his imagination. He unwillingly creates an image of Tom at the receiving end of severe brutal punishment, begging for Mathias to come and save him. His arms and legs are being carelessly snapped in half and his ribs continuously smashed in with a solid metal bar. Cuts and gashes repeatedly appear on his flesh after the tip of a long whip connects with his back. He screams out for Mathias and begs for

God to make it stop while hanging from his wrists that are bleeding beneath a tight rope as his feet dangle two inches from the dirty floor that is covered in the poor boy's blood.

Mathias suddenly comes back to the room. His chest is thumping so fast and is now becoming dangerous for the technology in his brain that is powered by the normally steady beat of his heart and if not controlled will painfully claim his life. He curls over from the unbearable and unnatural pain and tries desperately to calm himself down by taking slow and deep breaths. He finally forces the disturbing images out of his powerful mind and remembers that Tom is safe and well.

'You see, Mathias, this is why I could not tell you about this . . . your life is too important . . . you have a greater purpose and your life is one that we cannot risk losing. . . if you go and fight for this boy while you are not ready, they will attack your heart, so I am begging you, please do not do this . . . not yet.'

With red cheeks and dark bloodshot eyes, he slowly lifts his head as sweat continues running down his face and he almost mumbles in reply as it is a struggle for him to even breathe. 'You promise me he is safe?' he growled.

'I promise.'

'So when can I go and bring him back?' he quietly asked.

'You will know when the time is right, my dear.'

He subtly nods in agreement before asking the question he has been itching to know the answer to for longer than he cares to remember. 'Do you know who is responsible for his disappearance?'

She shuffles in her seat to reposition herself, exposing her discomfort having been asked such a question. 'I'm going to be honest with you . . . but you're not going to like it.'

His eyes open wide and his jaw slightly drops. He can't believe he is about to discover the truth. She glares at him motionless and silent for a short moment. The few seconds of suspense are more intense to him than anything else and finally, she reluctantly answers him. 'It was Barry.'

He drops his face in the palms of his hands, knowing that he should never have ignored his instincts and blames himself for allowing the boy of whom he admires so much to be placed in serious danger. 'I knew it,' he growled. 'I fucking knew it.'

She stands up and cautiously walks towards him; she reassuringly places her delicate hand on his shoulder and crouches down in front of him. 'You have to emotionally detach yourself from this. If you don't . . . then you will never be able to help him.'

'I'm gonna kill him,' he snarled.

After a few seconds of consideration and repeatedly filling his lungs, he eventually agrees that she is right. He stands up in front of her and reaches his open hand down, she places her hand inside of his and both of her knees shake and click as he carefully helps her rise to her feet. 'Thank you . . . you're very sweet,' she said.

'What do I do, Your Majesty?' he continued. 'How can I just sit back and let this happen?'

'You will have your chance, I promise you that All I need from you, in fact what all of us need is for you . . . to stay alive.'

He turns his back to her and begins to walk away. 'I'm sorry' she caringly said, for which Mathias stops and turns to face her once again. 'So what now?' he asked, ignoring her apology.

'I fear that the president has devised a plan,' she replied. 'There's been some unusual activity but if there is something going on, it has been hidden and hidden well.'

Mathias knits his eyebrows together in confusion, 'but I thought they were contained by the Neflium.'

'Yes . . . they are contained but we cannot take the country . . . we must not.'

'But that's crazy,' he advised.

'Trust me, Mathias . . . this is how this has to happen . . . You have got to believe me.'

'Then what's the point of all this if we are not going to fight back. Your own people are out there celebrating a false victory; they have been led to believe that the war is over.'

'This war is far from over,' she snapped, 'and my people know it.'

He closes his eyes, desperately attempting to clear his mind. He lifts both hands to either side of his head and gently caresses his temples with the tips of his fingers, followed by a growl of frustration. 'There has to be something we can do to stop this.'

To Mathias's surprise, a cute, squeaky voice enters the conversation. 'Maybe there's something I can do to help.' He feels a sudden rush of love trust and an overall happy feeling, and instantly notices the immediate change of emotion. 'Was that the baby?'

He slowly walks towards the cot and steps around to the side, watching carefully as Gracie comes in to view.

You're supposed to be asleep,' said the queen.

She is lying on her back looking up at him with her big beautiful blue eyes, as though she is reading his past and future like a book. He attempts to reject her power but cannot deny the strength of her abilities so he finally gives in, allowing her to introduce herself to his soul, leaving him unable to explain this amazing feeling and suddenly hears her voice from deep in his mind. 'Hello,' she asked, 'can you hear me?'

'Yes,' he replied. His eyes well up and a tear rolls down his cheek and suddenly nothing else matters but the feeling itself. He sniffles and rubs the back of his shaky hand across his nose while clearing his throat.

'My name is Gracie . . . remember this feeling. Lock it in your mind because it will save your life when you need it to most.'

He feels his heart suddenly beat at a calming steady pace, instantly making everything seem different. His abilities are operating at full capacity and he can see the life in absolutely everything. His vision penetrates the solid walls around them and spreads out for hundreds of miles in every direction. He can hear thousands of different conversations all happening at the same time. A bird flies past the window and the flap of its wings sound so clear to him like it's massively amplified. Cars and all kinds of vehicles with roaring engines drown out the constant voices. He notices a strange feeling beneath his feet and his vision retracts at a rapid speed bringing him back to the room. He curiously looks down and watches a distorted ring spread out from around the base of his feet like a ripple on the surface of still water, followed by another, continuing over and over again. He is drawn to her eyes once more and searches her memories but he almost loses himself in a sea of visions that are happening right in front of him. She captures his curiosity when he spots someone that he thinks he may know. A beautiful woman far prettier than he has seen before. He blinks three times and shakes his head, forcing himself back to reality.

'Are you okay?' asked the queen.

'I think so,' he replied, while focussing on a blurry image of Gracie's cot. His mind is finally clear and is thinking straight for the first time in what seems like forever 'Thank you, Gracie,' he said under his breath.

The queen steps in front of him and blocks Gracie from his view. 'I never told you her name.'

'No,' he replied in amazement, 'she did.' He steps around her and continues the conversation with Gracie. 'Who was that woman I saw in your memories?'

'I wish I knew,' she replied. She drops her eyes and stares in the far corner of the room. She rolls her head to the side, appearing upset as though she is about to burst in to tears. 'She is always there. I can't seem to get her image out of my mind.' She rolls her head back to him and they lock eyes once again only suddenly quite surprised. 'Wow . . .,' she said. 'You're good at this, aren't you . . . but why did only she stand out for you? If you don't mind me asking.'

Mathias gulps and searches for an answer. 'I just think I know her from somewhere. . .'

'Well. . . I'm sorry, I can't tell you more . . . I just have one question,' she curiously asked in her heart-melting voice. 'I saw two young children in the deepest depths of your mind, they were almost concealed from me so I pushed through the barrier and when they saw me, well . . . they welcomed me.'

Mathias thinks he knows what she is talking about and if it is about the same children, he wonders why that memory is so well hidden. 'What were they wearing?' he asked.

'They were both wearing baggy jumpers with a hood attached and over their heads. I think it's a young boy and girl, only the young girl appears to be holding a large silver handgun.' He looks at the queen wide eyed and extremely impressed, for which she replies by merely raising her eyebrows in agreement. He believes that the child holding the gun was Tom's girlfriend and feels ashamed to talk about her. 'Um . . . I'd rather not say.'

'That's okay,' she said. 'I was just curious.'

The queen noticing that he is feeling a bit uncomfortable and has no more to say on the subject can see that he is ready to leave but knows that he cannot escape the connection with Gracie and feels that he can't leave her side in case something happens to her. 'Why don't you go and get a drink and something to eat. Abdul. . .' she yells. The door immediately pushes open from the outside and Abdul pokes his head in under the large door frame. 'Everything okay, ma'am?' he asked in his abnormally deep voice. 'Yes,' she replied, 'could you please get some food and drink for our guest'

'Of course, ma'am.'

Mathias stands in front of them and bows his head to the queen, but before turning to leave, has one last glance at Gracie and tells her with his mind that he will see her soon. They both smile at the same time and he politely exits the room.

As soon as the door closes, the queen begins asking questions. 'What was that all about, who are these adolescents in his mind?'

I think they are the reason why his vision is clouded and why his abilities are restricted only. . .' She turns her head and glances at the door. 'I don't think they are human.'

'Not human?' she asked, sounding shocked. 'But you said they were children.'

'Yes but their eyes were white all over, no pupils no irises and no veins . . . they looked like giant pearls and their souls appeared somewhat dark and evil.'

The queen glares at her, fearing the safety of Mathias and hopes that they are not in his mind to try to make him become something he isn't. 'What do they want with him,' she asked

'I don't know, but the feeling wasn't good.' She reaches her arms up to her as though she is asking to be picked up. The queen leans in the cot and gently lifts her out, giving her a huge hug and slowly twisting her shoulders from one side to the other. 'I can't explain the feeling of what I saw . . . but I can show you,' said Gracie. The queen feels her heart rate increase quite dramatically as her nerves begin to grip her. Gracie gently presses the palms of her tiny hands against her temples and closes her eyes tight. She penetrates her mind and reveals her thoughts. Gracie instantly disappears from her vision as she shoots through a small red tunnel, moving at phenomenal speed like being sucked into a worm hole. Suddenly to her surprise she is standing in a dark street with abandoned cars all the way along and broken glass covering the ground. Two young children with hoody jackets on are standing in the street twenty yards in front of her and facing each other. They turn to face her at the same time and rise from the ground, floating steady for a second or two before flying head first in her direction and rapidly close in from both sides. Their arms are extended towards her with their fingers curled in like the long skinny hands of an old witch. Their faces are virtually skinless, exposing their decaying skulls, with white wavy hair and deep hollow dark holes where the eyes should be. They scream with a terrifying ear-burning sound that inflicts so much fear into her and forces her out of Gracie's imagination and back to her body. She is rendered speechless, breathing fast and heavy as a stream of tears roll down her cheeks.

CHAPTER 3

Kyle is sat on his own in the middle of a pub at a round, oak wood table and matching chairs. He appears to have drunk far more than he can handle. His head is drooping forward over a half-empty pint of Stella while gripping it tight in one hand with his elbows resting on the table to support his swaying body.

His phone begins to ring, and with great difficulty, he searches every pocket he can find, looking embarrassingly confused as to why he can hear it but not see it. To his surprise, he discovers it in the inside pocket of his jacket and pulls it out holding it two inches from his face. He closes his eyes tight and opens them wide, over and over again.

After focussing as hard as he possibly can, he discovers that the number is not displayed and the caller is unknown, so he carelessly switches the phone off and tosses it aside. He releases a long sigh of pure boredom while lifting up his glass and sinking the rest of his drink in one. When finished, he slams it down on the table and exhales loud and slow. Suddenly, his phone rings again and after a moment he slowly and suspiciously picks it up, he focuses on it once again with difficulty and it is still displaying no caller ID.

He waits for a short moment while he decides whether or not to answer it but his curiosity gets the better of him. After pressing the small green icon, he places it to his ear. 'Hello,' he curiously slurred.

'Kyle . . . is that you?' asked the voice, with urgency in his tone.

'Who's this,' he demanded.

'It's Mathias . . . I really need to speak with you.'

'Why?' he slurred, 'what's so important that you had to interrupt me during my therapy session. . .' Nothing is said for few seconds. 'Well. . .' he said impatiently.

'I know where Tom is,' said Mathias.

'Tom who?' he carelessly asked.

'Come on Kyle, you must remember . . . Tom . . . and his uncle Paul.'

'Oh yeah, the kid and his fat uncle,' he remembered. 'How are they?'

'Paul is still in a coma and has been since we were in America six months ago, Tom went missing at the same time.'

Kyle then finally snapped to attention 'What? I didn't know Paul was in a coma . . . and certainly didn't know Tom was missing.'

'It's okay,' said Mathias. 'None of this is your responsibility . . . but I need your help . . . are you still in touch with your squad?'

Kyle chuckles to himself in the hope that he may have an excuse to get them all back together and suddenly sounds a bit more sober. 'I'm in touch with them all apart from Barry, but he's always been a bit of a wild one.'

Mathias feels that he has the right to know and decides to break the news gently. 'There's something I have to tell you . . . now when I tell you this, it's important that you stay calm.'

Kyle replies, sounding amused, 'Just tell me.'

'Barry beat the life out of Paul and took Tom to America and is now under orders of the president.'

He closes his glazed eyes in disappointment, sure that he knew something was wrong but couldn't quite put his finger on it, but through loyalty alone, he can't help but argue in his defence. 'That's utter bollox, I don't believe it.'

'This is information direct from the queen, so you can believe what you want . . . I just thought you should know.'

Kyle hastily changes the subject knowing that it was him who gave the order to get them both home safely. 'Where are you anyway.'

'Don't worry about that . . . I'll be in touch again soon, oh, and I suggest you sober up, you've got company.' The phone suddenly goes silent and switches off again, leaving a dark blank screen. He lifts his empty glass and aimlessly takes a swig of nothing. He looks at it in disappointment and lifts it above his droopy head as high as he can. 'Barman,' he shouts, followed by his eyes involuntarily closing. A hand takes the glass out of his and places it back down on the table in front of him. 'I think you've had enough . . . don't you sir?'

Kyle opens his eyes and smiles. He lifts his head and slowly turns around, finding himself face to face with Kieran, Rob, and Kevin, who all solute him at the same time, 'What are you lot doing here,' he slurred

'We heard about Barry,' said Rob.

Kieran and Kevin nod their heads in agreement, each looking shocked in their own way.

Rob continued. 'He rang me this morning . . . at first I was pleased to hear from him but then he told me the reason he called.'

He locks eyes with Rob in disbelief, yet even though he is furious with him, he swears to the core of his heart that Barry wouldn't do this unless he had a damn good reason to embarrass him so badly. 'So it's true, then?' he asked.

Kieran enters the conversation from behind Rob. 'Who told you about it?'

Kyle struggles to look him in the eye as his are bloodshot, heavily glazed and beginning to close. He ever so slightly sways from side to side watching everything spin in front of him. 'Mathias called me a minute ago,' he said, just before dropping his head forward and snoring for a short moment. Rob reaches his arms out and claps his hands together two inches from his ear, for which Kyle instantly lifts his head, 'Four pints please, barman,' he turned and looked at his men, 'do you guys want anything?'

'Sir, please,' Rob pleaded, 'this is serious . . . What did Mathias say to you?'

'I don't know, probably the same thing he said to you.'

He lifts his glass and once again tries to drink from it, followed by him slamming it on the table and losing his temper, 'Barman,' he shouts 'where's the fuckin' service 'round here?'

Everyone in the pub looks in their direction and shakes their heads.

'Sir . . . we did not abandon the queen's protection for this . . .,' said Rob, 'we're on our own now . . . so what the fuck are you doing, mate?'

They all look at each other with concern as Rob stands and casually walks around the other side of the table and sits in front of him. He rests his elbows on the oak surface and interlocks his fingers. 'Barry said that he had a message for you.'

'And,' he replied, like he couldn't care less.

'He said he has Tom and to come and get him if you've got the bottle. . . He also asked if his fat uncle is dead yet.' Kyle finally receives another pint of Stella, gently placed on the table in front of him by the barman. He smiles and reaches for it, but Rob quickly snatches it before he has the chance. He quickly necks it and slams it down in front of Kyle, followed by releasing a long sigh of satisfaction. Kyle simply glares at him with his eyes wide and mouth open, continuously inhaling from the pure cheek of it. He finally exhales like blowing out a candle and shaking his head from side to side.

'He also said,' Rob continued, 'if that jumped up, bossy little prick has the balls, then tell him I look forward to demoting him,' which finally grabs his full attention. 'And who's he talking about?' he shamefully asked, yet secretly knowing what the answer's going to be.

Rob sits back in his chair and drops one hand down to his side, while turning and looking at Kieran and Kevin, who are both standing tall but also feeling very disappointed

'Well, by the sound of some of his choice words,' said Rob, 'we think he means you, sir.'

'So you think I'm a prick then?' he slurred.

He looks up at Kieran and Kevin who simply shrug their shoulders, then slowly turns his head, keeping his eyes fixed on them for a moment longer, then looks at Rob, who is doing exactly the same.

Kyle aggressively stands and holds both hands out either side of him like he's enticing a fight but seriously struggling to stay on his feet. 'None of you are denying it are ya?'

Rob quickly stands and slams his hands down on the table, that makes Kyle jump and once again grab his attention, leaving him stood completely still with his arms open like a statue. 'The point is, sir . . . are you ready to go back to America and finish what we started?' He drops his hands to his side and appears to be thinking hard. He looks at each of them individually, recognising the suspense in their expressions and carelessly drops himself back in his seat. 'Get me some coffee,' he proudly ordered.

They all smile at the same time and Kevin immediately heads for the bar, leaving a moment of strangely uncomfortable silence. Kyle drops his head forward and ignores them as though they are not even there. Rob repeatedly taps his fingertips on the table, and Kieran begins whistling after putting his hands in his pocket. 'So how have you been?' asked Rob, to break the silence, only not realising that Kyle had almost fallen asleep again. He bangs the ball of his clenched fist on the table, making a loud thud that once again brings him back to the room. 'Sir. . .' he barked, 'wake the fuck up.'

Kevin places three cups of black coffee in front of him and steps back to Kieran's side with his hands behind his back as though standing to attention. Kyle reaches for the hot cup and carefully lifts it. 'So what do we do first?' asked Rob.

'First,' he announced, while holding the cup as steady as he can, 'I'm going to drink my coffee,' he burns his lip and spills some down his top from the shock; 'Fuck it,' he growled, before placing it back down and wiping his hands down his front over all the other stains that look like beer, urine, and possibly vomit. 'And then,' he continued, 'we arrange a meeting with the queen somehow, to find out more about what's going on.'

Suddenly his phone rings after being switched off the whole time. He lifts it to his face and through his blurry vision focuses on the screen that reads no caller ID, so he answers it and holds it to his ear. 'Is that you again?'

'So you're ready to challenge America then, are you?' Kyle curiously looks around the room. 'Where are you?' he asked, followed by a hick-up. 'How do you know what I said.'

'That's the good thing about mobile phones,' said Mathias, 'they can be used as listening devices even when switched off.'

Kyle puts the phone in front of his face and looks at the screen with an extremely confused expression. The phone clicks making the sound of a picture being taken accompanied by a bright flash. 'This phone is shit,' he moaned, before holding to his ear once again.

'You said that you want to arrange a meeting with the queen?' said Mathias.

Rob, Kevin, and Kieran all get a text message at the same time; they pull them out of their pockets and open a picture, revealing Kyle looking more gormless than ever.

'So . . . drink your coffee and head for the palace . . . I'll meet you there,' Kyle glances at Rob who quickly stops giggling and stares at him, waiting to find out what's going on.

'But we're miles away . . . it might take us awhile,' he mumbled.

'That's fine,' he replied. 'Just be as quick as you can.'

He looks at his phone and watches the screen go blank and switch itself off, followed by him quickly turning it back on. He locks eyes with Rob looking hopeful while placing it back in his pocket. 'Please tell me you've got your car?'

Rob simply smiles in return, having waited so long to for an excuse to put his well-known driving skills into action.

Rob pushes open the two large double doors from the inside and walks through into a small gravel parking area, followed by Kieran and Kevin who each have one of Kyle's arms around their shoulders, dragging him out like his body is lifeless. He rocks his droopy head towards Kieran and breathes heavily right in his face. 'I love you, man,' for which Kieran immediately turns away and clenches his face like he's just sucked on a lemon. Kyle looks from left to right in a confused manner. 'Well . . . where is it then?' he sarcastically asked.

'Over there' said Rob, pointing at a rusty old Camper van.

Kyle laughs out loud. 'You've downgraded a bit, haven't you?'

They continue walking towards it and to Kyle's surprise it pulls away, revealing a shiny, light-blue, and virtually brand new Nissan sky line, with very real looking flames up the bonnet and down both sides that fade out as they near back. The spoilers are low and the wheel arches are wide, with a dramatically dropped suspension. The tyres are jet back and low profile with nine spoke, gleaming chrome alloy wheels. 'You lied to me,' said Kyle, in a jokey tone, 'now all you have to do is get us there.'

'Just get in,' said Rob, repeatedly chucking his keys in the air after bleeping his car unlocked. Kieran straps Kyle in the back seat and he almost instantly falls asleep. They all climb in followed by Rob roaring his engine into life. He wheel-spins off the mark and glides around the exit with a high-pitched, ear-piercing squeal, making Kyle roll to his side and face plant against the window.

CHAPTER 4

Peter is sat in his assigned gaming chair, with his eyes fixed on the large screen in front. He is operating a standard RCD in the official training facility and making his drone perform actions that are humanly impossible. It is climbing one of three very tall and identical reinforced solid stone walls and leaping from one to the other, digging its powerful fingers beneath the surface with its deadly grip. It drops down from fifty feet and lands on bended knee with one hand flat on the floor at its side, echoing a loud thud of metal striking metal that spreads throughout the entire facility with a rumble. It rises to its feet and stands as still as a statue. The shoulder blades spring out revealing small openings as two small guns rise up either side of its head and move around in all different directions at their own individual pace and stopping for a short moment on all different kinds of targets.

Peter can't help but express a cheeky grin, as a small sheet of glass attached to a thin metal rod extends out from his seat from either side of his head and bend around in front of his face, covering his eyes, with a display of everything his drone can see.

A tiny white circle with a cross in its centre shifts back and forth across the lenses as he flicks up two small red covers with the sides of his index fingers, revealing a white trigger hidden beneath; he gently places his first knuckle over the top of each one and prepares to shoot to test the weaponry, but he is disturbed by a recognisable voice that calls his name so he immediately removes his fingers and flicks down the protective covers. The two sheets of glass rapidly retract and disappear in the headrest as he sits forward slightly and looks to his side only to find himself face to face with William. 'What do you want?' he asked, with a clear lack of interest.

'Look,' said William. 'I know you and I have never seen eye to eye but. . .'

Peter quickly jumps up from his seat in a threatening manner and stands almost toe to toe with him, challenging him with his posture alone. 'You killed my friend . . . you and me will never be cool . . . you're a bully and a murderer.' He moves even closer before continuing. 'So let's get one thing straight here . . . you . . . and I . . . will never be friends.'

'I am aware that you will never forgive me for my behaviour and I deserve everything I get,' he steps back and opens his arms out, as though surrendering himself for his shameful actions. 'I abused my position as the commanding gamer, but. . .'

'Don't you dare begin to make excuses,' said Peter while poking him in the side of his head with the tip of his index finger that forces him to tilt his neck one side.

'Don't you think I'm suffering enough?' he pleaded.

'You think you're suffering do you? I'll tell you about someone who suffered shall I?'

William simply glares back at him for a short moment, looking extremely ashamed of himself. 'My friend Ben,' Peter announced 'doubt you would remember him though . . . probably not important enough to be placed as another notch on your belt.'

'It wasn't like that,' he barked, 'I was following orders.'

'Fuck your orders,' he shouted, while pushing his face forward and stopping two inches from his nose, leaving William speechless.

Peter turns and begins walking away, only William cannot afford to let it end like this. 'I need a favour,' he asked, with anticipation.

Peter immediately stops and turns to face him once again; he looks and feels shockingly surprised from the sheer cheek of it. 'You've got a nerve haven't you . . . after everything you have done . . . you're asking for my help.'

William remains silent in the hope that he will give him a chance to explain. 'Yes.'

'Alright then,' said Peter, 'I'll entertain your stupidity.'

William immediately comes out with it, before he loses the chance. 'Myself and a few others had a meeting with the president.'

Peter raises his eyebrows and ever so slightly drops his jaw, 'Why?'

'The US defence has devised a plan to bring down the giants.'

'So what's that got to do with me?' he arrogantly asked.

William steps towards him and puts his hands behind his back with his heels together, surprisingly standing to attention. 'I told him about you and your abilities and . . . he wants you to lead the army.'

'Forget it,' he replied after a moment of consideration.

'We need you, Peter,' he said begrudgingly. 'You're the best gamer I know and I don't think we're going to pull this off without you.'

Peter stares back at him with narrow eyes as the curiosity slowly grips him. 'Why do I get the feeling that you're up to something?' He releases a sharp sigh with no believable way to answer his question, so he quickly moves the conversation forward. 'Are you in or not?'

'Fine,' said Peter, still looking at him in the same manner, 'but this changes nothing.'

William drops his head back and looks up at the high ceiling in shock that he actually persuaded him to agree and secretly thanks the gods for making this happen.

'So what's first,' asked Peter.

William begins to feel a bit more at ease and wants to get out of there before he says something that could change his mind, so he attempts to give him a short explanation.

'After the president learned of your existence, he ordered a meeting with just the two of you, but then decided he would be back tomorrow to discuss the plan with the secretary of defence and wants you, me, and Jack present . . . the meeting is being held in the conference room tomorrow at 1400 hours.'

'I'll be there. . .' said Peter, 'but before you go,' he snapped, stopping him from leaving, 'why is me doing this a favour for you? And don't lie to me.'

William suddenly appears startled, and his voice has a very noticeable shake, 'Because the president didn't know about you so . . . I told him everything.'

'Everything?' he asked.

William glances at the door, asking himself why he didn't just leave the very moment he agreed. He slowly turns and looks at him as sweat beads begin glistening on his forehead 'Yes . . . but I was just trying to. . .'

'I know what you were trying to do,' Peter interrupted. 'You attempted once again to have me killed, but if I had to guess, someone must have mentioned the in-house vote or told him of my gaming abilities, leaving him no choice but to accept it . . . does that sound about right to you?'

William opens his mouth to desperately defend himself but shamefully decides against it after realising there is no point in even attempting. 'Yes,' he replied, trying hard not to advertise the fact that he has in fact been caught out. 'You are still in though, right?' he pleaded

'Yes,' he replied with resentment in his tone, 'but I'm not doing this for you.' He pokes him in the middle of his chest. 'In fact you . . . had better stay the fuck out of my way.'

He pushes him aside with the back of his hand and swiftly storms off, leaving him standing alone in the centre of the training room. 'Oh and Peter' he yelled, as he neared the exit, 'don't forget . . . 1400 hours and dress nice.'

Peter ignores anything else he has to say and leaves with pleasure, as he feels he could not tolerate him for one more second.

CHAPTER 5

It is a quiet evening with a gentle cool breeze and the sun is approaching its lowest point in the sky. The lights that brighten Buckingham Palace are glowing in the shadowy areas that make the structure look welcoming. A blue Nissan skyline pulls up outside the main gates and parks next to a huge concrete water feature that is continuously flowing. Kevin pushes his head forward from the dark behind; revealing his face in the light of the front seats between Rob and Kieran. 'So what now?' he asked, 'surely we can't just walk up to the front door and knock . . . can we?'

To all of their surprise, Mathias drops from above at a phenomenal speed and lands directly in front of the car with his back to them. He places his left foot forward and pushes his open palms towards the large, heavy, black gates. They slowly open inwards, creating sparks at the joins that force the springs to snap and the high power pressure pumps to burst. They suddenly swing fast and smash against the inside of the palace courtyard walls, leaving them both hanging by merely a thread.

He proudly walks through and signals them to follow but as they enter the premises, it looks virtually abandoned. There are security cameras placed all around the premises that are purposely located to be made blatantly visible. Every single one ever so slowly begins following them as each lens twists back and forth, focussing carefully on the uninvited guests.

A large steel black door in a shadowy corner bursts open and hundreds of large men dressed in dark black flood in to the courtyard, each carrying a black machine gun. They sprint around the edge walls in an orderly fashion that continues until they are completely surrounded, then all at once they stop and turn to face him in unison. 'Aim' shouts one of the men. They all aim their weapons at the intruders, holding their guns at eye level and focussing down the top of the shiny barrels.

'Put your hands on your head,' shouts the voice.

'We're here to see the queen,' Mathias announced.

'I will not ask you again, sir . . . do as I command.'

He reluctantly puts his hands on his head, 'For fuck's sake,' he whispered, 'I don't have time for this shit.'

The man swings his weapon behind him on the shoulder strap and cautiously walks towards him. When he finally reaches him, he puts his hands behind his back and cuffs him.

'You know you're making a big mistake here, don't you,' said Mathias.

The man now, feeling safe, having restrained him, suddenly sounds cocky and arrogant, 'Tell it to someone who gives a fuck.' He aggressively pushes him from behind, only Mathias doesn't budge at all, and to the man's surprise, he forces himself two feet back. 'What the fuck,' he subtly snarled.

Some of the men snigger as he tries to push him again and again, until he is crouched down behind him and pushing his shoulder into his lower back, like a rugby player in the middle of a scrum. The surrounding men are struggling to hold back their laughs but one or two physically can't take it anymore and bury their faces in the thick shoulder pads on their jackets.

Squad three are in the car assessing the situation, but also can't help but laugh at him.

The struggling man stands tall and releases a long sigh after placing his hands on his hips and embarrassingly walks around to the front of him, 'Would you follow me please.'

Mathias holds back his smile. 'Certainly,' he replies, sounding more smug than ever.

They both head for the main entrance of the palace and as they near the large thick and heavy double doors, they pull open from the inside revealing his fragile queen standing in the centre of her top and most trusted security.

'What's going on?' asked Mathias.

She steps forward to address herself but Abdul puts his abnormally large hand on her shoulder that stops her in her tracks 'It's okay, Abdul,' she said reassuringly, 'we have to talk about this.'

He reluctantly removes his heavy hand and bows his head while stepping back. He then glares at Mathias with a deep frown and expresses a subtle growl that warns him not to break her trust.

Mathias immediately spots the tense environment and wonders why he is being treated as a threat. He looks back at the car and squad three simply shrug their shoulders, also confused as to why there is such hostility between them. He turns to face the queen once again and a strange feeling he has never felt before spreads through his body. It is so intense that his speech is unexplainably restrained for a short moment. 'I need to speak with you in private, Your Majesty.'

She takes a step back as suddenly she is overwhelmed by her nerves.

'Are you okay, Your Majesty?' he curiously asked.

'Yes dear . . . we just have to be extra cautious.

He knits his eyebrows and steps back from her to happily advertise that he is no threat.

'Look,' she said, 'we believe that some of the most notorious American assassins have crossed our boarders, and if our intelligence is correct . . . they have some new and unique abilities that are hard to believe.'

'What kind of abilities?'

'It turns out they can impersonate any one they chose and are able achieve this down to the last detail . . . they sound the same, look the same, and in some cases even smell the same. . .I don't know how they have done it but . . . as I am sure you are aware . . . this could potentially be an extremely powerful weapon.'

Mathias bows his head and reveals his open palms at his side 'I assure you, ma'am . . . I am me.'

'Oh bless you, darling, it's not you that we are worried about . . . having said that . . . can you prove that you are in fact you?'

'Certainly,' he replied, with no hesitation at all he reveals one open palm out in front of him in her direction and leans forward as though pressed against an invisible wall. All of the men surrounding her gulp at the same time and to their surprise a handgun spring's out from the holster under each of their jackets, floating six inches in front of their faces and aiming at each man directly between the eyes.

'Okay. . .' she said, 'that's quite enough Mathias.'

The black handguns gently slip inside their jackets and are accurately placed in the slots, leaving each of them in shock and not surprisingly rendered speechless.

'My apologies your majesty . . . do you have a suspicion of someone in particular?'

'I'm afraid so,' she sighed, 'one of squad three.'

'Which one?' he asked in disbelief.

She takes a deep breath in the hope that she is wrong. 'Kyle.'

Mathias looks back at the car and sends his vision forward as though Kyle is two inches in front of his face. He glares deep in his eyes and attempts to read his mind, only he is blocked somehow. 'What?' He whispered. He turns to face her in shock and remains silent, wondering how he has stopped access. 'You could be right . . . who told you of this?'

She steps forward and stands tall and proud with her hands at her front and fingers interlocked. 'Gracie warned me.'

'Oh,' he replied, sounding convinced. 'Let's see what happens.' He signals them to come over and they cautiously climb out.

'What are you doing?' she quietly barked.

'Trust me, Your Majesty . . . I've got this under control . . . wouldn't you rather know for sure?'

'I hope you know what you're doing,' she snapped, sounding extremely unconvinced. She turns and walks back into her home, followed closely by her security. Mathias also walks in behind them with squad three in toe and Kyle as the last person to enter. Before he pulls the heavy door closed behind him, he has one final glance around the courtyard and nervously gulps as the strength of her protection is more nerve racking than he expected.

They walk through a huge landing area with a ten-foot-wide set of red stairs in the centre and an unnecessarily large diamond chandelier hanging low and wide from the high ceiling. The walls a varnished dark wood that is so clean it reflects like the marble affect. The carpets are a soft red with a golden trim placed six inches in from the matching walls.

They walk down one side of the dominating structure of unusual steps and enter a large corridor with pictures hung accurately every few feet along both sides. They all aimlessly stroll through, admiring the strange but beautiful detail in the sculptured walls as they finally enter the opposite door at the far end of the hall. The room is small in comparison with the main hall and the queen quickly stands in front of a large fire place. Her long blue dress that hangs two inches from the floor looks so soft that it appears weightless and she feels good but she is almost positive that Kyle is not him and is reluctantly putting her trust in Mathias.

As squad three enter the room, Kyle closes the door behind him and suddenly looks as though he hasn't touched a drop of alcohol. 'Excuse me,' he said from the back. They all turn and face him in unison, apart from Mathias and the queen, who lock eyes in agreement, 'Do you have a rest room I could use?'

Mathias slowly turns and glares at him with fire burning in his eyes, for which Kyle simply shrugs his shoulders 'What?' he mindlessly asked

'Yes' she snarled 'down the end of the hall, last door on the right' for which he immediately bows and hastily exits.

The queen looks at each of them in a suspicious manner 'Excuse me' she said, pushing Abdul's large hand off her shoulder. 'I'm just going to powder my nose' and she quickly leaves through a different door giving him no choice but to let her go. Now they are both out of sight of Mathias, so he attempts to follow her, only Abdul steps in his way and looks down at him like a hungry beast eyeing up a snack.

Kevin nudges Rob to secretly get his attention and Rob subtly leans one ear closer to him, under the impression that he is about to say something intelligent. 'Who'd of thought the queen was in to coke . . . she's powdering her nose right now.'

Rob chuckles under his breath and Mathias immediately frowns at them both with a threatening stare, making them both suddenly stand to attention and not say another word.

After a few minutes of silence while they all patiently wait for her to return, she finally re-enters. 'Sorry to keep you waiting, gentlemen.'

Kevin nudges Kieran and whispers in his ear, 'The queen doesn't normally apologise . . . does she?' for which he snapped under his breath in return, 'Shut up.'

He looks back at him in shock and turns to face his queen once again before calmly standing to attention.

'Now,' said the queen, 'What is it you want?'

Mathias stands directly in front of her and looks her up and down, under suspicion that something is different, so he quickly scans her but still can't quite put his finger on it.

The silence is disturbed by Rob tapping Mathias on his shoulder from behind 'Where's Kyle?'

'Is he not back yet?' she gasped. She places her hands over her open mouth in shock. 'The Phoenix,' she panicked.

She speedily leaves the room and storms along the hall towards the rest room but stops half way up. She pulls a picture away from the wall that opens like a cupboard door hiding a small silver safe. She quickly enters the code and snaps it open only to reveal an empty box. She steps backwards out of shock, covering her open mouth with her fingers as the realisation forces her eyes open wide. She steps back clashing with the wall behind and gazes hopelessly as the shadowy cube within the safe begins moving further and further out of her reach as the reality sinks in.

'Your Majesty,' yelled Mathias, from the doorway at the end of the hall, making her turn and glare at him in shock with sheer terror in her eyes, and suddenly, she looks more pail than ever 'the Phoenix. . .' she cried, 'it's gone . . . I warned you, Mathias . . . retrieve that Phoenix,' she ordered, 'and bring it back to me.'

'Forgive me, Your Majesty . . . I should have. . .'

'There's no time for that,' she impatiently interrupted, 'bring it back and we'll call it even.'

'Consider it done, Your Majesty.'

He turns to face what's left of squad three who are standing and awaiting orders. 'Right then, gentlemen . . . It looks like we . . . are going back to the U.S.'

'Oh shit,' said Rob, 'not again.'

'I'm afraid so,' he replied, sounding fearless. 'But first . . . we need to find the real Kyle.'

Rob steps forward and stands tall and proud directly in front of Mathias. 'I think I know where to find him.'

'Good,' said Mathias, 'but this time, make sure it's him.'

They all hastily leave and bow their heads to the queen as they exit. 'I'll be in touch,' said Mathias, before pulling the door shut behind him.

The queen smiles to herself with a satisfied grin, before realising that she is surrounded by her security who are all staring at her, wondering how this has happened. 'Back to your stations,' she barked.

Abdul squints his eyes with concern and becomes overwhelmed with a feeling of fear that he can't explain and suddenly becomes even more afraid for her safety. 'Are you okay, Margaret?' he asked.

She ignores him and sits down in a tall back chair and effortlessly lifts her right leg over the top of her left, pulling down the bottom of her dress to cover her thin delicate shins. She gingerly places her hands at the end of each arm of the chair and lightly caresses the material in a circular motion. She looks up at Abdul who has blatantly ignored her orders and raises her eyebrow while turning up her top lip. 'I said . . . back to your stations.'

He remains still for a few seconds and continues observing her. 'Are you sure you want me to leave?' he asked, neglecting the arrogance in her eyes. She fills her lungs and exhales a long sigh of irritability. 'Just leave,' she ordered, 'and do it quietly.'

He bows his head and places his huge hands in front of his chest as though praying. 'My apologies, Your Majesty . . . as you wish.'

He reluctantly leaves the room and gently pulls the door shut behind him. She dramatically rolls her eyes, elated to finally be left in peace. She bum shuffles in her seat, making her drop slightly deeper in the overly soft cushion. She drops her hand down by her side and reaches into a concealed pocket near the bottom of her dress and carefully retracts her hand with a flimsy grip around the Golden Phoenix. She lifts it for a closer look and holds it six inches in front of her face, admiring its artistry, and wonders how something so small and fragile can contain that much power. She pinches her left ear lobe and the sound of a phone ringing echoes deep her ear. 'What have you got for me,' said a man's voice in a deep American Accent that only she can hear. 'Mathias is on his way to you.'

'Oh,' replied the voice in shock. 'How long do we have?'

'I'm afraid I couldn't tell you . . . could be days, hours, or even minutes for all I know.'

'So the plan worked then?'

'I believe so, Mr President . . . I have sent Mathias to retrieve the Phoenix.'

'Don't you have it?' he nervously asked

'I have it right here, sir . . . and you're not going to believe this, but, I am sat on the throne.'

'You mean you're the queen of England?' he asked in shock.

'Yes, Mr President,' she said with a smile. 'Queen of England, at your service.'

'Ha ha, good work, soldier,' he acclaimed.

'I will arrange transport and have the parcel sent your way,' she proudly stated. 'Has preparation began on bringing down the Neflium?' she asked.

'Yes,' said the president. 'Any minute now . . . I'll keep you posted.'

The president abruptly hangs up his phone, leaving silence in her ears as she confidently fills her lungs and pushes her shoulders deep in the luxurious comfort and once again admires the room's character with an arrogant grin.

CHAPTER 6

The night was cold and peaceful, leaving behind a thin sheet of frost that covers everything with a sparkling white but now it is early morning and the sun is due to rise at any moment.

A faint buzzing sound accompanied with a small yellow continuous flashing button catches the president's attention from the corner of his eye. He pleasurably taps it to stop the irritating buzz and turns the flashing yellow to a steady calming green before announcing himself. 'Mr President speaking,'

'Good morning, sir, this is the board room. . . I'm sorry to disturb you, but I have a Natalia here to see you, she has been fully debriefed and has been awarded clearance.'

He opens his eyes wide as the excitement rushes through him. 'Oh!' he said, sounding surprised. 'She is earlier then I thought.'

'Would you like us to make her wait?' asked a random member of the board.

'That won't be necessary,' he said, while suppressing a yawn. 'Send her through.'

A few moments pass and the door pushes open from the outside. 'Right this way, Madam,' said a man's voice standing in the doorway while holding it open with a firm grasp around the shiny golden handle. A short chubby lady with long straight brown hair and a distinctive curved jawline walks in. She immediately locks eyes with the president and involuntarily gulps as her nerves noticeably begin to get the better of her, yet somehow she instantly finds the courage to speak. 'Good morning, Mr President,' she said politely.

'Good morning . . . you must be Natalia . . . I've been expecting you.'

She reaches in to her pocket and anxiously retrieves a small container about the size of a matchstick box and places it delicately on the table next to him. A black leather chair with chrome arm rests next to the president automatically turns to face her, inviting her to be seated.

'Please sit,' said the president, extending his arm out and welcoming her to make herself comfortable. She sits down feeling ill at ease and tries to remain as elegant as possible, only misjudges the height of the chair and drops the last inch or so that shocks her from the unexpected judder. As soon as her weight is off her feet, the chair without warning turns back to the table, 'Ooh,' she said, sounding slightly comical, 'that's clever.'

The president, appearing eager to get on with the meeting, lightly places his fingertips on the edge of the table and waits patiently for her to calm down and relax.

'So,' he said after a short and intense moment. 'What do you have for me?'

'I think you will be very impressed,' she said confidently.

He leans forward a little and rubs his hands together, unable to conceal the buzz any longer as he is dying to find out more about this so called brilliant plan. She slowly and attentively slides the small container towards him and gently presses the tip of her index finger in the centre. A red line appears across the top and she rolls her finger from one side to the other for her finger print recognition. A sudden click makes her jump and she jolts her hand away in awe. Feeling marginally embarrassed, she brushes her hair from her eyes in a geeky fashion and her puffy cheeks shift from her natural skin tone to a penetrating red.

Two hollow lines that cross in the centre gradually materialise, dividing the tiny surface into four even squares that each spring open at the same time, revealing the inside of the box. She gingerly reaches in and pulls out a tiny metal bug about the size of your average fly. It has miniscule transparent wings and a thin curved body with a miniature camera where the head should be. She holds it up in front of her face, ever so gently pinching it between her index finger and thumb, and admires its tiny mechanics for a moment before continuing 'This . . . Mr President has been named as the RCI which stands for Radio-controlled Insect.' She cautiously places it in the centre of his open and awaiting hand as he fixates on it in amazement.

In the underground facility of Robotics and home of the gamers that have earned their name by becoming the best professional drivers of the drones, thousands upon thousands of children stand waiting in this vast facility, watching a screen that is so large that it can be seen by everyone, regardless of how far back they are.

Lucian is stood next to Peter and nudges him with his elbow to get his attention 'What's going on,' he whispered.

Peter turns and looks at him in a confused manner. 'What?' he asked. 'Don't you know?'

'Know what?' said Lucian.

He leans towards him like a gossip that can't wait to share what he's heard. 'We are finally bringing down the giants.'

'Really?' he asked, suddenly sounding excited. 'How?'

Peter simply smirks at him and turns to face the front. 'Just watch,' he said with confidence.

The huge blank screen begins to flicker as fuzzy white horizontal lines flash repeatedly all over, and after a few seconds, it reveals a live feed of a huge green field that is covered with hundreds of gleaming silver hollow tubes that are poking out six inches from the ground.

'What am I waiting for?' asked Lucian, who suddenly knits his brows. 'And how do you know so much anyway?'

Peter looks him up and down as though judging him then turns to face the front once again. 'Being the Commander has its perks,' he grinned.

'Ooh look at you, mister. I'm the best gamer that ever lived.'

Peter glares at him looking furious. Lucian maintains eye contact, pulling a similar expression. Suddenly, they both laugh and Peter grabs him in a head lock. 'Get off me,' he barked as Peter rubs his knuckles up and down across the top of his head. Lucian finally escapes his grip and pushes him away, making him take two steps back and jumps on him with a huge smile and begins shaking him vigorously. 'You might be the commander but you're still my bitch.'

'All right all right,' Peter whined.

One of the older gamers in front of them turns and interrupts them. 'Excuse me, sir, but you might want to see this.'

They both immediately stop playing and stand tall with their hands behind their backs and face the front.

A faint buzzing sound that gets increasingly louder echoes through the concealed speakers, filling the facility with a threatening rumble and silencing anyone that is still talking. At that very instant, thousands upon thousands of tiny metal insects burst out from the end of each pipe and quickly fills the air above creating a thick and dark cloud that rises like smoke from an active volcano.

Natalia sits quietly in her seat, resting her hands on the table with her fingers interlocked and ever so gently twiddling her thumbs. She glances all around the room feeling very uncomfortable and nervously searching the room for something to fixate on while the president continues admiring the unique mechanics. She eventually speaks and finally breaks the uncomfortable silence that seems to be effecting only her. 'They each have a set target that has been programmed into them and immediately fix to it, making it virtually impossible for them to be removed.'

He finally hands it back to her, carefully placing it in the centre of her palm. 'The attack will begin momentarily, soon you will be ruler and you will save this world from itself.'

Her phone rings from in her pocket and she quickly pulls it out as though she was expecting the call. 'Excuse me, sir,' she apologised. She holds it to her ear and listens intently. A few moments pass as the president glares at her with anticipation but she remains silent throughout the entire conversation and ends the connection with a subtle grin before tapping the screen and placing it back in her pocket. 'The mission has begun, sir . . . by sunrise . . . America shall once again be free.'

All of the mini mechanical insects suddenly and amazingly spread out in all different directions and almost instantaneously fades out in the darkness of the early morning. The magnificent swarm amazingly gets smaller and smaller and quickly disappears as each and every one heads for their target, which just so happen to be, the huge rotten bones on the cleverly targeted giants that have surrounded America by order of the queen of England.

The magnificent beings, better known as the Neflium, continue as normal, patrolling the edge of the country under the night's dark sky and selfishly stomping through the shallow waters with specific orders to remain there and under no circumstances can they retreat.

The tiny RCIs buzz and fly at great speed before landing softly on the bones, placing themselves accurately throughout the bodies of each and every one. They dig their claws in and press their tiny bodies firmly against the surface, followed by a microscopic screw that drills in the bone from its centre and firmly attaches itself.

Natalia places the small box in her pocket. 'Quite impressive, don't you think?'

'Absolutely,' he replied. 'So how do they actually work?' he eagerly asked.

She replies immediately and confidently shares her knowledge. 'I'm glad you asked . . .each one contains a single drop of a heavy, colourless, and oily liquid called nitro-glycerine,' she slowly pronounced, 'it was first discovered in 1847 by an Italian chemist named Ascanio Sobrero. It is the hottest form of explosive in the world, reaching heats of 5000 degrees Celsius and when ignited by a single spark it creates a self-sustained shock wave that propagates through the explosive nucleon at thirty times the speed of sound.'

The president continues gazing at her in amazement, shocked at how this unsuspecting woman truly knows her science.

'For more than two hundred years, it has been used medically, mainly for heart conditions such as angina and chronic heart failure. It was even used for construction back in the old days for mining industries as dynamite. We are now also using it to keep our drones active, a small amount is inserted into the fluid routs of each and every one and circulates them from head to toe to keep them at their strongest and once inserted they will never weaken. A single drop is enough to level a small building,' she proudly stated. 'The power of this fluid is astonishing yet easily contained, and our weapon specialists believe that this is the best and most controlled procedure to bring the beasts down.'

He opens his eyes wide and slightly drops his jaw now that he is compelled to believe that this shocking plan will indeed work. 'So where are these explosives now?' he curiously asked.

'By now they should have fixed to their assigned corpse ready for detonation.'

'This is perfect,' said the president, 'and definitely not what I was expecting.'

She smiles in return, elated to be the lucky individual to share this good news with him. She reaches in another pocket and pulls out a small flat square of a solid transparent material with the numbers one to nine laid out across the surface like a calculator and each one lit up in a bright green with the word *Enter* along the bottom 'This. . .,' she said proudly, 'is the detonator.' She hands it to him carefully and places it in his now clammy palm, happily excepting her invite to take a peek at something that at this very moment is extremely precious.

'So . . . can we detonate now?' he asked, with excitement in his tone.

'Not yet, Mr President . . . the sun is due to rise in the next few minutes. I have been advised to wait for daylight, so they are all at their full strength. Doing it this way, will not only claim their lives but also destroy their pride, and will remind that tiny country's precious little queen that we are not to be messed around.'

With an arrogant grin, he leans back on his spinning chair and crosses his arms to proudly display his liking of her.

Lucian stretches as high as he can, balancing on tip toe to see over the top of the slightly taller children standing in front as he frantically searches for any gaps to get a better view before eventually giving up. 'This is shit. I can't see anything past these fat heads in front.'

Peter, who is standing next to him, turns to face him and humorously grins. 'What's the matter, short ass?' he said while messing his hair in a degrading fashion. 'Are the normal sized people too tall for my little homunculus.'

'What's a homunculus?' he regrettably asked.

'A perfectly formed miniature human being,' he laughably replied.

Lucian giggles sarcastically for a short moment and without warning stands straight faced and silent. 'Very funny,' he sulked.

'Oh come on, I'm only joking.'

'Yeah, yeah,' he whined, 'whatever . . . If you weren't my superior, I would have broken your jaw for that.'

'Ooh,' said Peter in a taunting fashion, knowing that he is actually beginning to get the better of him.

'Shush,' Lucian snapped, 'something's happening.'

Peter immediately turns and faces the front, giving the giant screen his full attention. Suddenly, an instant silence descends upon the vast facility, as the hearts and minds of every person present fills with hysteria and passion as they gaze in anticipation.

Peter tilts his head slightly, in Lucian's direction and whispers, 'The sun is rising . . . not long now; this is going to be unforgettable.'

Lucian turns to face him once again with concern in his worried eyes before facing the front. 'I thought you didn't agree with Americas take on this war,' he attentively whispered in a prudent manner.

'Ssshh,' he snapped, before looking around and suddenly appearing shifty, which then leaves Lucian intensely silent.

'Look,' Peter whispered, after a short moment of exasperation. 'I'm just a gamer, same as the rest of you . . . who's going to listen to me?'

Lucian replies sounding positive, although his posture displays otherwise. 'I think you would be very surprised, but that's just my opinion.'

It suddenly dawns on him that given his position, he could potentially lead his fellow gamers in an attack of rebellion against their leaders, but after a moment of consideration, he shakes his head in disbelief after almost instantly deciding it would be a reckless move to attempt.

'Do you really think so,' he asked, purely out of curiosity.

'Yes,' he whispered. 'Why wouldn't they . . . thousands of these gamers feel the same way you do about all this and me being one of them.'

Peter shrugs his shoulders in agreement before Lucian continues. 'None of these kids have seen a gamer with abilities as . . . extreme as yours. You just need to find some form of leverage that would benefit them and they would follow you to hell and back . . . if they had to of course.'

'I can't believe we are even considering this,' he silently barked.

'When this is over,' said Lucian, 'there's someone I think you should meet.'

'Who?' he asked.

'We'll talk later . . . but for now, just think about what I said.'

They both stand silent for a moment only Peter can't help but continue the conversation. 'You say I can command these gamers,' he whispered, 'but look at what they've done to William.'

'They have never respected him,' said Lucian, 'they obeyed him because they were told to. . . earn their respect and gain their trust and this army could be yours to command, I guarantee it.'

'This is insane,' he argued quietly. 'How could I enforce that kind of influence . . . I wouldn't even know where to start.'

Lucian simply grins in return, having more confidence in him than he will ever know. 'Leave it with me,' he said assuredly. 'I have a plan . . . but for now, shall we just enjoy the show.'

Peter nods in agreement, desperately trying to hide the sudden rush of adrenaline and attempts to continue as normal by watching the screen with everyone else while Lucian continues searching for a gap to get a better view before the action starts.

The sunlight gradually spreads across the land, creating solid shadows from all the surrounding structures, vehicles, and street signs. The dark and clear sky slowly changes to a calming blue, revealing only a few small white fluffy clouds that glide slowly through the thin air high above. The cold slowly begins to fade out as the natural heat from the bright morning glare penetrates the cool steady mist of the night's chill.

As the warm heat infiltrates the empty shells of the giant corpses, the transition instantaneously begins as their muscles, nerves, organs, and veins manifest out of thin air and are finally concealed by their thick leathery flesh. The magnificent mutation begins with their feet and gradually rises, covering their giant skeletons and ends by concealing the skulls of each and every one.

Once fully regained, they each fill their lungs as deep as they possibly can, furiously inhaling the fresh air to satisfy their desperate need to breath, followed by each of them releasing a long aggressive roar in unison, that rumbles the ground beneath their huge feet and alarms every living soul for hundreds of miles inland. And so... the day time patrol begins.

They all glare across vast land, sending their perfect vision deep in the heart of American soil, searching for any changes that may have accrued that could potentially jeopardise their very existence, only everything seems calm and normal.

Natalia smiles at the president while admiring him as her leader, and still trying to absorb that she sat in the company of the most powerful man in the world.

'The daylight has reached its full strength,' she said calmly. 'Are you ready, Mr President?'

With enthusiasm, he casually replied, 'More than you will ever know.'

She leans forward and rests her elbows on the table with her fingers interlocked before anxiously gulping. 'The code is 020413,' she said slowly.

He carefully types the numbers in and hovers his index finger over the top of the bar labelled *Enter*. He glares deep in her eyes, overwhelmed with anticipation.

'Whenever you're ready, Mr President. . . Your future awaits you.'

He closes his eyes before filling his lungs and exhales long and slow then finally, he presses enter.

One of the larger giants from the ancient race known as the Neflium instantly explodes from the inside out. Fragments of disintegrated organs, shattered bones, and blood are forced out through its thick dark skin that splits into thousands of pieces, leaving a hot mist of steaming blood where the huge proud being stood with honour.

Huge limp body parts land on the dry sand as the blood is slowly washed away by the reoccurring waves of ocean water that rolls repeatedly over the remains of its stripped lifeless limbs.

One of its fellow giants in earshot heard the horrific explosion and immediately gives it his full attention. It takes a short moment for the realisation to sink in but before he has time to react, the motion is duplicated and continues over and over around the outside of the massive country like a wave of dominos.

The calm blue water that surrounds one of the largest continents on earth gradually changes to a penetrating red that gets increasingly darker and spreads through the cold water like paint in a clear solution.

'Did it work?' asked the president in sheer suspense, but suddenly, the ground rumbles beneath their feet and leaves them both rendered speechless.

The president places both hands flat on the table and immediately he sits up straight. He fixates his eyes on the backs of his hands and refuses to move an inch. Physically unable to hide his nerves, he remains as motionless as a statue throughout the deep rumble that after a couple of minutes gradually fades out. Silence descends upon the large room as he slowly lifts his head and locks eyes with Natalia, who can't restrain her voice any longer and confidently grins, 'I think it did, sir.'

His racing heart begins to ease and once again beats at a steady pace. In shock, he slowly drops his eyes back to his sweaty hands, like a suffering patient of severe trauma, and watches the condensation expand outwards on the shiny surface from the sudden change in body heat.

The deafening sound of an entire country celebrating in unison gradually becomes increasingly louder as cheers, screams, and gunfire spreads wildly across the country, only drowned out through the thick walls of the White House. 'Wow,' said the president. 'In all my life . . . I have seen and witnessed some amazing things . . . things that were thought to be impossible, but now . . . I have truly seen it all.'

Natalia simply smiles in return to his comment.

'So what now,' he asked politely.

Natalia can still feel her hands shaking, yet continues to conceal her adrenaline and does so with ease that surprises even her. She fills her lungs to control her breathing and once again finds the courage to continue. 'Firstly . . . I would like to say, congratulations, Mr

President, you have an entire country behind you, and you have proven to every one of them that nothing will stop you from achieving your goal.' He continues gazing in her eyes, arrogantly enjoying her comments. 'I, for one,' she continued, 'am honoured to be an American.'

'I thank you for your kind words, Natalia,' he smiled. 'You have moved me.'

She slowly begins to lose herself in his eyes, as through the adrenaline, fear, and respect that he commands and sheer arrogance that he expresses so freely has unexpectedly made her horny somehow, so she shakes her head and clears her throat before continuing. 'There is a camera crew awaiting your arrival in the briefing room, the crowd is small and intimate and the feed is linked to every channel in America. I think your fellow citizens could use a few words of inspiration.'

He nods in agreement before casually rising from his seat and heads straight for the door to share the good news with his people. 'Of course,' he said proudly. 'I expect there is a lot of very confused people out there.'

Natalia jumps from her seat and stands directly in front of him with her hand on his chest that stops him in his tracks. He frowns at her in disbelief for which she immediately retracts her hand. 'Forgive me, sir, but there is something you should know.'

'Go on,' he snarled.

Realising she has crossed the line, she immediately comes out with it. 'There is a handful American citizens who we believe may be forming an alliance of rebellion in an underground facility that we are yet to locate.'

'How many?' he growled.

'A small crowd,' she said, assuring him there is nothing to worry about.

'Thank you for the update,' he said, 'but don't worry, I will have them dealt with.'

He attempts to leave once again only she continues to speak. 'With your permission,' she firmly asked, making the president roll his eyes as this is now the second time he has tried to leave. 'Would you consider allowing me the opportunity to assemble a team and destroy these traitors for you?'

She drops her eyes at his crutch and slowly steps forward in a seductive manner, and places her hand once again in centre of his chest before looking up in his cold and emotionless eyes. 'It would be a great honour,' she said softly.

He nods in agreement and hastily exits the room, leaving her alone and in silence with nothing but her own disturbing thoughts.

CHAPTER 7

A loud and echoing American female voice calls out across the silence of the Huge Gamers facility and immediately catches the attention everyone.

'William and Peter, please report to the main control room. I repeat William and Peter to control room.'

Lucian grabs Peter's arm as he tries to leave. 'What do they want with you now?' he asked.

'I don't know,' he replied. 'Meet me in my dorms later and I'll let you know . . . until then,' he said caringly, 'stay out of trouble.'

Lucian lets him go and hopes to god that he is going to be alright. 'Be careful,' he yelled as he catches a final glimpse of him through the crowd.

Peter reaches the control room, it is a large, smooth, and shiny black door made of solid and virtually impenetrable reinforced steel. Being the new commander, he enters without fear or anguish only to find William is already inside and standing to attention in front of Natalia, who is sat on a large black leather reclining chair. 'Hello Peter,' she said as he enters the room. 'I'm sorry to take you away from the entertainment but the president has a job for you.'

Peter looks her up and down suspiciously, and having never seen this woman before, he feels unsure whether to trust her or not. 'And who might you be? If you don't mind me asking.'

She rises from her seat with a smile and slowly walks towards him. 'Of course,' she said, with admiration in her tone. 'You don't know me and have never seen me before, well let me put your mind at ease before you judge me too fast . . . my name is Natalia and the president has asked me to assemble a small unit to complete a very important mission.'

'And what is that exactly?' he asked, sounding critical.

With a smile, she glares at him in silence for a few seconds before replying, 'I like you, Peter, you really are quite the character.'

'Well I've never seen you before . . . so if you wouldn't mind telling us why we are here.'

She walks back to her chair and sits back down and beams at them both in confidence. 'Would you like to sit down,' she politely asked.

William and Peter look at each other at the same time and turn to face her in unison. 'I think we'll stand,' said Peter.

'Suit yourself. The president wants you to kill a group of rebellions who are threatening our glorious revelation. He wants you to remind them that traitors will not go unpunished . . . but first you are to get to the White House and help Nikki bring down Mathias. Do you accept this great honour?'

'Do we have a choice?' said Peter immediately.

'No . . . not really,' she arrogantly replied.

William interrupts. 'Then I guess we accept.'

'Good . . . then that's settled.' She rubs her hands together and stands up. 'Follow me, gentlemen,' she ordered.

'What? Do we have to leave right now?' asked William, with his eyebrows knitted.

'I'm afraid so my dear, or would you rather work the sewers . . . if you're too afraid.'

'I'm not afraid,' he immediately barked.

'Good,' she replied. She pushes the door open and holds it wide with the side of her foot, revealing the corridor on the other side.

'There are two containers in the courtyard,' she said proudly, 'each holding a single gamer's chair with headsets on each one, place your earpieces on and await orders, also . . . don't be alarmed if you sense movement. We must take any precaution necessary, and keeping you mobile reduces the risk of having you tracked . . . these new young challengers appear to be quite intelligent.'

They leave the room and head down the long corridor and remain side by side all the way. The high ceiling and walls are so white that it's hard for them not to strenuously narrow their eyes. The floor is a dark jet black with a shiny marble-like surface and the contrast in colours makes the whole thing look almost transparent. Peter has fixed his eyes on the larger-than-necessary thick metal double doors at the far end. His mind is focussed and clear, thinking purely about what it is he must do and ignores his surroundings completely, while William simply wonders along with a cocky strut. They walk a long way before William decides it's a good idea to break the silence. 'You're not scared are you?' he sarcastically asked.

'You wish,' said Peter.

William rolls his eyes after releasing a short snort of derision. 'I can't believe they've put us two together for this.'

'You should be honoured,' said Peter, with a grin, knowing full well that it will wind him up.

They both push the huge double doors open at the same time and continue along an identical corridor.

'Give over,' he barked. 'You just sound like a twat now.'

Peter simply grins as he unexpectedly turns away pushing a door open on his left side and carelessly walking through, followed by William who almost forgot where they were headed and hastily jogs a few steps to catch up. They continue onwards through a large warehouse with hundreds of boxes on solid metal shelves, stacked up over and over reaching heights of hundreds of feet right the way along. They continue walking in silence through the crammed eerie stockroom. They finally reach the opposite end and come face to face with a huge shutter that is big enough to harbour a small plane or allow massive delivery vehicles to enter and exit at the same time. After a short moment, the door begins to rise and reveals an enormous empty courtyard that spreads far and wide, accommodated by two lonely trucks that have a small container on the back of each one.

Out of the blue, two men in high visibility jackets approach from either side. They are both wearing hard hats with baggy white trousers and light-brown leather steel-toe-capped boots and both holding a clipboard with a single sheet of paper attached that loosely flaps in the breeze.

William and Peter glance at each other in suspense. 'Something doesn't seem right,' Peter curiously stated.

William locks eyes with the man approaching and feels his heart begin to race. 'Finally, we agree on something,' he replied.

'William,' yelled the man on their left.

'That's me,' he responded, holding his hand in the air.

'Right this way, sir,' the man requested.

William turns and locks eyes with Peter in a slightly cocky fashion now that he has successfully hidden his nerves. 'How about a race,' he challenged.

'And what would that prove,' he replied, after releasing a sigh of impatience.

William steps forward and invades his personal space by placing his nose inches from his cheek only Peter continues gazing at the wide open space and patiently awaits his predictive insult. 'It would prove how much of a loser you really are,' he snarled.

Peter calmly turns his face towards with narrow eyes as though he has excepted his juvenile challenge. 'Like I said before . . . only one of us here knows how it feels to lose.'

'You cheated,' he barked in defence

Peter smiles and once again glares out at the open space. 'You need to learn to let go . . . or at least move on.'

'Just stay out of my way,' he warned, before following the man.

'So,' said the other man, 'you must be Peter . . . Right this way, sir,' for which he happily follows as to him, William is an insufferable boar that he cannot endure for one more second.

Total darkness and sheer silence is interrupted by the faint sound of talking; only the voices are so mumbled that no words can be made out but it ends with a loud and sudden clunk.

Two stiff metal doors slowly swing open with a loud grind and creak that echoes through emptiness within, and as the daylight reveals the inside of the container, the lights automatically switch on.

Peter, who is standing in the centre of the expanding opening between the doors, watches closely as the inside is gradually revealed, making his jaw slightly drop open.

There is a single gaming chair in the centre, with a screen in front that dominates the whole edge wall of the inside. The chair itself is made mostly of gleaming chrome and covered in buttons of all different shapes and sizes, and lit up stylishly in a green flourescent glow. The joysticks and soft-cushioned seat is covered with dark soft leather and overall, it looks to be the most inviting gaming chair he has ever had the pleasure of driving.

He eagerly approaches the seat and has a quick look around to work out what is what, and without hesitation, climbs in to test the soft cushions and smiles as the comfort surprises him. There is a small headset on the top of his backrest that begins to flicker with blue lights and his attention is drawn immediately to the light. He places them over his ears and waits patiently while caressing the tops of his joysticks with the pads of his thumbs.

CHAPTER 8

The president enters through a huge white door on the side of a staging area with a dark blue background on the far wall. A large American flag hangs free from the high ceiling behind an oak wood podium desk top. There are three standing microphones at neck height at his front and two small American flags on white rods, standing upright on both top corners.

'Right this way, Mr President,' said one of his top members of security, who welcomes him as he walks on stage.

Bright camera flashes begin immediately but he neglects the urge to smile, or show any form of pleasure over what their technology has finally managed to achieve.

The cameras that are connected to the live feed focus in on him and with the latest gadgets he is made to look perfectly groomed and airbrushed.

He strolls to the centre of the stage looking calm and collected with his eyes fixed on the huge flag, simply admiring the symbol of his proud country and finally faces the large crowd, placing his mouth inches from the microphones.

'My fellow citizens, people of America. We stand here once again united and free, as we fight off terrorist attacks against our country. Those giants,' he said, while pointing at the door, 'were resurrected by the queen of England to contain us. But our ever-expanding technology cannot be contained,' he yelled.

'America will not bow down to this resurrected race of giants . . . or any other race. They had their time here. . . We will not surrender to terrorism,' he barked, while banging the ball of his fist on the desk top. 'Not now. . . Not ever. If the world has learned anything about our country, then they will know. . .' He takes a deep breath before yelling once again. 'America will not be brought down one small nation. . . a nation that seems hell bent on stopping our god-given right to create a peaceful world . . . a world with one ruler, which would mean, for all of us. . . no more war. Have I not proven that I have our nation's best interest at heart, by taming the sadistic rulers who only ever want war?'

He places both hands on the table and drops his head while filling his lungs as he searches for his next words. He stands up proud and tall with his head high and arms open.

'All I want . . . all we, want . . . is peace and harmony throughout the world . . . and if we stand together . . . united, as we always have . . . we can win . . . we will win,' he passionately yelled.

He immediately turns and arrogantly heads for the exit, ignoring the bellow of the few chosen members of paparazzi that call out in desperation to get their questions answered.

A member of his security stops him in his tracks and whispers in his ear, so he nods in agreement to whatever was said and hastily leaves the room. The man quickly approaches the podium desk and silences them at once.

'The president will not be answering any questions at this point. However, a security issue has arisen and I am told to advise you that the White House is to be evacuated.'

Everyone suddenly begins to panic as they jump from their seats in shock. 'What's going on?' they shout. 'Are we in danger?'

'Please,' the man yelled, 'will everyone just leave in an orderly fashion.'

At this point, the panic has already spread as they all suddenly scramble for the door and step on those fallen in a desperate attempt to escape.

CHAPTER 9

'Okay, boys,' said Natalia's voice, in Peter's and William's ears, 'Mathias is on approach to the White House. Protect that building; let's show Britain what we can do.'

William smiles in a cocky fashion and feels more eager than ever to get started, while Peter simply drops his head and shuts his eyes to focus and gather his thoughts. He feels his heart race as he fills his lungs due to an unexpected sense of apathy towards his target.

He knows deep down that this is not what he wants to do, but turning back now would only make things worse, so he reluctantly turns his back on his dignity and swallows his pride, having once again accepted that he cannot disobey his orders.

'Good luck,' said Natalia. 'Activate in 3 . . . 2 . . . 1.'

They both lift a protective cover on the top right of their built-in control unit, revealing a bright red padded button and they immediately press down on it hard and firm. A small transparent lens on a thin flexible rod extends out from their headsets in a smooth motion and tenderly presses against their right eye before fixing themselves firmly in place.

Four bright red eyes light up in the darkness and through the sight of their drones, the inside of a container is displayed on their screens. A high-pitched whining sound reverberates off the thick metal walls as they power up, followed by a sharp burst from a mechanical hydraulic pump that indicates full power has been achieved and the drones immediately straighten their artificial spinal cords and expand their thick metal chest plates.

'The White House is twenty-one miles north of your position,' she continued. 'You have approximately seven and a half minutes. . . It's time to truly test the new drone. This game is yours, gentlemen . . . Natalia signing off.'

They both step forward to opposite ends of the container. William performs a hard punch on the door's centre, while Peter's drone kicks with the large solid metal base of its right foot. The two large metal plates shoot out at a phenomenal speed, crashing and deflecting through the pathways of hundreds of identical containers and they both exit in a coordinated manner before briefly glancing around at the immediate surroundings.

They are identical drones and stand a massive thirty feet high. The mechanics are protected well, beneath the solid metal plates around the arms and legs that are built to mimic an extremely muscular human form. The chest plates are wide and thick, covering the delicate wires beneath. The stomach and waist are constructed with metal belts that overlap from chest to hips for maximum flexibility that are cleverly designed to imitate the developed abs of a body builder.

With no further delay, they rapidly sprint off the mark, reaching speeds of 120 mph in a mere few seconds and continue moving faster as each second passes, making the limbs of each one appear as a blur to the naked eye.

On their approach to the city, Peter sends his drone's perfect vision forward and can see the general public going about their everyday lives, only each of them are oblivious to what is coming.

He decides to back off a little with a deep concern for the many defenceless pedestrians and after a very brief moment of consideration he shoots off in a different direction hoping that William will follow, only William, not to Peter's surprise, cares for nothing but winning this unnecessary race, so he speeds up even faster and selfishly ploughs through the city centre.

Cars, buses, and other vehicles swerve to avoid the huge and rapidly moving drone. Crashes occur repeatedly from the blind panic to get out of the way as it passes, leaving a trail of destruction, chaos, and death.

The huge metal feet as wide as a truck pound against the road surface and crack the thick concrete after each and every impact as trees, buildings and vehicles are carelessly crushed and demolished.

William grips his control sticks tight as the intensity builds up inside.

A single small white circle with a cross in its centre representing a target darts back and forth across his lens and stops for less than half a second on everything it can, to register in advance, anything that could potentially slow him down.

Peter continues sprinting around the edge of the city, glancing through the buildings and massive skyscrapers at which point he spots William's drone tearing through the built-up area without a care in the world and shakes his head in disgust. He locks his target on the White House in the far distance and flicks a switch on the side of his control pad. At that very moment, his drone speeds up even faster, reaching almost double the speed as masses of rubble mud and dirt flick up behind, leaving a long trail of dust that stretches back for miles.

A high-pitched whine that begins softly, as a sudden mechanical serge of immense power gets louder and louder, ending with a bang that rumbles the floor like the blast from an exploding grenade. His drone leaps from the ground forcing rubble and dust hundreds of feet in the air from the tremendous amount of pressure of the final impact. It leaps so high that he clears the tall buildings by almost double.

As he glides through the air, it feels like everything is moving in slow motion. His eyes remain fixed on the White House and as he nears the large gardens, moving at a phenomenal speed, he prepares himself for the landing and crashes into the path that runs through the pleasant green grass that surrounds the president's home. The large metal feet shatter the solid concrete, creating huge cracks that spread beneath like a monstrous spider's web.

Peter feels his container rock from side to side as though he is being lifted in the air, but after a loud bang that echoes through the emptiness within, he is finally still again and thinks nothing of it.

Peter does a quick scan of his drone's vitals and everything seems normal. He looks around in search for William who is still nowhere to be seen, only his attention is drawn to what sounds like chaos and suddenly William's drone sprints from behind a mass of buildings, leaving behind a trail of devastation.

He locks eyes with Peter's drone and swiftly sprints even faster, heading straight for him.

'Ha ha, beat you,' said Peter, in a competitive tone.

William acknowledges his cockiness but says nothing in return. Out of frustration and envy, he narrows his eyes and forces his joysticks as far forward as they can go. His drone leans forward for aerodynamics as it shoots like a gliding arrow creating a high-pitched whine from the sudden increase of speed that shocks even him. In astonishment, he leans back from his screen and widens his eyes in disbelief. 'Now it's my turn,' he whispered.

'William,' he said sounding cautious, 'what are you doing?'

To Peter's surprise, the drone leaps headfirst and dives in an unplanned attack to finally take his revenge and destroy Peter for wrecking his life and shattering his dreams that he has worked, bled, and suffered for, even committed murder in cold blood to become the commander that Peter simply snatched from him and gloats about it every chance he gets.

Peter effortlessly steps aside and humorously watches him smash through the main doors of the president's official home of residents and forces a large cloud of rubble and dust out in the open.

'What the fuck,' said Peter, as he knits his eyebrows in awe. 'William . . . what happened?'

Receiving no reply, he edges forward through the thick cloud of dust in a very cautious manner, believing that some kind of malfunction or misunderstanding had accrued.

'William,' he called again, 'where are you?'

Peter's drone is suddenly lifted from behind, and to his surprise, thrown through a solid wall and immediately followed by the opposing drone that grabs his ankle and slings him through yet another wall. Upon landing, Peter's screen flickers and he tries to once again to check his vitals for damage as he attempts to sit forward and stand but finds himself forced back down to the floor as William's drone appears in his view looking down at him with his large metal foot on his throat.

Peter attempts to grab his knee, only William stops him and grips his drone tight around the wrist before stretching his arm to its full extent.

In the excitement of everything happening, William leans closer to his screen with joy as he glares in the bright red eyes of Peter's desperate drone.

'Mathias is my kill,' he growled, 'and you are not taking this away from me.'

He suddenly pulls his twisted arm as hard as possible and with great difficulty he finally detaches it from the shoulder join that snaps with a loud ding of metal, and sparks repeatedly as its vital fluids squirt out.

'No,' shouted Peter. 'What have you done . . . Mathias will tear you to pieces without me.'

The huge drone leans down and grabs the other wrist while pushing his foot deeper in its throat and once again rips it off, leaving Peter's drone with no defence at all.

'We'll see about that,' he growled with satisfaction.

William's drone stands tall and proud with a lifeless metal limb dangling in the deadly grasp of both hands, and looks down at him feeling more empowered than ever.

'You're going to regret this,' said Peter. 'You're out of your depth.'

William cannot help chuckling to himself before his arrogant reply of certainty.

'Don't make me laugh . . . I've fought Mathias before and if I wasn't interrupted I would have beaten him then . . . and I will beat him now . . . mark my words.'

'Good luck,' he replied, sounding uncertain.

Without further delay, his drone repeatedly swings Peter's own limbs at his drone's defenceless body and continues hacking until there is nothing but a limp hand remaining of each one. He carelessly slings them aside while dropping to bended knee and continuously punches the body anywhere and everywhere. He begins ripping off chunks of reinforced metal by the handful and watches in utter bliss as the large body gets smaller after each part is savagely torn away. He then places his huge metal hands either side of its head and forces its knee deep into what remains of the chest to hold it steady and rocks the head from side to side before finally tearing it from its shoulders. The red eyes flicker for a short moment before the artificial life finally slips away. He proudly rises and crushes the severed head into a mangled ball of metal. He carelessly throws it through one of the only remaining windows and kicks the limp body across the room before exiting the building. After proudly stepping through the large hole in the White House wall, he stands tall and immediately searches for any signs of the alleged attack. He prepares himself by posing his favourite fighting stance and holds the position, awaiting the arrival of Mathias.

Peter yanks his headset off and angrily tosses it aside. 'What a fucking idiot,' he growled to himself. He leans back and takes a deep breath while running his fingers through his hair, purely out of frustration.

'I need some air,' he said quietly.

He climbs out of his seat and approaches the entrance. There is a large lever in the centre with a rubber grip pad on the end. With great difficulty, he lifts it, producing a loud clunk that indicates the door is open and he pushes it hard, only to find himself forced back in by a strong gust of wind. He pushes again with his entire mite and the door slowly swings open, creating a gap wide enough for him to squeeze through. He glances around for any signs of life but no one's to be seen, through his search a shocking realisation hits him as he spots a vast and bright horizon in the far distance that almost blends with the clear blue sky above. In a hopeless gaze he comes across some white railings that runs all the way along both sides of him and approaches them with caution, only as he draws near he slips on the damp wooden floor. His heart begins racing, certain that something is not right here, and gulps from the sheer anxiety of not knowing what follows.

His suspicion becomes even more aroused as he carefully stands up and continues heading towards the edge. The sun is blazing hot with not a cloud in sight and the intense glare shimmers off the solid wood surface making his vision appear murky. After a steady stroll, he finally reaches the rail and grips it tight with both hands while leaning slightly over the edge, and to his surprise he finds himself on a large boat miles out at sea and they are shifting through the rough waters at tremendous speed. It doesn't take long before answers are needed, so he begins his next mission, to find out what the hell is going on.

CHAPTER 10

The queen is sat on her huge soft-cushioned sofa in her private room. She is still and silent, gazing in to the huge fire place with an empty mind while patiently waiting for Gracie to waken from her long nap. She glances over at the cot in the corner of the room and fills her lungs from the sheer boredom as the silence is beginning to feel unbearable for her.

Gracie finally begins to stir and the queen's attention is immediately on her.

'It's about time,' she arrogantly snarled.

She walks over to the door and locks it with the dead key and slides across the large bolts at the top and bottom with a noticeable clunk. She slowly walks past the cot, glaring at Gracie in disgust. She reaches over the small round table next to the sofa and tenderly presses the small yellow button on the built-in speaker, that changes to a calming green.

'Please do not disturb me,' she ordered. 'Gracie and I would like some private time.'

'Of course, Your Majesty, you shall not be disturbed,' said a very pleasant young female voice.

She casually walks towards the old-fashioned cot in a sluggish manner and for some reason looks overly pleased with herself as she slowly raps her delicate fingers around the cot's sculptured bar in a creepy fashion and glares down at her.

Gracie ever so slowly and with noticeable difficulty opens her eyes and struggles for a moment to focus. When her sight becomes clear, the queen is standing over her, gazing into her large blue eyes with a caring smile.

Gracie smiles in return before yawning unexpectedly. She lifts her arms high above her head while pointing her tiny toes and stretches her entire body with a groan of pure indulgence. She wakes up feeling safe, in the comfort and protection of the one person she doesn't have to trick to ensure her safety.

She locks eyes with her once again and curiously tilts her head to the side but suddenly, and all at once, the good feeling vanishes and is replaced with a tormenting sense of danger that spreads rapidly through her entire body, from head to toe.

To her unexpected horror, the queen's face mutates, inflicting terror in her heart and appearing creepy like a ghost. Her skin turns white and her eyes sink in her skull, leaving two black and empty holes that hollow into darkness. Her nose folds in on itself as her mouth opens wider then humanly possible, making her lips stretch and tear in both corners, revealing nothing but darkness inside, followed by a long snakelike tongue that extends out and licks all around her face before it slowly retracts.

Gracie's heart beats faster than ever, so to escape the horror, she closes her eyes as tight as she can and for as long as she can bear; after a short while, she cautiously reopens them one at a time in the hope that the image has gone and thankfully she looks to be normal again.

Gracie seizes the opportunity to read her mind before she mutates again, only finds herself locked out somehow. 'Who are you?' she asked, with a clear shake in her voice.

The queen aggressively wraps her bony fingers around her ankle with a firm grasp and lifts her in the air. She dangles her upside down and holds her inches from her face. The tight grip is painful for her but she refuses to give this unwanted intruder the satisfaction by saying so.

'I'm what most would call . . . your worst enemy,' she growled.

Gracie's heart continues pounding faster than she knew it could. Her hands and feet turn hot and clammy while sweat beads protrude from her skin as her head is now starting to ache from the blood flow she's not use to, but she bravely shows no fear and holds eye contact for as long as she physically can. 'I'm not afraid of you,' she proudly stated.

The queen simply laughs in her face before arrogantly glancing over to her left, which in turn makes Gracie look, only to see a small box made of solid oak wood, with a matching lid leant against its side.

Her eyes well up uncontrollably, 'Are you sending me somewhere?' she asked, with a heavy lump in her throat.

The queen replies by merely nodding.

'Where?' she squeaked.

'Back to where you belong,' she snarled.

Gracie remembers her fear of small spaces and promised herself that no matter what. She would never allow herself to be put in that position again, even if it killed her, but through fear and shock, she has forgotten she has power, so at this point she is merely a defenceless baby, 100 per cent dependent on those who love her.

'Are you going to kill me?' she asked, in a manner that is begging her not to.

The queen laughs once again with a presumptuous snort. 'Kill you? No no no . . . You're too important to kill . . . however . . . I can promise you one thing . . . you will experience more pain than your precious little body can take.'

Gracie tries to be strong and holds eye contact to show no fear but after a short moment her eyes fill with tears and she shamefully sobs in desperation.

She holds Gracie at arm's length and walks towards the box while selfishly enjoying her pain. Gracie immediately starts to panic and frantically tries to get away, only proves to be too small and weak to make any kind of impact.

'Please,' she cried. 'Please don't put me in there.'

'Shut up,' she growled, hoping to god that no one can hear but her warm tears begin streaming as her worst fear is about to become reality.

'Please,' she cried again. 'Whatever I did, I promise I won't do it again. Please,' she begged, 'I'm sorry.'

'Shut the fuck up,' snarled the queen, while trying to peel her off her hand. She lowers her in but she continues hysterically trying to grab something, anything, as her fear is now controlling her.

The lights begin to flicker and everything electrical in the room turns on and off. Her ear piece whines at a deafening rate, forcing her to quickly rip it out.

'Get in there you little bitch,' she snapped, before finally dropping her and making her knock her delicate head on the solid edge.

'Well that's disappointing,' she said, sounding genuinely disheartened. 'I thought you would have made it a bit more difficult than that.'

Gracie looks up at her through her big blue eyes that are now bloodshot from all the tears, but the queen slowly pulls the lid over the top.

'Please,' she begged, in one final attempt to sway her.

'Pathetic,' the queen humorously whispered, before the ray of light is finally blocked out, leaving her alone in complete darkness without so much as a breathing whole for air.

'Please,' she whispered; 'Please. . . ' but after no further response she curls up in a ball and whimpers in silence.

She picks the box up and proudly heads for the door, unaware that the eyes of the Phoenix hanging around her neck have lit up in a burning red as it is suddenly stretched from her neck, forcing the ribbon to break as it shoots in the fireplace, stopping dead against the far wall. To her surprise, the cold logs at the bottom suddenly burst into flames, at which point the queen finds herself stunned and paralyzed from any movement, but with very limited use of her feet alone, she slowly and unwillingly turns around to face the massive flames head on. Her eyes are wide and full of terror and her pupils have shrunk to virtually nonexistent. Her complexion changes to a very light pail and her lips turn to a dark blue as the veins throughout her entire body swell and become extremely visible. Her colourless skin begins streaming with beads of sweat all over, making her instantly look soaked from head to toe.

Within the flames are two dark black and hollow eyes appear within the vague outline of a very large man. From beyond her control, her entire body violently shakes, as a deep growling voice rumbles through the floor boards beneath her feet.

'Put the box down.'

She gently places the box on the floor at her side and rises once again, only she does so with great difficulty and stands motionless.

'Who are you?' asked the voice.

'Jamie Valco,' he immediately replied, finding himself unable to lie as he struggles for breath.

'Why are you here?'

'I am here to impersonate the queen' he replied, after further struggle for air, 'and surrender England to America.'

A huge figure made purely of fire slowly steps out of the burning flames. He crouches on his godlike entrance and once through, he stands tall, pushing out his large chest as though filling his burning lungs that makes him glow even brighter. He locks eyes with the cruel impersonator and glares at him for a short moment before relentlessly walking towards him.

Jamie Valco wants to run and scream the building down, he wants to more than anything he has ever wanted but he physically cannot move a single muscle. Unable to break eye contact, Jamie's head slowly tilts back on the gatekeeper's approach as he gradually towers over who looks to be the queen.

'Where is the queen?' he snapped.

'In the abandoned dungeons,' he murmured.

The gatekeeper looks him up and down, secretly admiring the shocking resemblance. He leans down and places his burning face inches from Jamie's nose, but he finds himself unable to do anything, but stare back.

'Your soul is dark,' he humorously growled, 'just the way I like them.'

He wraps his huge hands around his chest and locks her tiny arms at her side before carelessly lifting her from the ground. A thin layer of burning hot flames spread out from the gatekeeper's hands and gradually covers the intruder's entire body from head to toe. He screams continuously while kicking his legs and throwing his head from side to side, doing anything he physically can to escape the agony. The gatekeeper watches him closely for a moment and grins, as though his screams from the excruciating pain are satisfying him somehow, then after a brief moment, he slowly turns and walks back towards the scorching flames.

He accidently taps the box with his massive foot of fire but having caused no damage whatsoever, the box simply tips, making the lid pop off, followed by Gracie, who rolls out on top of it. She immediately shields her eyes from the sudden brightness of burning fire and unbearable heat that leaves her vision obscured.

Jamie's skin has now virtually melted off completely and the flesh beneath is changing to a charcoal black that is quickly peeling from the bone as each piece splats on the floor leaving a trail of smoking and sizzling flesh. His eyeballs burst and the juice seeps down what is left of his face which at this point is mostly bone, yet Jamie, the man with no morals, is still screaming.

His soul tries to escape, but like his body, it is trapped in the gatekeeper's firm grasp. He enters the flames with what is left of Jamie in toe and the magnificent fire expands to almost twice the size but only as a flash. Gracie falls back in shock as all at once they disappear and do so along with the flames, leaving the desperate screams of Jamie echoing through the silence of the vast empty chimney breast.

The door bursts open and Abdul runs through followed by two other men who look more lost than ready to protect her.

Gracie is staring at the enormous fireplace with her eyes fixed on the still glowing Phoenix, while Abdul quickly darts around the room in a desperate attempt to find his queen. The two men nervously glance around holding their guns at arm's length and have absolutely no idea what they are looking for.

Charlotte walks in from the back of the room and immediately spots Gracie on the floor looking scared and shaky, but most importantly, unprotected. She looks more beautiful than ever, her hair is glowing in a golden blond and her long blue dress is perfectly fitted to her unique tall and slender shape but as she darts between the two men they jump out of their skin and instantly point their guns in her face with a squeal.

'Put them down you idiots,' she ordered, making them both immediately drop their weapons in embarrassment.

She picks Gracie up and cuddles her close with nothing but love and she wraps her tiny arms around her as far as she can and squeezes her tight while burying her teary face in her neck.

'What happened, Gracie?' she lovingly asked.

Abdul is still panicking in a blind search for his queen and is getting more anxious by the second. Not thinking, he angrily darts for

Gracie and attempts to grab her but luckily Charlotte quickly snatches her away.

'Where's Margaret?' he barked, having now lost his temper.

'What are you doing?' Charlotte shouted.

Gracie gently touches Natalia's face and she instantly relaxes, feeling no threat whatsoever from Abduls anger.

'It's okay,' Gracie said to her, 'he's just scared that's all . . . he would never hurt me.'

She looks over at Abdul who is sweating from the unthinkable fear that he may have lost his queen, the one person he is sworn to protect and his only real purpose for living.

'She's in the abandoned dungeons,' she gently advised. 'Hurry, and take a medic with you.'

Abdul puts his hands together as though praying. 'Thank you,' he said happily, before hastily exiting the room followed the two other men. Charlotte also tries to leave but Gracie stops her. 'Wait,' she said quietly. Charlotte looks at her in silence, wondering what she is up to.

'We can't just leave it here' she said.

'Leave what here, sweetheart?'

Gracie merely points at the fire place, making Charlotte glance over, only to spot the Phoenix glowing more golden than ever before but it's stuck to the far wall above a pile of fresh wood that is laid out on a long bulky grill and ready to burn.

'Did you see the gatekeeper?' she asked, sounding shocked. Gracie replies by merely nodding her head. She gently places her on the huge soft sofa but gives her a big squeeze and a kiss on the head before letting go.

'Stay there, angel, and don't move, okay?' she worriedly ordered.

She walks over to the Phoenix and cautiously leans in to retrieve it but it pops out with no struggle and she grips it tight. Without delay, she straightaway picks Gracie up and cuddles her close again.

'Let's return this to the queen, shall we?'

Gracie smiles and cuddles her even tighter and they both casually exit the room.

'Did you hear a wimpy sort of scream in that chimney,' asked Charlotte, as they disappeared around the corner.

CHAPTER 11

Rob, Kieran, and Kevin, are walking along a bright hall, with large square lights above that are laid out every ten feet all the way along. Every door they pass is large and heavy, made of dark oak wood with a long grey handle and a single pain of glass up high, that are all covered with small white curtains.

They are all wearing dark black and matching shirts with bulletproof vests wrapped tight around them that have the words *squad three* across their backs in large white and bold letters.

A group of doctors and nurses walk past and glare at them in a cautious manner and turn the heads of every man woman and child that crosses them.

They suddenly stop and turn on the spot in unison before proudly entering one of the rooms. When they walk in, they spread out in an orderly fashion and lock eyes with Kyle, he is sat opposite Andrew who is seated on the other side of a single bed that is comforting an unknown man who is covered from head to toe in bandages. He quickly stands in a startled sort of way, yet secretly felt happy to see them.

'What the hell are you lot doing here?' he barked, trying to keep the noise down.

'Right,' Kevin interrupted, while holding his hands in the air like he's just been amazed. 'Now I am officially freaked out.'

Kyle looks at him confused as though he's asking what he's done wrong.

'We were with you yesterday,' he continued, 'well . . . not with you but someone who was being you.'

'What?' he asked while shaking his head.

'You were drunk,' he continued, 'and we went to Buckingham Palace and spoke to the queen,' he steps forward from the back and waves his hand in front of Kyle's face, like a child watching to see if they can make the eyes move on a statue. Kyle simply glares at him, as though witnessing someone on the turn to insanity right before his eyes.

'That's amazing,' Kevin continued.

Rob grabs his shoulder and pulls him back to stand behind with Kieran and immediately stands tall with his hands behind his back. 'Sir . . . we need to ask you some questions.'

'For God's sake, relax, man,' Kyle ordered.

'Thank you, sir.' He drops his shoulders and stands at ease, while Kyle returns to his seat. 'Andrew, you remember Rob and the other two,' he carelessly pointed before dropping his hands in his lap.

'Of course I do,' he proudly announced, 'the heroes who made Mathias possible.'

'Well . . . we helped,' said Kieran.

'That's right you helped . . . now for the last time. What are doing here?' Kyle snapped, getting more frustrated by the second.

'Mathias knows where Tom is,' Rob reluctantly announced.

Andrew immediately inhales as a rush of excitement shoots through him. 'Have you found him?' he asked.

'Matthias thinks he may have.'

'Wait a minute,' said Kyle. 'How did he find out where he is?'

'The queen told him,' Rob answered

Kyle is holding his index finger in the air and frantically looking from left to right as though he has come to a conclusion. 'You said I was with you, right?' he asked, making them all nod in agreement, 'and I took Mathias with us to the palace, right?' They all nod again in unison. Kyle's eyes widen as the realisation sets in. 'Shit,' he snapped. He turns and looks at Andrew who is staring back at him in suspense. 'The queen ordered that under no circumstances am I to take him there, and you were just telling me about this new technology that America has.'

'What's that?' Kieran interrupted.

'It can give you a new identity. It looks like a harmless bracelet but it's an amazing piece of gear. It's got tiny needles all around the inside that injects the DNA of whom you want to impersonate and you can be whoever you choose.' He stands still for a moment, gazing at the floor in deep thought before locking eyes with Rob. 'Have you got your car?'

'Yes, sir,' he proudly announced, 'But before we go, sir, we need to know that you are you.'

Kyle goes to walk past him but stops next to him and turns to look at him before back handing across the chops. 'There's no time . . . now get in the car and take me to London.'

He walks away leaving Rob rubbing his jaw.

'Call us if he wakes up,' he said to Andrew before disappearing around the corner.

'Is that proof enough for ya,' said Kevin as he quickly leaves to catch up with Kieran. He frowns at Andrew looking pissed off but also feels satisfied that he is in fact him.

They all walk out through the main doors of the John Radcliffe Hospital in Oxford and into the main car park located at the front. Kyle, Kieran, and Kevin approach a blue Nissan skyline with flames that run along both sides and fade as it nears the back end. The spoiler on the back is high and sleek and the alloys have a sparkling shine with low-profile tyres and tinted windows. It bleeps twice as the hazards blink and the locks pop up. 'You really are a tart ent ya,' said Kyle, while reaching for the handle of the passenger door. They all climb in and strap their belts, with Rob as the last one to enter. He rocks his jaw from side to side and looks at Kyle sat next to him. 'You didn't have to hit me so hard,' he moaned. 'You could have just said.'

'Shut up, you tart, and get me to London,' said Kyle humorously.

Rob, who feels pissed off, puts on his belt and revs after dipping the clutch and putting it in first gear. He glances at Kyle one final time, hoping that this time he is going to scare him. He then wheel-spins for a moment and rapidly shoots around the corner, leaving an instant dust trail after the deep growl from the roaring engine quickly fades into silence.

CHAPTER 12

America's main gaming hall is still full with thousands of young drivers who are all talking amongst themselves while eating lunch. Many of them have left and gone back to their dorms or simply gone about their day however they normally would, exercising or training or even in the games room playing snooker or ping pong.

Lucian is still in the enormous facility along with many others, waiting to hear something from Peter. He has remained there since he first left and refuses to leave through loyalty alone. Having waited so long, he is moments from giving up and heading to his room but the large screen begins flickering again and immediately snatches his attention. After a short while, the screen reveals a picture of an old man with white scruffy hair; his short white beard looks perfectly groomed and he is wearing a freshly cut grey suit.

'Is it on?' he repeatedly asked, followed by him suddenly standing tall while straightening his tie and clearing his throat.

'My name is Marcus Chapson,' he said proudly. 'I am head of security for the grounds of the White House and I am pleased to announce that the president has allowed us to display full footage of his home of residents. Ladies and gentlemen, what you are about to see is America's technology at its best. As I speak to you now, Mathias is on approach to the White House and the president is there. But before any of you run off,' he said, stopping some of them from darting to their gaming chairs. 'Nicki is there and I assure you that the president is in good hands, in fact, her creators are so certain of her, they want everyone to witness it and enjoy America's response, so sit back, relax, and enjoy the show.'

The screens flick through different images and different rooms all over the building, showing nothing but emptiness and silence throughout.

The hall gradually fills with more and more gamers and almost immediately becomes cramped in there. Lucian is standing somewhere in the middle, getting shoved and pushed as the older gamers rush to the front for a better view. He refuses to take his eyes off the screen in the hope that this may have something to do with his best and most trusting friend. As the camera flicks through, it finally stops on an image at the front of the building that reveals the grounds from a bird's-eye view. The image changes again to the main entrance and focuses in on the collapsed wall. In front of it, is a thirty-foot drone, standing fast, and ready to fight.

'That must be Peter,' said Lucian cheerfully, while joyously pointing at the screen and being told to shush from an older gamer standing behind.

William is sat in his luxurious gaming chair with his eyes fixed on the large screen in front of him. He is holding a fragile grasp around his joysticks waiting patiently for the arrival of Mathias, only he is beginning to feel a bit more relaxed than he should as he buries his finger deep in his nose and wipes it on his shirt. His drone has a built-in radar that can detect any unusual activity for miles out, and operates in a 360-degree radius. It is displayed in a small box at the top right corner of his screen and not to his surprise, it begins flashing, as a small red dot appears from out of the blue. It is speedily moving towards the centre and shifting at phenomenal speeds. His drone sends his perfect vision forward and locks on to the target in question. After a short moment of intense focus from the super-strength lenses, he locks on to Mathias and watches him in the far distance drop in from high above, landing approximately six miles away from the White House. William shuffles deeper in his seat and nervously straightens his back.

'Here we go,' he said to himself in excitement. He begins walking in the general direction, feeling happy that he has a minute or two, so he can emotionally prepare himself for possibly the battle of his life, only he stops in his tracks as Mathias has appeared not eight hundred yards away on the grounds of the White House and is calmly walking towards him.

'Creepy fucker,' he said, sounding slightly alarmed.

William continues walking towards him and gradually increases his speed. He moves faster by the second until he is running at full pelt, while Mathias casually struts and appears unfazed by his presence. William grips his controls and prepares himself for glory. He is about to seize his moment and finally destroy Mathias, believing deep down that when he does, he will be renamed as the Commander of Gamers.

Mathias can feel the world moving beneath his feet, he can feel the natural powers that travel through the Earth, and can feel the presence of all kinds of life from all around him. He places his foot for the first time on the welcoming green grass and every stem all around him leans in his direction, creating a shape that expands outwards like a slow-forming crop circle, and the effect is repeated after each step he takes.

William grips his controls tight, making his knuckles appear white and his concentration is fully focussed on beating the most important opponent of his entire career.

'Now you're gonna get it,' he threatened, before diving head first to destroy him after every mechanism had been set to attack mode. Mathias reveals his open palm and continues as though his opponent is not even there.

To William's surprise, and in the blink of an eye, his drone is pulled apart, severed, and detached as every nut, bolt, wire, and reinforced plate shoots past him on both sides and scatters in two equally divided piles of useless parts. William's screen suddenly switches off, leaving a blank screen in front of him.

'What?' he barked. He immediately starts flicking it on and off in the hope that it may have been simply some sort of malfunction

'No no no, this can't be happening,' he panicked, before finally giving up. He rips off his head set and angrily slings it at the wall, shattering the small glass lens on impact. He aggressively jumps from his seat and begins pacing up and down while stomping his feet like a spoilt brat and gripping clumps of his own hair from the undeniable frustration that he is unable to express.

Lucian glances around at his fellow gamers in a confused manner and can see many of them pulling the same expression and shaking their heads, feeling baffled.

'Something's not right here,' said Lucian, as the few gamers in earshot that heard him agreed and nodded. 'Peter's not that stupid, he's smarter than that.'

They continue watching as Mathias cautiously approaches the large shattered hole in the White House wall and he carefully steps through the unsettled dust and spraying water that crosses his path from both sides. He immediately scans all around him for any signs of movement but the entire building seems abandoned, which is forcing his curiosity to become more aroused by the second. A spark from beyond the next wall that is also barely standing grabs his full attention. He is drawn to it immediately and proceeds with caution, as he edges round the corner and is faced with nothing more than what remains of a huge drone that has been savagely torn to pieces.

Satisfied there is no threat, he heads for the stairs, sending his amazing vision through the walls and scans each room he passes like an x-ray. He spots a tiny camera in the top corner turn slightly, while the miniature lens adjusters twist from side to side and focus in on him, creating a sharp display of his face that purposely makes him aware he is being watched. He glares at the camera as it zooms in even closer, revealing his glazed eyes that appear perfectly focussed, as though he is staring through the actual mechanism and gazing into space. He closes his eyes tight for a moment, before flicking them open. His eyes are white all over, as though they've rolled back in his head, followed by tiny bolts of electricity darting towards the centre of each one and gradually, it creates a pupil made of electricity that slowly expands.

His sight enters the lens and turns blank, yet in his mind, he is travelling at warp speed through the electrical system and can see through every single camera located in the White House.

While retracting his vision, a single room on the top floor alerts him, right before his neck jars backwards and staggers slightly, as though his mind was thrown back in to his body, so he immediately darts for the room in the hope that he may have found Tom.

As he nears the suspicious room, a heartbeat becomes more noticeable to him. It pumps more powerful and true than he thought possible and has never known a human heart to function like it. He scans the room on his approach and can see a beautiful woman in a long blue dress sat on a chair with her legs elegantly crossed.

He finally reaches the large white door and stands proud, feeling certain that he is prepared for anything. He glances to his right and left down the empty corridors to ensure that this is not a trap and cautiously proceeds by grasping the gleaming golden handle.

To his surprise, a sexy black and leather knee high boot with a five-inch heel bursts through the solid oak door and smashes him in the chest. He is forced back at phenomenal speed as he crashes through four solid brick walls and finally stops dead against the reinforced edge wall of the building.

Large cracks expand from the point of impact and instantly spread from the centre to every corner, leaving a spider web effect behind as he drops to the floor. He lands on his hands and knees feeling mildly frustrated and glares at the floor in suspense while he tries to understand what just happened

'Okay,' he said, under his breath, in a competitive tone.

He calmly stands up and dusts himself off; only his attention is caught when he spots a faint outline of a woman staring at him through the row of man-sized holes and can barely make her out through the thick unsettled dust. He narrows his eyes as his unique focus penetrates the small cloud so that even the colours of her eyes are bright and her face is perfectly clear.

'Nicki!' he muttered, as his eyes widen and jaw drops. 'It can't be.'

She slowly turns and walks away, disappearing behind what is left of the wall, leaving Mathias stunned and lost for words. His heart begins pumping fast and increasing by the second, which sends a sharp and unbearable stain from the burning nerves that continuously spasms up his spine and throughout his entire brain.

He tries harder than ever to fight his pain, but even with his formidable abilities, he cannot deny his emotional attachment to her. Unable to fight the pain any longer, he drops to his knees and his veins swell all around his body, as his blood is violently rushing through him faster than it should.

He presses his open and clammy palms either side of his head as his temples are pulsating under immense pressure as the veins that cross them have now swollen to almost three times the size. Beads of sweat begin forming from head to toe and almost instantly they begin dripping off the end of his nose and chin.

A door to his right in the unfamiliar room bursts open with a loud and sharp crack that surprises even him. His reaction is extremely slow as he tries desperately to stand; only pushing through the unforgiving pain barrier is so unbearable that it is physically impossible for him to so.

She is standing in the doorway composing a typical fighting stance with her good foot forward and both fists tightly clenched. She casually walks towards him and stands over him in a threatening manner, satisfied that he is now immobilised.

He struggles greatly to look up at her and can barely keep his eyes open through the salt water streaming down his pail cheeks.

'Well that was easier than I thought it was going to be,' she sniggered.

'What have they done to you?' he mumbled, while gasping desperately for air.

She holds eye contact but unexpectedly looks very confused and feels kind of sorry for him; however, she cannot allow herself to feel or care; it would go against everything she has trained to become. She fights off any urge to feel or care and ends the moment with a swift kick to the side of his head. She moves faster than Mathias had ever thought humanly possible, but for him, the pain has gone as he descends into darkness.

CHAPTER 13

A magnificent containment ship has pulled in for dock at an unfamiliar, native land. The green fields spread for hundreds of miles and the forestry is dense, wild, and natural—a clear view of Mother Nature at her very best.

William has wondered for hours through the long corridors inside and has not encountered a single person but to his surprise a white door by his side is pulled open from the outside by a man dressed in a white sailor suit. The sun is bright and hot, forcing Peter, who is standing in the doorway, to shield his eyes, for a moment before gazing at the beautiful view that immediately has his undivided attention as never before has he seen such wondrous landscape. He has absolutely no idea what is going on and feels more confused and lost than ever before. Several reasons cross his mind, is this a test? Or have I received a promotion somehow? Or even, have I been kidnapped? But nothing in particular is a reasonable explanation. He decides to just go with it and exits politely, as the man in white welcomes him ashore. The dry air fills his lungs as he inhales deeply as the nerves he is withholding are becoming a struggle to hide.

A long wide and grey slope is attached to the docking station in front of him, and at the bottom is a large group of young gamers, twenty or thirty to be precise, most of them Japanese but generally mixed of all races and they are all patiently and enthusiastically awaiting his arrival.

He begins walking towards them and glances over to his side; while doing so, he witnesses the containers being unloaded by huge drones, each one is carrying a large metal unit and some carrying two. As they reach the bottom, everyone around stands in silence; he catches eyes with most of them, but they all look just as anxious as he does. A small Japanese boy at the front with short black hair and thick round glasses smiles and welcomes him with a handshake.

'It's a pleasure to meet you,' he said, sounding typically foreign. 'I'm Cailan.'

Peter shakes his hand and is lost for words. His adrenaline begins to ease and finally he gains the nerve to speak. 'I'm Peter,' he replied.

'We know!' he said proudly.

Kids from the back are all trying to stand taller than each other to get a look and see if it's really him.

'You're . . . kind of a celebrity around here,' he said with a smile.

'Why?' he eagerly asked.

He assuredly places his hand on his back. 'Follow me,' he kindly asked. 'I'll explain everything on the way.'

He follows them, yet still feels he shouldn't, but his curiosity has always got the better of him and he simply can't deny that he is excited about potentially being famous.

'Do you know a gamer called William?' Cailan asked, hoping to find out first hand if the rumours are true.

'Yes,' he replied, 'of course.'

'Well, we have challenged him with our best and brightest and none of us ever got close enough to him to cause any damage, I mean, it's like he is always one step ahead and doesn't miss a single move . . . honestly . . . he's the best gamer I have ever known, and everyone here would say the same . . . but . . . then you came along,' he said, with passion in his tone, topped with a hint of envy.

Peter looks at him and can see the admiration in his eyes as he glances around at all those following in front and behind and suddenly feels welcome in a way that he can't explain.

'What's it got to do with me?' he asked.

'You beat him in a one-on-one battle in the church yard,' he replied, which suddenly catches his full attention.

'How do you know that?'

'We watched the whole thing . . . we saw you rip him to pieces like he wasn't even a challenge for you . . . it was quite amazing, my friend.'

They walk for a while longer in silence, as Peter feels he shouldn't be asking too many questions, so he is left with nothing else but to glance around in discomfort and simply take in the beautiful views all around him in amazement, as he's only ever seen such images in magazines.

'Stop here,' said Cailan politely.

They stop next to a short tree in the middle of a strange-looking area covered in dry soil that looks overly suspicious. A large round circle appears on the surface all around them as the ground slowly and steadily sinks beneath their feet and gradually gets faster on the unexpected descent. They drop through levels of all kinds, each displaying a different field of technology. Some are working on gaming chairs with a style he has never seen before, others are creating drones and working on new weaponry and all other kinds of gadgets, the likes of what he never knew existed. They finally reach their floor and come to a sudden stop. One of the children opens the only door and walks through, holding it wide for the rest of them to enter. They all flood through and do so in an orderly fashion, only a select few stay behind Peter, knowing that he still feels apprehensive about continuing.

'It's okay, Peter,' said Cailan. 'I promise you there is no danger here . . . trust me my friend.'

Peter reluctantly walks through, followed by the rest of them who refuse to leave his side. He is led down a long and dim-lit corridor, with doors all the way along both sides and made of solid steel in a gun-metal grey. The entire structure has a kind of eerie feeling that he can't explain, yet considering everything so far, he feels obliged to follow on.

At the opposite end, there are large and matching double doors that open automatically on their approach. When he enters, he looks around yet another large facility, but there are pairs of drones scattered all around, padded with protective sparing gear and fighting with each other. The first thing he is drawn to notice as the commander of gamers is that no effort is being made and everything is so basic. Where he comes from, training is pushing your drone to its full ability, aiming to achieve the impossible; training is taking yourself out of your comfort zone, so that when the time comes you can always be

ready, but it is not his place to say and he's never really been too quick
to judge.

As they near the opposite end, they approach a matching set of
double doors. A few of the young lads have wondered off to continue
their work, but many of them happily remain by his side, each feeling
more than honoured to be accompanying him. They walk between
two giant square platforms, with three ten-inch-thick solid metal
chains all the way around; they appear to be massively oversized
boxing rings, and from this moment on, he knows where they are
going wrong.

The doors swing open revealing hundreds of gaming chairs
laid out equally across another vast but dark facility, the chairs are
immobilised and in the upright position, they look to be very inviting,
and part of him is desperate to play. He continues looking around
and spots a dark-shaded alcove over to his right and swears he can see
a figure of someone tucked inside. 'Who's that?' he asked, pointing
at the shaded area that looks suspicious. Cailan glances over at the
shadow in question and in a respectful manner, he immediately begins
to back away. 'Okay, people,' he said happily, 'it's time for us to leave.'
He places his hand reassuringly on Peter's shoulder before nodding
assuredly. 'Peter needs to talk to . . . the boss.'

He shows them all out before leaving the facility and as the last to
follow, and Glances at Peter one final time before the doors close.

He turns to look again at the dark corner and narrows his eyes.
Nothing is said for a moment, but for him, he is starting to feel scared
again. The suspicious character finally steps forward into the light with
open arms, only Peter finds himself lost in sheer confusion, staring in
the eyes of Natalia. 'You?' he said in shock.

'Welcome to the rebellion!'

Peter puts both hands up in front of him as though backing away
from a physical conflict, revealing his clammy palms while shaking his
head in awe. 'Whoa whoa, wait a minute,' he snapped. 'What's going
on? I mean . . . what are you doing here?'

There is a small desk just at her side, with a white stool either end.
She pulls one out and reaches her open hand out towards it, inviting
him politely to be seated, only he doesn't move.

'If you give me this chance to explain,' she hopefully asked. 'I promise . . . you will understand.'

Given there is no real reason not to trust her, he decides to give her the benefit of the doubt, so he cautiously sits down and does so in kind of a dainty manner, as now his curiosity is tearing him to pieces. Overall, he is more interested in knowing why they would go through so much trouble to get him there.

'My gamers,' she continued, while pulling out the other stool and sitting down, 'have fought and fallen over and over again. We gave our best, but nothing seemed to work . . . but then you came along,' she said in disbelief, 'and I assure you . . . that when you showed up . . . you arrived with quite a bang, and you certainly lived up to your expectations.'

He simply stares at her feeling slightly stunned and doesn't know what to say next.

'You beat William,' she said boastfully.

'Yes but. . .'

'Nothing else matters,' she interrupted. 'We have seen what you can do,' she leans forward and rests her elbows on the desk while interlocking her fingers and filling her lungs in preparation to speak. 'We want you to train us,' she asked.

He sits up straight and leans on the table in a sort of cocky manner before continuing.

'And this is why you kidnapped me?' he asked, sounding more intrigued than anything else.

'Yes,' she replied, after nervously filling her lungs once again.

'Does anyone know I have gone yet?'

'Only one person knows that you're missing . . . and where you are.'

'Lucian!' he immediately answered. 'But I can't believe he wouldn't tell me about this,' he disappointedly whined.

'Try not to look at this as betrayal of your friendship,' she advised. 'That boy admires you more than anyone else.'

'Really?' he flatteringly asked.

'Yes, Peter . . . your entire fan base is run by him.'

He raises his eyebrows in disbelief and leans back while placing both hands on his head, trying to decide if he feels cheated or honoured.

'He is the reason you are as famous as you are. He is the reason you are an icon to us . . . so you see, Peter . . . this is why you are here.'

His eyes drop and he hopelessly gazes at the table, he slowly begins losing himself in deep thought before Natalia leans forward in to his view to gain eye contact in a hopeful sort of way.'

'Teach us, Peter,' she quietly begged, 'lead us.'

After an intense moment of consideration, he shakes his head and stands up to leave but after realising he is possibly stranded thousands of miles from what he recently called home and with no way of getting back without help, he stops in his tracks and glares down at her.

'I'm not what you are looking for,' he argued 'what you need is a miracle.'

She holds eye contact and believes deep down that she is doing the right thing and nothing is going to change her mind. 'Well you're the closest thing we have,' she said, sounding as though she is beginning to lose hope.

He turns to walk away, only he can't deny that he is curious about all this. He stops in his tracks once again and gazes at the floor, while throwing the pros and cons back and forth in his head. He deeply fills his lungs and exhales loudly. He cannot believe he is even considering this, let alone doing it. He turns and faces her once again with narrow eyes and Natalia finds herself able to look now where else but directly back at him. He finally agrees by merely nodding his head with an unnatural grin. 'I just have one question,' he quickly asked, stopping her from rising from her seat and immediately locking eyes with him for the last time.

'Why did you kidnap me?'

'Apparently,' she replied, 'and from a reliable source, you were going to be hard to persuade.'

'And who said that?' he snapped. Feeling the need to defend himself.

'Who do you think?'

He right away thinks of Lucian and many emotions run through him at the same time, deciding if he's mad at him or just disappointed, or does he even feel thankful for forcing him to take this leap he so craved. 'How long do we have?' he promptly asked, suddenly sounding like part of the team.

'My Intel has informed me that the president has dispatched over half of his army to England and that they are all travelling by boat, and although the boats are fast, it's a long way to travel, so I would say we have a day, maybe two.'

'What am I supposed to do with two days?' he whined.

'Like I said . . . you're the closest thing we have.'

After a moment of further consideration, he finally agrees and at least knows now what he has to work with. 'Okay,' he said confidently, 'we had better get started.'

'Thank you,' she said proudly, with appreciation in her tone. 'Everyone is dying to meet you.'

She pulls out a small flat microphone that looks more like a mobile device and holds it up to her mouth while squeezing a little black button on the side. 'Gamers,' she announced, as her voice echoes through the entire facility. 'We have Peter . . . I repeat . . . We have Peter . . . all drivers report to the games room . . . we've got work to do.'

Her words alone were inspirational enough to spread cheers across every level in the facility. She looks at him with admiration in her gaze and smiles, feeling thankful for his time and trust.

'So what now?' he asked, as he steadily becomes more nervous by the second; he suddenly feels the pressure of living up to this powerful name that has spread through the rebellion all around the world and has made him feel more honoured than ever before.

'Just wait here,' she said politely. 'They will all come to you . . . and trust them, they are good people.'

CHAPTER 14

The president is waiting patiently in his underground bunker. It is built with ten-foot-thick reinforced walls and a lead lining that makes it invisible from radar scanning, it is fitted with a matching door that is hidden in the wall, only this entrance is invisible to the naked eye and drops into the floor for entry.

He is sat on a thick metal chair with a black, leather soft padded cushion. He is simply twiddling his thumbs and appears to be lost in deep thought but feels overall safe in this impenetrable room that can only be located by those who know where it is.

All the lights and electrical equipment in there suddenly switch on and immediately alarms him. He quickly sits up straight and looks around in shock, hoping that Nicki is still alive and it is safe for him to leave, as he was assured that he would remain safe and she would not be beaten by Mathias. A monitor in front of him flickers for a moment and finally reveals an image of Nicki's face. 'Mr President,' she stated. 'If you can hear me, sir, everything is safe. We are in the torture chamber and Mathias is restrained.'

He decides that he has no choice but to trust her, before walking towards the corner of his bunker and out of nowhere a small hollow square at head height opens up, no bigger than a ten-pence piece and he cautiously leans towards it like staring through a secret peep hole. A tiny sheet of laser projects out in a vertical line and scans his eye from one side to the other. The miniature machine inside then quickly retracts and switches itself off as the hole completely disappears. The shape of a door moulds on the smooth surface in front of him before slowly dropping in to the floor. As he walks through, the walls around him are so thick that the exit is almost a tunnel, so with caution he proceeds forward, and does so around each corner he approaches.

The gamers are all watching closely as the president warily continues through the building and finally reaches an elevator on his right that opens without command. He slowly enters as the doors suddenly and unexpectedly close behind him with a loud bang of metal against metal that makes his heart skip a beat. He nervously edges away from the doors and to his surprise the descent begins, it doesn't last long but the feeling itself is almost unbearable for him regardless of its durability. It promptly comes to a sharp stop and without any command at all the doors open in front of him. His heart is racing as the adrenaline inside is becoming uncontrollable, forcing his knees to feel weak, leaving him unstable on his feet and he involuntarily gulps before exiting the elevator with a slight wobble in his step.

Nicki is patiently awaiting his presence and welcomes him with a very formal greeting. She is standing tall and proud with her hair beautifully straightened over her lifted roots, and even after dragging Mathias's limp body all the way to this creepy room, she still looks fresh and perfect; even her long shiny blue and fitted dress is as good as brand new with not a single mark or scuff.

The room is shadowy and poky and lit by the dim glow of open flames rising from small round concrete bowls that are each sat in the open palms of metal hands that appear to be protruding through the old-fashioned brick walls right the way around. The floor is rough, bumpy, and damp, cold beneath their feet and grubby in the corners with a thick layer of dust that has settled on everything.

In front of him is a large desk that looks a bit like a huge podium stand with all kinds of buttons that are glowing in different colours and fitted in all different shapes and sizes. On the far right are four long threatening levers that display thousands of volts that dramatically increase after each notch they pass. Overall, everything is presented to intimidate and appears to be in perfect working order. He calmly lifts his eyes and glares in the direction of the far wall, only to find himself peering directly in the heavy eyes of Mathias.

He is suspended in mid air by thick heavy chains, with his wrists and ankles locked at the joints; both hands and feet are clamped tight and firm inside balls of solid, reinforced metal that makes it impossible for him to even wiggle his fingers and toes.

The president grins in disbelief before cockily reaching his open hand out towards the beautiful woman to formally introduce himself. 'You must be Nicki.'

'Mr President,' she replied while shaking his hand before standing tall and feeling honoured to even be in his presence. He curiously turns and walks around the control unit and stands directly in front of Mathias, admiring the restraints that appear to be inescapable. 'How did you capture him so easy?' he asked while gripping the thick chains to test the tension.

She finds herself feeling flattered and can't help but release a very subtle gin. 'It was simply a matter of persuasion, sir,' she replied exalted.

He turns and stands at the side of Mathias and arrogantly glares in Nicki's eyes before gripping a handful of the dry and dirty hair of Mathias. He yanks his head back hard and fast, trying his hardest to look intimidating.

At this point, Mathias can barely hold his eyes open any longer and his body is almost as limp as a corpse. Out of nowhere, his veins appear in dark blue all over his body as though his skin is becoming transparent somehow. His mouth is dry and has never felt so sore and his lips are cracked all over, covered in clotted blood that portrays darker against his pale skin.

He slings his limp head forward and once again stands in front of him, after a moment of silence from the sheer tension he snobbishly shoves his face to the side before slowly turning and walking away. 'You have caused me nothing but trouble,' he bitterly stated. 'So what do we have for this waste of air?' he asked, suddenly sounding enthusiastic.

'I'm glad you asked, sir.'

Sounding boastful, she continues, 'The restraints are connected to an illegal power point that up until recently was presumed as defective, thanks to a special few in the gifted school. This forbidden power line is once again active, it has the ability to contain and pass millions upon millions of volts through a single unit and would assuredly destroy thousands of our own drones with nothing more than a short sharp connection.'

'Why don't you just shoot him?' he interrupted.

'I'm afraid bullets don't work, sir, believe me, Mr President . . . I've tried but nothing like that seems to affect him.'

'Nonsense,' he barked, before quickly pulling out a large black handgun from a holster hidden beneath his jacket. He instantaneously shoots him three times, twice in the chest and once directly between the eyes. He stops and is immediately drawn to Nicki after she delicately placed her soft and warm hand on his extended arm.

'Honestly, Mr President, there's no point in wasting perfectly good ammo on him,' she turns her body slowly in a titillating manner but holds her eyes on his for as long as she can before seductively leaning over the desk and arching her back to advertise her availability.

The president gazes at her from head to toe and finds that he is physically unable to tear himself away. She flicks her hair to one side, revealing her long and slender neck before grasping one of the levers, she wraps her fingers delicately around the silver rod and flirtatiously moves it up and down while softly rocking her body back and forth, divulging an intimate moan under her breath.

The president finally comes back to reality after sensing he is about to lose control and give in to his urges, as he is rendered powerless to sheer lust for her that he can't seem to contain any longer.

She looks at him once again and modestly giggles. 'Don't look at me . . . look at him,' she jokily voiced.

They both look up at the same time and she quickly snaps the lever down a notch as hundred thousand volts instantaneously pass through him. He slings his head back, making his neck crack and spasm; every muscle in his body is strained to full capacity and every bone and joint is placed under so much pressure that the flesh deep beneath his skin is tearing and splitting, forcing his bones to bend, almost to breaking point. In sheer distress, he clamps his jaw, forcing his teeth to grind as he growls from the unbearable agony.

The president poses an arrogant grin purely out of impatience, only decides that the pain is not good enough and the frustration is making him angry. He wants to see him die more than anything but the delay is getting more intense by the second until finally he snaps.

'We're not here to tickle him for fuck sake,' he snorted and aggressively barges Nicki, only she doesn't budge at all. He embarrassingly pretends he hadn't noticed and yanks all four levers down to almost three quarters of the way. At this point, all his limbs are conducting over three million volts at the same time and circulating his entire body in search of an exit. His heart is beating so fast that the chip in his spine is tremendously overpowered and is now glowing in a bright red from the heat, that should be melting through his brain yet amazingly it remains fixated and active.

The president watches intently and almost admires his courage but enjoying his pain nonetheless. He begins to feel a rush of satisfaction, only decides he wants to torment him a little longer before their final goodbyes. Nicki has stood at his side in silence, free from emotion and blind to sorrow, yet merely ignorant to regret, as her tech is unable to completely reject her human half. To her confusion, the president slowly and gradually decreases the voltage by egotistically clicking the lever rite down to zero, leaving Mathias unconscious. 'What are you doing?' she asked, for which the president glares at her with a threatening scowl. 'Is there a problem?'

'No, sir . . . it's just that he's not dead yet.'

'I know,' he snarled. 'I just think we should have a little fun.'

Through her body language alone, he can see that she is in complete disagreement but also knows she is powerless to divert him from the arrogance that somehow makes him happy, so he simply ignores her subtle beg to get this over with.

'Bring me the boy,' he demanded.

'Sir . . . I don't think.'

'I said bring me the boy,' he snapped.

She fills her lungs in discontent as a display of personalities that differ in many ways and clearly doesn't want to take part in whatever he has planned for him. Under duress, she gently pinches her earlobe and patiently waits in suspense for some kind of response.

'Yes, hello, this is Nicki. I'm with the president in the abandoned torture chamber and he has ordered the presence of the boy . . . make it quick.'

She ends the connection by once again pinching her ear and swiftly turns on the spot to face him. With her hands at her back and heels together, she poses a false smile with reluctance to participate in his sick games.

'How long?' he impatiently asked.

'About ten minutes, sir, give or take a few.'

'Okay,' he nodded, 'then we shall wait.'

'Mr President,' she subtly begged, 'I don't think this is.'

'I said we wait,' he angrily interrupted and fixates his eyes on hers with a glare of daggers that silences her.

'As you wish,' she gently replied in resentment.

CHAPTER 15

Peter is stood with his back to a large whiteboard covered in random doodles; he is facing a small room full of young gamers that each appear to have rank in command and has the full attention of each and every one.

They are almost crammed in discomfort, only the sheer respect and honour they have for this esteemed gamer is overwhelming for Peter, leaving him no choice but to overlook the admiration in their eyes as they intently watch their idol and study his each and every move.

He nervously looks around in fear of leadership but also with the discomfort from this unusual place that unexpectedly tore him from his comfort zone, then through the empty silence, someone from the back jokily clears their throat.

Now that his physical perspiration has become visible, he suddenly notices the shake in his breath intensify, which in turn makes it even harder to find his opening words, but through the stares, he locks eyes with Natalia at the back and she simply nods as a reassuring gesture.

To the surprise of them all, Cailan proudly stands up from somewhere in the middle of the group. 'May I say something, Peter,' he respectfully asked.

Feeling disappointed in himself for being too gutless to continue, he gulps from the anxiety and embarrassingly nods in return, unknowingly authorising him permission to speak.

'Thank you, sir . . . I just wanted to say that, well . . . everyone here admires you, sir, and we all understand that this must be very hard for you, we brought you here with trickery and deceit, but only through lack of other option.'

A few of them giggle in agreement knowing that he was in fact harder to apprehend than they originally expected, so after placing his fist against his heart, he ends his words of praise with hope and trust in his tone. 'Everyone here loves and respects you my friend, to a level you may never understand, so please relax and just be yourself because believe me when I say, that's the person we need right now.'

Cailan's words make him feel a bit more at ease, so he prepares to speak but is interrupted once again. 'Yeah . . . you've got this,' said another voice from the back.

After quickly throwing ideas back and forth in his mind, he finally reaches an angle and attempts to approach them as an equal as appose to a commander.

'First things first . . . your training so far has been used at a level of misguidance, so if you want to win this thing then we must intensify your method.'

'Excuse me, sir. . .' interrupted another voice in defence of his strategy. 'Our gamers have mastered the art of hand-to-hand combat and each of us have trained and perfected three different styles.'

'Yes, I know,' he agreed, 'but when I teach your gamers what they are really capable of, it will open a whole new world of gaming, they will realise their true potential . . . you see, what you're forgetting is there are no limits in this digital world. Your gamers have been held back by rules and regulations, but in this world of no limits, the one rule is . . . there are no rules and no repercussions; we are merely children playing so we must make them believe that it is in fact just a game. . .' realising he has stunned them to silence in surprise of his well-deserved knowledge, he confidently continues, 'this is the reason they use children . . . it takes the realism away and replaces insanity as entertainment. The last thing you want is drivers sat in gaming chairs because they have to be, they have to want to be. They will crave the rush and yearn for the hunt, but most importantly, they will discover their courage, and believe me when I say, that in a child, it's not that hard to find. With the help of everyone, we are gonna get this army battle ready to make our final stand . . . so what do you say we get started?'

Remembering they are on a very tight schedule, he quickly glances at his watch. Every one of them has been silenced by his words of wisdom, and without warning, applaud quickly spreads. 'There's no time for this,' he yelled, but no one listens, so with whistles and cheers, they proudly continue. The honour he can no longer hide is finally revealed to his audience as he suddenly cracks a smile and over the applaud he shouts at the top of his voice, 'Let's go and blow some shit up.'

'Yeah,' they all yell as they jump to their feet in a playful manner and virtually sprint for the door.

Peter is left standing in front of Natalia and like any child would he finds himself waiting for words of praise, only she remains speechless by his courage and simply gazes at him in shock.

'So what do you think?' he asked.

'The only words I can think are, well, your parents must be very proud,' she lovingly stated.

He immediately drops his eyes and slowly turns away, as though he's concealing shame or torment of some kind. Right away she feels his pain, but with good sense of awareness, her immediate reaction is to comfort the boy and raise his spirits.

'Well I'm sure wherever they are,' she gently continued, 'they would be very proud of you.'

'Thank you,' he quietly replied after releasing a slight whimper.

The difficulty of not knowing what to say next has silenced her once again, leaving her glancing around the now shady room in discomfort. 'So . . . are you ready to check out our drones?' she finally asked, for which a cheeky grin slowly expands across his face.

'In fact,' she continued, 'we have actually created a drone, especially for you' she gloated. The realism immediately grabs him as he excitedly stares in her eyes for more. 'And its creators believe . . . you won't be disappointed.'

Through shock, he continues maintaining a steady gaze, though struggling to hide the apprehension that is rapidly growing inside.

Pleased that Peter is now feeling happy and hopeful once again makes her more proud than ever that she was able to cheer him up, yet she remains astounded that this genius, this champion that everyone respects and loves is just a child.

For a moment, she attempts to understand the pressure of his position in command, as simply being a child is hard enough without this extra stress, so with a loving heart she cracks a smile.

'Come on,' she whispered, 'let's go and meet your drone.'

His mind suddenly and unexpectedly becomes cautious once again after a random thought arouses his curiosity, only her continual stare and posture of unquestionable certainty exposes her strong personality, which immediately reminds him she can be trusted.

'I just have one question . . . did you have anything to do with bringing down the giants?'

Her smile suddenly collapses and she immediately drops her eyes, only to slowly raise them in shame. 'Yes . . . the RCIs were actually our idea.'

'I don't understand, they were contained so, why did you give the president that power.

'I know,' she replied, 'but you must understand, living two lives has its perks, but it also has its disadvantages . . . I have had to watch first hand that sadistic psycho slowly destroy the very cause I fight for, being powerless to cruelty is heartbreaking, but if we can save that country, the country I love, that's all that matters to me . . . I regret my decision, believe me, but now we're here, and there's no running from it. I was always told to keep my friends close, but my enemies closer, though I never really understood that reference . . . until now.'

He continues searching her eyes for ridicule or deceit, but after seeing the shame and regret she is forced to live with, he finds himself feeling more concerned than anything else.

'I have to say,' she continued as an impulse to quickly change the topic, 'I'm very excited to see what you can do . . . it's a very exciting time,' for which she clenches her fists in celebratory manner. She then gently places her hand on his shoulder and leads him towards the door. 'You're gonna love your drone, and the other gamers are dying to meet you.'

After a short walk, they end up pacing side by side down a long and wide corridor. The high walls are a perfect white with not a speck of dust in sight and with no windows or doors all the way along, suddenly makes him feel slightly claustrophobic. The high ceiling is plated with unusual gleaming silver, with feature lights behind square sheets of glass, evenly spread from one end to the other. The floor is layered in a gun-metal grey, with a glasslike shine that creates a beautiful marble effect.

As they approach the white doors at the opposite end, they automatically open, releasing sharp burst of pressurised air and reveals yet another large room. This one is shaped hexagonal with work tops all the way around and random tools scattered on every surface. The rest of the room is completely clear, apart from a large, silver cylindrical structure that stands alone in the centre and fixed to the reinforced ceiling and floor with freakishly large bolts all around making the content of its purpose extremely well protected.

'What's that?' he curiously asked.

'That,' she proudly replied, 'is an impenetrable lock up, accessible only by those with rite to enter.'

He slowly and curiously creeps all the way around it in search for an entrance, only no visible access is blatant to the naked eye. After pacing the full circle, he stands once again at her side, so left feeling stumped, he crosses his arms for answers.

'Go ahead,' she taunted, 'touch it.'

For reasons he can't explain, a nervous rush spreads through his body and with caution, he slowly lifts his arm. His fingertips finally make contact before firmly pressing his clammy palm flat. Without warning, a loud and deep monotonous voice makes him judder in surprise and quickly snatch his hand in awe.

'Access granted,' said the computer.

The outline of a large square door increasingly manifests in front of him and disturbingly drops inwards, releasing a short, sharp burst of pressurised air. The huge frame divides down the centre and both halves steadily separate, sliding perfectly along the curved inside edge. It is filled with thick white mist that completely conceals the content and as the haze begins to clear, his eyes slowly widen as Natalia grins with pride 'Allow me to introduce . . . the Falcon'

The mist finally clears, revealing a jet black and chrome robot, with the general build no bigger than a typically proud athlete. After scanning it from top to bottom, relishing on the unique style and curves that complement the shape and posture, making this machine look far superior in comparison to the common style he has always worked with. No longer able to restrain himself, he slowly and cautiously edges towards it.

'It's so small,' he passionately expressed. 'How have they done this?'

For which Natalia raises her brows in a modest fashion, 'Wait till you see what it can do.'

'I have gamed with the best the world has to offer, and perfected the art . . . this is gonna be cool,' he grinned.

'Do you want to see your gaming station?'

His eyes immediately light up with joy, and although he appears calm and collected, he is suppressing the passion within that makes him want to jump and scream like a child on Christmas morning. He reaches out his hand and gently places it on the Falcon's shoulder, before speaking, as though talking to a fellow human being. 'Pleased to meet you, Falcon, I'm Peter, your driver.' He fills his lungs and expressively exhales.

Introducing himself to a mindless machine could be seen by many as insanity, but it's simply a tradition amongst gamers, something that so many would never understand, so he proudly continues, 'I'm looking forward to gaming with you my friend.'

Right at the very moment, he turns to leave, both eyes flash once with a very dim glow and he snaps his eyes back in amazement. 'Did you see that?' he quickly asked, only to be disheartened by her unfazed reply. 'Yeah,' she said calmly, 'I'll get our technicians to take a look.'

For only a moment longer, he curiously gazes in the empty transparent eyes that distort his wavy reflection, giving him a huge head and a tiny little body. After Natalia gently tugs his arm, he finally tears his eyes away and with Natalia urging him to move on; he is almost nudged out the door in matter of urgency. He glances back once more as the pressurised doors close behind him, sneaking one last peak before his drone is snatched from view.

CHAPTER 16

Squad three speedily dart around the huge water feature located at the main gates of Buckingham Palace, squealing the burning tyres from side to side to maintain control before briskly skidding to a stop and placing the front bumper millimetres from the gates dividing bar. The first thing Kyle notices are the gates, and why they look as though been repaired, as these high walls have never sustained any damage whatsoever.

'They repaired that well,' he said sarcastically. 'What happened?'

'It's a long story,' replied Kevin from the back.

Kyle immediately climbs out of the passenger door, moaning about Rob's insane driving. 'If I die because of your stupidity, I swear to god, I'll kill you,' he growled before aggressively slamming the door. Rob simply shrugs his shoulders and whines in a high-pitched tone: 'What did I do?' He looks at Kieran and Kevin in the backseat for a reply of some kind, only they are both wide eyed and stunned to silence, holding hands in the centre and the other with a firm grasp on the door. Their sphincters are squeaky tight and knuckles are glowing white, while gripping their exit in preparation to attempt moving 'bah bah' mumbled Kieran after attempting to speak before he was ready. Rob rolls his eyes and immediately feels unappreciated for his efforts, so after a loud sigh, he too climbs out in a huff, leaving them both in silence. Not a moment more passes before Kevin releases a long and blatant fart that is sure to leave a mark.

He looks over the top of the car and can see Kyle in the distance, standing in front of a royal guard who is refusing to allow them through. So with Kyle being Kyle, he waves his arms around in frustration and reiterates his rites in rank of command. The guard simply stares at him as blank as a board and doesn't move a single muscle, only a spot of Kyle's sliver lands in his eye, resulting in an irritating twitch that he's too proud to wipe away, but now with Rob sharing the frustration, he too walks over to explain the situation.

'Stop right there,' the guard demanded, but with a snort of derision he continues.

'Sir, I said stop,' he yelled, while snatching out a small handgun from under his jacket and with the other hand revealing the flat of his palm.

Kyle quickly grabs his gun and immediately liberates him of possession, before aiming it directly at the side of his head and firmly pressing it against his temple, leaving the guard stunned and speechless

'Now that I have your attention,' he said calmly, 'we really need to speak with Queen Margaret.'

'I believe you,' he nervously uttered, 'but I . . . I can't let you through.'

'What's going on out there?' asked a man's voice through his radio.

Rob's first instinct is to uncouple it from his belt and instantly press the small red button on the side, to announce their presence. 'This is squad three, we urgently need to see the queen.'

'Hold on a moment,' replied the voice, and after only a second or two, the gates begin to open. In an extremely cocky fashion, Kyle swiftly flicks the gun around his trigger finger and with a diminishing wink, he hands it over, for which the guard cautiously takes it back.

'See . . . no dramas,' he grinned.

'Follow me please, sir,' he embarrassingly replied.

'Pull it together, bitches. . .' said Rob, after climbing back in his car. 'We're entering royal territory again, so snap out of it you pair of tarts.' The engine roars to life once again, and he very slowly rolls forward behind Kyle as he fearlessly proceeds unarmed. The huge gates slowly close behind them, as Rob quickly pulls his keys from the ignition, leaving silence throughout the entire courtyard. They all cautiously climb out with a spur of hesitance, though Rob does his best to stand proud for his honour, his efforts appear wasted after watching Kieran and Kevin struggle to keep their balance with wobbly knees.

The queen is sat not two feet from her telly, with her unblinking eyes fixed motionless on the screen and covering her mouth in sheer terror.

A loud knock on the door alarms her as she judders and stares at Abdul with her hand on her heart. He slowly pulls the door open and Kyle immediately steps through, only he is forced to stop in front of him like a toddler to his daddy. 'Take it easy with her,' he warned, 'she's in a very fragile state.'

'And she couldn't be in better hands,' he replied.

Abdul cautiously opens the door and slowly steps aside to allow him access, only Kyle stops once again after seeing the fear in her gaze, as a single tear escapes her flooding eyes and as he steps closer for a view of the screen, he too is stunned in trance, with fast expanding pupils.

Two thousand ships almost a mile long are approaching the half way mark and headed straight for them, each loaded from deck to roof with highly charged and battle-ready drones. Every able driver of America's strength is grasping the controls and gazing at nothing more than the back of the drone stood in front.

After witnessing the giants as Britain's first shocking defence, every one of them are more skittish and jittery than ever as the dread of not knowing what they may be confronted with is more terrifying to them than anything else. Most of them are reluctantly seated, silently disputing why they must remain staring at a still picture in discomfort when they still have twenty-one hours before reaching their destination. In the eyes of their leader, they are all overlooking the fact that they are at their most vulnerable, only boredom to a child is something that creeps up without warning, so much so the excitement has run out and their attention is gradually slipping away.

Kyle finally tears his sight from the television and catches the queen's watery eyes. 'How long?' he asked.

'I am told, we have twenty-one hours before they reach our shores.'

With a heart full of hope, he fixates in desperation, praying to the gods for some good news. 'Mathias?' he asked, only to be daunted by her reply that is merely an uneasy shake of the head.

Charlotte promptly walks in with Gracie in her arms having a loving cuddle for comfort, pressing her warm cheek against her chest and she stares at the queen in disbelief, as all hope begins fading in the distance, but for a moment, nothing is said.

The rest of squad three enter the silent room; they avoid eye contact through the passing of Abdul's terrifying glare as he growls under his breath and once safely past they stand tall with their hands at their backs. Unaware of what's going on, they curiously glance at one another in confusion and shrug their shoulders for an update of some kind. Kyle fills his lungs and exhales aloud before filling them in, only the queen interrupts before he has chance.

'The full power of America's strength is heading for our shores.'

'Can we win?' asked Kyle.

She sits up straight in her recovery seat and drops her delicate hands in her lap before shamefully lifting her eyes at Kyle. 'Put it this way . . . he has sent one drone to every living person throughout the hole of England.'

'So what's he plan on doing?' Rob asked, for which Kyle immediately snaps. 'They mean to wipe us out . . . It'll be like Britain never existed.'

'Well what are we gonna do then?' he panicked, 'and where's Mathias?'

'We don't know,' snapped the queen.

Charlotte carefully leans over her and gently places Gracie in her arms for which she nervously snuggles in; right away, the queen feels a sudden sense of stress relief and finds that she is unable to hide the awareness of such a peaceful emotion. The physical touch of this amazing and powerful child is something she will always cherish and respect, in every way that makes her human. With a nervous gulp, she locks eyes with Charlotte and gently nods. 'It's time . . . the gatekeeper awaits . . . I can hear him calling me,' she said quietly, after fixating on the door like her prayers have just been answered. She wraps her bony fingers around the Phoenix with a tight grasp; the red ribbon hangs weightlessly over her white knuckles as she carefully lifts her feet over the chair's extendible leg rest before shimmying to the edge. Charlotte wants to help her more than anyone, only knowing her stubbornness is undefeatable, there's just no point, because when her mind is made up, there is no going back, so she finds herself helping her to her feet and making sure she is stable before letting go; Kyle also tries to help, after watching her back straighten with a click and a crack and wobbly knees. Victim to her own frustration, she finally stands proud and irritably pushes everyone's hands away in annoyance.

'I don't think you should really be moving yet, ma'am,' said Kyle, after snatching his hand away in awe.

'Oh tish tosh,' she grumbled, 'I might be old but I'm not dead.'

Her extremely posh voice makes the old saying sound humorous to them, but they hold back their grins and maintain solid composure while admiring her courage to continue.

CHAPTER 17

The president is panting, sweating, and growling with every gasp, from the continuous punching on the rib cage of Mathias. He is leaving no marks or no bruises, but can't deny that he is highly entertained. With one final combo of random strikes all over his body, he ends it with a final blow to the very centre of his face, forcing his neck to crack, leaving him staring at the dirty ceiling above with his mouth wide open.

The president swiftly tugs the sleeves of his shirt and sarcastically straightens his tie. 'Few more minutes,' he stated, 'soon it will all be over my friend.'

The air is warm, dry, and dusty; the burning flames in the palms of the surrounding statue hands have heated the room from top to bottom in a temperature that grows increasingly unbearable.

The door suddenly bursts open with an almighty crack and slams against the old brick wall behind, causing a downfall of dust and rubble from between the aged and tired stone. With great difficulty and tremendous pain, Thomas struggles over the threshold with a heavy limp, as the hot and dry heat stings the small cut under his eye. Nicki unexpectedly shoves him from behind; he desperately tries to stay on his feet, only he shamefully drops to his knees at the toe of the president's glossy and shiny shoes. He amusingly crouches down in front of him, balancing on tip toe, before aggressively grasping a large clump of his dry and matted hair, and cracks his neck back, forcing him to look in his cheerful eyes for which he finally cracks and sobs in desperation. The president sarcastically shakes his bottom lip with a derisive sniffle, before releasing his hair with a nudge. 'Pathetic,' he snarled. 'Mathias,' he yelled, making him slowly and painfully open his heavy eyes; he battles through the throbbing thump in his head as the severe pain is now too much for him to bare. 'I have a gift for you . . . hero'; he finally lifts his head and immediately locks eyes with Thomas. Right away his pupils dilate as his gaze widens with a shocking gasp. 'Tom,' he groaned, in the struggle for air. 'Is that really you?'

Tomas proudly attempts to stand with honour, in the presence of his idol and respectfully straightens his back as much as possible, to show no fear and prove that he will no longer cower. Mortified that the boy is that ignorant, the president kicks the back of his legs, forcing him once again to his knees, followed by a swift back hander to the face that sends him almost six feet across the hard floor. He immediately follows and repeatedly kicks him in the stomach, chest, and face, until Mathias shouts at the top of his voice, 'That's enough.'

He carelessly steps over the almost unconscious boy and purposely clips his head with the toe of his shoe, before marching over and stopping not three feet in front of Mathias and aims his index finger right between his eyes. 'I'll tell you when it's enough.'

Tom begins shuffling round on the floor, having not moved a muscle for the last few seconds. Nicki watches him struggle to his knees, only after a moment she finds herself feeling sympathetic towards him. She suddenly wants to comfort him and protect him, assure him that he will be safe from any more harm, only, realising her human half is screaming to escape, she rejects it and buries it deep inside to refuse any emotional attachment to another soul; thankfully she is alerted to a ringing sound deep in her ear that only she can hear and she pinches her ear lobe; for a few moments, she is silenced, listening intently to whatever is being said and she pinches it once again to terminate the connection 'Mr President,' she yelled, 'I think we may have a problem.'

'What now?' he snapped.

'William has returned, sir, but Peter is still out there somewhere.'

'What?' he panicked. 'Then find him,' he ordered, 'and bring him back—'

'But, sir,' she interrupted, 'he's off the grid.'

The immense heat circulating around the entire room is getting hotter by the minute as the glare from the open flames reflects off his oily skin. He glides his clammy hands down his face in frustration before once again frowning at Mathias. He stares back, but only after taking his eyes off Tom for the first time since they walked in.

'Do you know anything about this?' he growled.

Matthias simply grins in return. 'Having trouble with something?' he asked, with a dry and painful croak in his throat, resulting in the president losing his temper.

'My ships,' he shouted, after banging the ball of his fist on the desk, 'are hours from Britain's shores and my gamers need a commander.'

'We have William,' Nicki stated.

The president is well aware that William is a loose cannon and that his army doesn't really have the respect for him needed to play the role of commander, so not only is this deceitful but he has no other choice but to secretly reinstate him. 'Do I tell my gamers about this?'

'I believe this is best under wraps for now,' said Nicki.

'And how do I do that?' he asked.

'The gamers are hours from battle, distracting them now would be a big a mistake, so put William in Peter's chair, he will lead them, and they will follow.'

Too proud to agree that her idea may actually work, he simply nods. 'Where is William now?'

'He's in quarantine, sir.'

'Why?' he snapped. 'Remove him at once.'

'Sir . . . there has been a huge misunderstanding, it turns out that William destroyed Peter's drone when they were both sent to intercept Mathias.'

'Intercept him where?' he snapped.

'Here, sir,' she confusedly replied, 'at the White House, sir.'

He glares at her as the realisation of what's happened sets in. 'Natalia leads a mission to attack and bring down the rebellion.'

'But sir,' she interrupted. 'No one is aware of such a mission.'

'Is she here?' he growled. 'She's got some explaining to do.'

She drops her eyes in the discomfort of being the barer of even more bad news. 'I'm afraid she's off the grid too, sir . . . We think he may have been kidnapped, sir.'

'She took him,' he growled. 'You must find him, and bring him back.'

She immediately stands to attention and nods in acceptance to his orders. 'Consider it done, sir.'

'Now,' he said proudly, after clapping his hands once and rubbing them together in excitement, 'Let's finish off this waste of air.'

He threateningly approaches Tom who is crouched over on his hands and knees in agony, only the president once again grabs a handful of his hair, and drags him across the floor, making the boy squeal in yet more pain. Tom grabs his wrist to try and take the pressure off his neck, as the president carelessly lifts him to his feet and stands him in front of the control panel.

'Pull the lever,' he growled.

He looks up at Mathias who simply nods to tell him it's okay and to do as he is ordered to save himself any more abuse, only he doesn't move a muscle and silently refuses. The president's grasp on his hair tightens as he glances at them both, as witnessing this strong bond first hand, makes any further torment only too easy.

'Pull the lever,' he repeated.

Mathias can't bear to see him so horribly abused any longer, so with a begging gaze, he pleads for him to do it. With honour, he proudly straightens his back and drops his hands to his side, courageously holding his chin up high and once again point blank refuses. The president slowly turns to Mathias, as a wide grin slowly spreads across his creepy face; to Tom's surprise, he violently and repeatedly slams his head, face first into the solid wood of the control panel. With a terrifying growl of fury, Mathias strains using every ounce of power he possesses, he roars with exposed teeth like a lion to its prey and fixates on the president.

The glare from the surrounding flames reflects off his glazed eyes that are almost hidden beneath his deep and offended frown. Suddenly, the massive chains begin to creek, creating a rumble of echo that vibrates through the thick steel deep within the surrounding walls.

The shock of what's happening startles the president into thinking he may escape, so after dropping Tom's limp body in a heap by his side, he urgently slams the control to full power and is immediately forced to shield his eyes from the shocking brightness that could easily blind the naked eye.

The massive channels of immeasurable electricity cover his entire body from head to toe in a frantic search for an exit, repeatedly circulating through every muscle and bone, causing every single vein and nerve throughout to spasm. His flesh is heated to such high temperature that he glows like the bulb of a lamp that brightens after each passing second. His muscles are massively pumped and swollen to almost tearing point as his clothes slowly begin to burn away.

An intense crackling sound from the clashing blasts of electric quickly becomes unbearable to hear, forcing them both to cover their ears. 'How long will it take?' he shouted.

'Nothing can survive this amount of power,' she replied. 'It will be over soon.'

The president physically can't handle the brightness or burning heat any longer and the deafening crackling is quickly getting the better of him. He waits only moment longer, hoping to see the life slip away from his cold and empty eyes and watch his body fall limp, leaving him as nothing more than an empty shell, only it is all too much to bare. 'I'm going up,' he shouted, while pointing up at the concrete ceiling. Nicki replies by putting her thumb up and quickly covers her ears once again. 'Call me when it's over.'

She once again nods before his hasty exit, but no sooner does the door close, Tom slowly and painfully opens his eyes; with severely strenuous pain, he lifts his arm to touch the side of his nose, only immediately snatches his hand away and quickly inhales through his clamped teeth. The cuts and bruises from his eyebrows mouth and cheekbones are leaking with blood that almost covers his entire face. With great difficulty, he reaches his bloody arm up on the control unit, smearing his red handprint across the surface. He struggles more than ever to his feet, and with shaky knees, he pushes the lever down to zero with a brave growl. He stands as tall as he can, welcoming any punishment with a gladiator's glare at Mathias and proudly watches the massive bolts of electricity quickly reduce to a broken connection.

In a flash, Nicki barges him to the side, sending him almost ten feet across the dirty, dusty floor and once again leaves him unconscious; she grasps the lever to slam it to full power only to be interrupted by the croaky voice of Mathias that arouses the curiosity from her human side. 'Why are you doing this?' he pleaded. 'Do you really remember nothing?'

With a motionless gaze on the control unit, she finds herself stunned; the buttons and levers slowly become a blur in her perfect vision as her mind's eye steadily sinks in to a very real flashback; she is sat in dim and shady room in front of a huge open fire and to her shear surprise, Mathias is sat right next to her. They both lean in at the same time and passionately kiss, while he gently strokes her warm cheek with the gentle seductive touch of his fingertips. Her eyesight is suddenly restored as she stumbles back in confusion and fixates on him in a state of panic; a strong feeling that only a human can experience radiates through her entire body, forcing her caring heart to flutter and almost bring a tear to her eye. Mathias may have found his opportunity to attempt communication and speak with her on a human level, only before his chance to breathe another word; she snatches each lever to full power once again and immediately covers her ears.

CHAPTER 18

In a vast and secret base for England's main defence, fields and fields of British gamers are all sat at their stations, heroically waiting to begin training for the final battle, to uphold the freedom that this great country deserves. Each and every one of them are patiently gazing at a blank screen, simply staring at themselves in the suspense and excitement of what's to come; suddenly, the face of Peter appears and he immediately breaks the silence in a confident tone.

'Hello gamers . . . I am Peter, as you all well no, an enemy capable of tremendous devastation grows ever nearer and every move they make will leave a trail of carnage that will give even the bravest of you nightmares . . . I have been given twenty-one hours to train you all, and transform you into superior gamers . . . to do this, in the recreational sense, would take years; however, I believe we may have found a way to make this possible, but before we begin, I want you all to sit back for a moment and try to remember the games you used to play with your friends, remember the feeling of winning, remember the rush of almost reaching your goal and doing so with in a hairs fracture of total annihilation, remember the adrenaline moments before your win, or the anger in your veins as you fail within reaching distance of the very end. With aggression and determination, you will breed confidence and bravery, but to face the most horrifying opponent and do so with no fear and maintain your talent to assist a successful mission that could potentially save the lives of millions, doesn't just make you a champion . . . this makes you a god, a digital being of great importance, a protector of man.'

His moving words are so meaningful and so well said that a wide smile spreads across each and every one of their faces, leaving silence throughout the vast stretches of gaming ground. Peter waits just a moment longer; to allow them all to assess their talent and decide whether or not they have what it takes to continue.

'As you can imagine, there will be a lot of prayers sung tonight, so as a God, in the digital world, it is your mission, your destiny, to answer those prayers, So I ask you . . . Are you ready to become more?'

The cheers gradually begin and slowly get louder. 'Are you ready to become the gamers in history that saved their country? Are you ready to be the first to make a stand against a ferocious hoard of beasts that claim to be immortal?' The cheers continue getting louder, forcing him to shout to be heard. 'Then let's put their name to the test.'

A wild applaud of unimaginable respect roars throughout the tremendous domain of the rebellions hide out. The honour of receiving such an incredible welcome forces him to pose a grin; for him, this is the best feeling a gamer could ever wish for and now he's had a taste of this newfound celebrity life, he has already decided . . . he likes it. He simply appreciates the emotion for a moment longer, as the cheers very gradually begin to fade. He suddenly holds up a small object in front of the camera and immediately catches their attention once again. 'This chip holds a unique and exceptional game that we use to train beginners.'

Before the rumours of doubt have chance to spread, he proudly continues aloud, 'Ah but don't be fooled . . . this game also holds a secret, this secret will be revealed upon completion of your task . . . that is . . . to stay alive. For your own good, play this game with an open mind, and be sure to give it everything you've got, believe me when I tell you, and I must stress this . . . put your heart and soul into this game, and I promise you all . . . you will not regret it; the missions, fights, and challenges you will be faced with are impossible in the real world, so as a reward, the first of you to complete this task, will be assigned a seat at the head table as advisers of defence and strategy for this war . . . I will speak to you in a few hours; thank you for listening and enjoy your game . . . good luck champions.'

Without further delay, the screen turns blank, leaving only a red line repeatedly darting across the bottom; all gamers shuffle in their seats and grasp the controls after quickly placing on their headsets. A deep and monotonous voice that sounds typically robotic quickly draws them in to begin preparation for battle. 'Choose your weapon,' said the voice, followed by rows of 3D weapons, floating in front of them and each one repeatedly spinning for a full display of a vast choice of weaponry, ranging from huge and powerful fire arms, right down to armour piercing blades of all sizes. Some of the more confident gamers don't even choose a weapon and put faith in their combat skills to prove that is all they need.

Peter leans back on his seat and interlocks his fingers at the back of his neck, stretching like he's been sat down all day. Natalia has been stood right next to him throughout, watching every move he makes in astonishment and admiring the bravery and courage, to stand against everything he has ever worked for as a new and transformed gamer, who never would have thought for one second that he had that kind of motivation in him. 'So . . . ' he said, after releasing a groan of satisfaction, 'How was that?'

The shock by his unbelievable approach to the gamers has rendered her speechless, yet with nothing but respect, she easily finds the words of appraisal. 'Perfect,' she said quietly, before clapping her hands like an excited child and thoughtlessly firing question after question about this special game, 'Why is it special? Is this what you had to do? Is it going to work?'

Peter is left slightly confused but also quite calm considering what the near future holds; he wants to answer all her questions but too many has thrown him off, so he simply gazes at her as she natters on. Realising she hasn't stopped since first opening her mouth, she is finally silenced. 'Sorry,' she said shamefully, while dropping her shoulders and gingerly placing her hands in her pockets.

'That's okay, besides . . . it's nice to see that I'm not the only one under pressure.'

With a confused shake of the head, like searching for an answer to a shocking question, she pulls out a stool from under the desk and sits down on the opposite side. 'I don't think you quite understand your position,' she rests her elbows on the table and interlocks her fingers 'We have dreamed of this moment . . . we have prayed to the gods for an answer and after seeing our queen's true power that restored faith in Britain, it would be wrong not to defend such a precious gift . . . yes America was contained,' she sighed, 'and the world was slowly beginning to take back their self-respect, to finally make a stand as a country, but then that crazy son of a bitch found a way to break free, not only did he breach, but he obliterated those giants and shocked the world. So we took destiny into our own hands and I believe we found what we need. Don't you get it, Peter, you're the answer to their prayers. In their eyes you are god's messenger, it doesn't matter if you speak out of line or mess up somehow . . . succeed or fail, every single one of those brave gamers will love and respect you, simply for being here, you placing your faith in them has given them a reason not to give up hope.'

Peter stands up in deep thought and slowly paces up and down while tapping his bottom lip with the pad of his finger. 'How has the strategy been planned?' he curiously asked.

'We're going to hold the line and defend the boarders with ability and strength, we'll fight fire with fire,' she proudly boasted.

'But there's too many . . . they'll break through,' he panicked. 'They'll flood them like a giant wave of ocean water.'

She has no idea how to reply as being almost blind to America's true strength has left her searching for truth. For a moment, she watches him closely, silently praying that he is as intelligent and tactical as they all hope. She leans forward with a gaze of pride. 'So what do you suggest?' He immediately stops pacing and turns on the spot to face her. 'Does the Falcon have weaponry?'

'The Falcon,' she proudly smiled, 'contains fire arms way beyond what any of us have ever seen before, they're small and sleek and so accurate that it is revolutionary. Even without fire arms, it's the greatest weapon and it's the future of robotics, he is elegant by design but lethal in the right hands; it's swift, silent, and agile, far superior to any other modern tech, so with gaming abilities as . . . formidable as yours, makes the Falcon a supreme masterpiece. He was created by the greatest young minds of our time, and they are proud to have you as his driver.'

With honour, he embraces this amazing feeling, only part of him can't seem to comprehend what they claim to have accomplished, so this is something he must see, to believe.

'I'll need to familiarise myself with him, I may need a few hours.'

'Of course,' she understandably replied. Before leaving, she nervously clears her throat and asks the question that's been on her mind since the day he arrived. 'Do you think we can win this?'

He slowly lifts his eyes and very nearly lies to make her feel better, but then decides that honesty is the best rout, so he replies with heavy breath. 'Their numbers are massive, and their battle strategies are extremely effective. When I became their commander, I gave them responsibility; I allowed them to complete missions for me and placed my trust in them as gamers. Unlike William who simply wanted them all as bystanders while he reaped all the glory.'

'So you're saying you made them better?' she sighed.

'You're missing the point,' he interrupted. 'I was their commander . . . in fact I still am, only I never knew the importance until now. They follow me, and only me, without their commander they're a viper with no head. Unless of course they act as I taught them, in which case we should at least know their tactics.'

'So you're saying we could win?'

'All I'm saying is, with what I've learned in the gaming world, nothing is impossible, but the sheer numbers tells us otherwise. If we base this battle on math alone then I would say not in a million years, but if we are tactical, confident, skilful, and fight as a solid unit, then we should at least be able to hold the line . . . I guess what I'm saying is, it's about time you call on that miracle you have so much faith in.'

She shakes her finger at him in an educational manner. 'I'll have you know, some miracles have been known to come true.'

'Those . . . are very wise words,' he agreed, 'but who am I to say whether or not this will work. All I know is that we are here, and we have to be ready to fight.'

She proudly steps aside, revealing the door behind her. 'Do whatever you need to do . . . the floor is yours,' for which he nervously gulps and cautiously steps forward.

CHAPTER 19

In a gloomy and dimly lit corridor running through Buckingham Palace, the queen stands with her fragile hand resting delicately on the smooth Golden handle of her private quarters; at the very moment of stepping forward, she suddenly stands as still as the dead, startled as to why she can hear the roaring fire within.

She has a strong feeling about what could possibly be awaiting her on the other side, so after nervously filling her lungs, she shakily exhales before very slowly pushing open the heavy door. The glow from the high golden flames gradually lights her face as the thin crack steadily widens. She peeps through and notices the heat against her rosy cheeks before bravely and casually entering.

After gently closing the solid heavy door behind her, she slowly and cautiously edges around the corner, fixating on the roaring flames as they gradually come in to view. she steps forward into what she is led to believe is an empty room and is startled once again as the gatekeeper is stood in the centre and appears to be in a trance, gazing at the high and intense flames.

The huge body of fire is perfectly balanced with a solid posture. His huge hands are proudly at his side as his bulky chest expands and shrinks after each long breath. His flames are golden yellow and he has chosen to present himself to her with a faceless mask to avoid her fearing him as much.

The gatekeeper is well aware of her extremely curious personality, he knows she is simply amazed by all forms of life in general, but far more interested in the rare and unusual beings of life from all levels of bizarre, from the weak and defenceless, right up to the reckless and courageous or simply the exceptional beings, with freakish power and extraordinary capabilities, she is undeniably drawn to the unnatural and is proud to bear witness to such rare happenings in the world, that only a very lucky few will ever come across.

She has witnessed firsthand the extraordinary science of the unimaginable come to life after revealing a gateway, for mighty and supreme spirits to rejoin within their rotten vessels of flesh and bone, and rise once again as an army of living corpses, each with their own unique and astonishing past that deserves nothing less than respect.

In the unseeing eyes of those blind from truth, these beasts could be an instrument of God himself, or simply a lost soul that has been blessed or cursed with immortality.

All this excitement from recent days has flooded her mind with so many questions and has left her nothing but thirsty for more, so much so that she would kill for the truth, no matter how delightful or horrific it may be, only now she is stumped and has no idea where to begin. This woman doesn't fear death or defeat, or even sacrifice but more that her curious mind of intellect and fact will never be fulfilled with the wisdom of unknown knowledge that she so craves, knowledge that she desperately wants to understand. She has no idea why this makes her feel the way she does, but if it feels this good, what's the point in denying it.

She was always told that knowledge is power, only one thing she has learned in regards to this, is that knowing too much, could pull you deep in to an ugly or fatal world that you are not meant for.

With all of these possibilities floating in the midst, she proceeds with an open mind and secretly accepts whatever fate awaits her. She quietly steps back against the wall causing a very slight thump as her heel taps the oak wood around the edge. The gatekeeper instantly turns to face her, leaving a rush of fear spreading through her entire body as a terrifying gust of wind rapidly floods the room from behind the flames and instantly messes her clothes and hair. She nervously gulps before slowly and hesitantly stepping towards him, fixating on where his eyes would be and continues with a distressed shake in her breath.

She stops in front of him as defenceless as a child and looks up at the giant man of fire as he towers over her tiny and fragile body.

Nothing is said for a moment between them but the silence is strangely unbearable for them both. Finally, he steps aside, and with the burning palm of his open hand, he graciously reveals the massive flames within the hearth. She gazes into the blazing fire and bravely confronts the unknown with pride. The flames suddenly rise even hire, releasing a burst of alarming heat, but she doesn't move, she simply holds her head high while shakily filling her lungs, and to her surprise, the scorching flames gradually begin to decrease before her very eyes. It slowly shrinks smaller and smaller until finally, it disappears completely, leaving nothing at all but the fresh and unburned logs lying on the grid in preparation to become ablaze.

Suddenly, the keyhole behind lights up with a bright orange glow, as do the eyes of the Phoenix that she is proudly wearing around her neck, revealed by two sharp circles of dark red that penetrate her clothes. Upon seeing the key slot, the realisation immediately consumes her as the fear of facing the unknown truth grows ever nearer by the second, only this strange emotion has been unexpectedly replaced by a delightful and harmonious sense of awareness, for which she secretly thanks the gods in a silent prayer.

She pulls it out and raps her fragile fingers all around it in a protective manner; it feels hot in her clammy hand but she pays no attention at all. She tugs it to break the join of the ribbon before gazing up at the gatekeeper and he simply nods in agreement to her actions.

Now knowing what he expects of her, she proceeds forward and very carefully leans over the logs; she then reaches her arm to full stretch and places the Phoenix in the glowing keyhole. A loud knock and clunk rumbles all around them as the huge chains that run through the mechanism within the structure grind and crash continuously as the thick and heavy solid wall behind slowly begins to rise. Once fully opened, the gatekeeper calmly walks in, scanning the room from top to bottom before turning to face her and welcoming her in with a hand gesture alone. Without hesitation, she does what he asks, only immediately after crossing the threshold, a loud cluck in the wall startles her as it quickly but gradually drops behind, forcing her to dart forward in shock. In the moment of panic, she decides whether or not to dive through what remains of the shrinking gap but her hesitation has left her no choice but to remain trapped with the gatekeeper for which she skittishly looks up at him with an intensive stare but his reply is a mere shake of the head.

For good reason, she is finding it very difficult to put her trust in him, but very briefly looking back over everything between them she remembers, he has not wronged her yet, so as she watched the last few inches of daylight quickly decrease as the final beam of dusty light fades, leaving the secret room dimly lit through his golden flames and also in complete silence as though floating in outer space where sound cannot travel.

He turns away from her in a very curious manner, casually walking to the corner of the room, and with the tips of his burning toes, he gently touches the very rim of the concrete surface. To her surprise, a thin line of flames darts both ways along the edge of the cold hard floor like trail of petrol has been ignited. The fast-moving snakes of fire follow the jagged edges perfectly, lighting the dark and shadowy corners with a pleasant glow. The two ends finally collide on the opposite side of the room, for which the gatekeeper unintentionally walks towards her in threatening manner, making her step back in trembling fear and stumble over a small round stool.

After the gatekeeper takes a couple of steps towards his very nervous queen, an unexpected transformation begins; it starts with his feet as they slowly transform and reconstruct into what appears to be a very opaque figure of man. The astonishing effect continues up his long legs, cancelling out the intense flames as it gradually rises. A radiant shimmer of brilliant white follows in the shocking change as the last flames around his huge head finally vanish, leaving his entire body shining like an angel from the heavens above. He continues slowly creeping towards her and after each step he takes, he begins reducing in size.

The queen now has her back passed against the dusty shelves behind, with her clammy hands on the fragile spines of the ancient books. The suspense of not knowing what comes next has rendered her silent while she fearlessly holds her head high. The size difference is quite dramatic, leaving him approximately five and a half feet tall, yet holding a bulky and solid posture. He finally comes to a stop a mere couple of feet in front of her and stands as tall as he can, as any proud man would when confronted with his queen, but with no respect for personal boundaries, he taps his heels together and rests his huge muscular arms at his side.

Still with no idea what to expect, she presses her body even harder against the overcrowded bookshelves in a desperate attempt to put some space between them. Alarmingly, the flesh of a man impossibly manifests around his body, it starts at the centre of his back and gradually conceals the intense shine as it continues around his front and meets in the middle of his chest, followed by a dark grey suit that immediately imitates moments after, and finally completes the mind-blowing mutation as the breathtaking and wondrous effect conceals his head from back to front, giving him a full head of dark brown hair and a clean shaven face that appears surprisingly friendly. He looks down at his bare feet and wiggles his toes in a humorous fashion, for which a pair of dark black and shiny low-heeled shoes appear around his feet.

She is immediately drawn to his strangely caring face and after watching his sky-blue eyes sparkle, she cannot deny for even a moment that she is not attracted to him.

He had no intention of frightening her at all, so he gently bows and holds out his hand in a loving fashion. After a moment, she places her fragile hand inside of his and he very gently pulls her away from the hard wooden shelves behind.

With confidence and a general good style of clothes, he gently lowers her fragile hand to her side before charming her with his deep and husky voice that she could quite happily listen to all day long.

'Good evening, Your Majesty, please forgive me for startling you, that was not my intention.'

Stuck in a chance of sheer disbelief, she finally tears her eyes away from his and glances around the shadowy room in discomfort. 'Why are we here?'

What she has failed to realise is that he is admiring her with a similar gaze; he smiles at her before pulling out one of the small antique chairs and with honour he invites her to be seated. He respectfully admires her every move but tries hard not to stare as she gently lowers herself down on the fragile stool, hoping that it will hold her weight.

'We are here,' he stated, 'because there are matters at hand that must be discussed, but also I cannot risk another set of human eyes witness me in mortal form.'

'So why am I aloud to see you this way?'

'Because,' he replied, 'your heart, soul, and blood is royalty and pure, your spirit is filled only love and respect, even for your enemies.'

'But why have you . . . um well . . . you know?'

'I have chosen to present myself to you in this way, because this is me at my most vulnerable. I am weak and powerless. I did this to show you that I mean you no harm.'

He gently lifts his huge arm and gently caresses her chin. 'I am your friend, your ally. I am whatever you need, and I will defend this ship with every ounce of strength I possess . . . this boat will sink if it is not commanded with royal blood.'

'Ship?' she curiously asked. 'Boat?' for which he immediately chuckles. 'It's a long story, besides, even if I told you, I doubt you would believe it.'

She simply smiles at him before very nearly losing herself in his dreamy eyes, so after the realisation slaps her chops, she shakes it off. 'So . . . do you have a name?'

He places one foot behind and humorously rolls his arm at his front while bowing, making her giggle like a school girl and daintily cover her mouth. 'My name is sir Cedric Osmond,' he proudly announced. He looks up in her mesmerised gaze with his puppy dog eyes before continuing, 'And it is an honour to meet you, Your Majesty.'

He stands up and immediately catches eyes with her and for only a moment his mind is flooded with a lifetime of memories as he drops his shoulders in submission. 'Your family gene is so strong . . . the resemblance is amazing, I mean . . . you look just like her,' he whispered.

She has absolutely no idea what he is talking about but she is still flattered by his comment that suddenly makes her blush. 'Who?' she asked while daintily brushing her hair from her eyes, for which he proudly announces with a high chin. 'Queen Charlotte, she was married to King George the third, the first royal to be born of England.'

He chuckles as the memories continue filling his mind. 'He certainly left a footprint on this world, let me tell you, and as for Charlotte, well, I could tell you some stories about her.'

He humorously shakes his head as though his memories are happening right before his very eyes, leaving him silent as a single tear of joy rolls down his cheek.

The queen can see him falling victim to the power of emotional attachment from his human side and almost immediately feels the need to comfort him. Suddenly, the realisation of what she can see almost startles her. 'Ah,' she heavily breathed, 'you loved her.'

He weeps for a moment as all kinds of emotions flood his body, making him almost growl at her comment, but he manages to keep any regret or anger issues hidden deep inside and maintains a professional appearance before his honourable reply. 'With every bone in my body,' he snarled.

'I'm so sorry,' she said. 'I didn't mean to upset you.'

After shaking off any feelings that could potentially weaken him further, he holds his head high and proudly continues, 'Not at all . . . let me bring us back to the reason I called you.'

He pulls out the other fragile-looking chair and carefully sits down opposite her, 'We have arrived at a very delicate time,' he sighs heavily. 'As you are aware, your enemy is on approach and is growing nearer after each passing second. We know that this will be a very difficult time for you, and to defend these lands with a military strike alone would be a battle for which you have very little success. However, there are many forces at work here. . .'

Her eyes widen as she suddenly begins to look hopeful once again, but then Cedric continues, 'It pains me to tell you that at this point we are forced to place our faith on humanity.'

'What are you saying?' she panicked.

He shamefully fills his lungs and exhales loudly. 'I'm saying that this is a battle of which we are not permitted to intervene.'

In shear disbelief, she slouches back on the creaky chair and gazes hopelessly in his eyes; her mind is suddenly lost in wonder as to how they are going defeat such a great and powerful enemy alone.

'Look,' he said politely. 'The human race has rapidly progressed, but not for the greater good. Your strength and weapons as a species are in fact your technology, from which you have created a certain kind of machine and freely given it capabilities way beyond your control. These machines began as a mere imitation of life. You then made them your help, which in turn made you lazy, and I find it very coincidental, that once you became too reliant on them, that was the point they became your weapons, and now your race has become reliant on a system, a manmade system, that has the ability to make its own decisions. From the advice of any gods that have ever walked this land . . . you must take a step back from technology. If this is not followed, the consequences will undoubtedly be catastrophic . . . this could be as serious as the complete annihilation of mankind.'

She listens intently to every word that is spoken and doesn't take her eyes off him for even a second, while he shares his priceless knowledge.

'Every single one of you knows that something isn't quite right about the world, only no one can seem to put their finger on the problem. Those that have come to this conclusion believe it with every bone in their bodies, but they have all become so reliant on technology that now, you could not function without it and for some strange reason that only your race will ever understand, you are allowing it to continue.'

'So your saying that the created will destroy the creator.'

'Most certainly,' he nodded. 'There have been seven ages of rulers that have inhabited this earth, and the eighth age is now well over due.'

'So what do we do,' she panicked, for which he undoubtedly replies, almost as though he was expecting the question.

'Slow down,' he warned, 'and be happy with what you have accomplished so far, because believe me when I tell you, the more you progress, the weaker you become.'

Knowing that a simple answer will not fix this, she hopelessly gazes at him. 'So how am I supposed to do this?' she pleaded.

He quickly rises to his feet, pushing over the antique chair with the back of his knees, and begins pacing back and forth, racking his brain, in search for the words of which he needs, to make her understand, but instead, he simply blurts it all out. 'I believe you have created a weapon,' he stops pacing at the opposite side of the table and looks down at her with trust in his eyes before continuing. 'I believe he is the one you call Mathias. He is an extraordinary machine, an indestructible human being, made of nothing more than flesh and bone . . . how incredible. This Mathias of yours . . . his weaknesses are known by his enemies, so with the right weapons, he could become an easy kill.'

'What if we can't find him?' she panicked. 'What if he's already dead?'

'Try not to worry too much about Mathias, you have friends in high places that are fighting for you as we speak.'

She fills her lungs and exhales with bloated cheeks. 'So why can you not help us?' she curiously asked.

He pushes himself away from the table having leant against it in a casual manner and heads straight for the huge bookshelves across the far wall. Knowing the room like the back of his hand, he immediately pulls out a particular one. It is so large and heavy that he almost struggles to carry it and unintentionally drops it down on the old table with a bang, making the layers of dust scatter all around, leaving the queen with an itchy nose and holding back a sneeze.

'Do you remember this book?' he asked.

With wide eyes, she admires the authenticity of the ancient work of art that is filled with information and unknown truth about the fascinating wonders of previous man.

'Of course,' she answered. 'That book was on this very table when I first discovered this place.'

'I left it open on a particular page . . . did you read it?'

'Yes,' she immediately replied. 'Why?'

'And did you read about the great seven?'

Beginning to feel worried, she knits her brows in fear of more bad news. 'Yes, of course.'

He once again sits down opposite her and rests his elbows on the table with his fingers interlocked beneath his chin. Before speaking, he silently prays to the seven gods that she will understand what he is to say, and finally, he breaks the hesitant suspense.

'As you are aware . . . You may only summon two of the great seven.'

'Yes,' she interrupted, 'and any further attempts would result in the Phoenix claiming my soul.'

'That is true,' he advised, 'but there is also a catch. . .' She curiously leans forward. 'If you do in fact summon a second, and they are defeated . . . your life force will then join the souls of your predecessors in the ring of eternity.'

She once again drops back on her seat, as the old chair creaks to the very point of collapsing and crosses her arms in a defensive fashion. He is about to continue, only she interrupts him once again. 'Look,' she snapped. 'If that is how it's meant to be . . . then I except my fate.'

'I am very sorry my queen, but it is just not your time. I will protect you with my last breath and trust me when I tell you that getting past me . . . is far more than just a challenge.'

'This is never going to work,' she whimpered.

The gatekeeper leans back and taps his chest with the palms of both hands, locking his wide eyes onto hers in a state of unexpected frustration. 'We must believe in humanity,' he snapped. 'We believe that the rightful heir will prevail, but if humanity can't even believe in themselves, then we may as well just throw in the towel right now.'

She gazes at him in shock, as being the queen of England, she is rarely corrected having been brought up with an in-depth political understanding and highly educated. 'You're absolutely right,' she sighed, 'forgive my moment of weakness . . . this is just so much to digest in one go.'

'A great enemy is invading your country with everything they have. They are throwing their very best at you, to rid you of this world, and if you are to defeat this enemy, you will be once again be feared throughout this floating rocks entire population, and this land must be feared'

'But why?' she asked.

'Because fear is the strongest form of respect . . . without fear you are just another human in command, but your formidable influence is worth much more than that.'

'But I am just another human,' she said proudly.

'Yes . . . but your ancestors stumbled across this gateway, which in turn has revealed a long and dangerous road to a great destiny for all those worthy of the crown. I'm afraid that this future, bestowed upon your family has fallen to you, but now you must once again prove your worth as queen and honour the eternal bloodline that awaits you in the afterlife.'

'Well,' she sighed, 'I suppose that explains the Phoenix.'

'The Phoenix is a symbol that represents eternal life, it is a mystic species that cannot die, it is the only living and breathing being with a heartbeat that is blessed with immortality, and now, you must defend it.'

'So what must I do?' she nervously asked.

'The only thing you must do . . . is put your faith in humanity . . . as we have, and let your future run its course.' He stands as tall as he can and salutes her with honour. 'Good luck my queen . . . may the Gods watch over you . . . and light your path to victory.'

With a struggle, she rises from the old creaky chair and stands in front of him, gazing into his dreamy blue eyes, followed by a wide smile that is beyond her control, as a peaceful emotion suddenly fills her heart. Without warning, the fire all around them disappears, leaving them both in absolute blackness and complete silence as her pounding heart thumps through the core of her body. Suddenly, and all at once, his entire body bursts into flames, forcing the queen to unexpectedly shield her eyes, but then the heavy wall begins to rise, revealing a thin and expanding light of the late afternoon sunshine through the bottom of the thick and heavy wall. She slowly and disappointedly heads for the growing exit, but the fear of fighting this battle alone makes her feel as though she doesn't want to leave.

'When will I see you again?' she asked, as she turns to face him one final time, but she finds herself scanning an empty room with no other life present but her, and her alone.

CHAPTER 20

Over the vast hills covered with endless miles of woodland, the low sunset creates huge shadows, darkening the areas of forestry that the fading daylight can no longer reach. The pink sky of the early evening enhances the few lonely clouds with a mesmerising vision of beauty. The vast beams of light reach out across the sky and absorb into what is soon to become a clear and captivating night sky that will sparkle and twinkle from the heavens above.

At phenomenal speed, a man-sized jet darts into view from a far. It is a black and pointy tipped cylindrical vessel with a mere six-foot wing span. It instantaneously comes to a stop, hovering above a small square landing site that has a bright red cross painted in its centre. The silent jet slowly and steadily rotates, leaving the nose end pointing straight up towards the sky above. There are two small circular flares at the bottom that are holding it perfectly balanced as it gradually nears the centre of its landing target and maintains perfect balance from a mere three feet from the ground. All at once, the smooth and cylindrical surface cracks into thousands of tiny squares; each one rapidly begins folding in on itself, like an extremely advanced version of origami. It quickly fades from front to back as each square disappears into virtual nonexistence and gradually reveals what lies beneath. The entire surface reduces over and over again and packs into a small square box protruding from between a set of metal shoulder blades. Once concealed within the casing, it sinks into the unique mechanics within and right away the artificial spine reforms and conceals the small opening. The Falcon then drops to the surface with a clear thud, for which he stands tall and motionless, ready and awaiting his next command.

Peter leans back in his seat, before releasing the white knuckled grip of his controls and almost shakily pulls his headset off in a stunned and speechless manner as the adrenaline-fuelled beat of his heart makes it difficult to bring himself back to reality.

'So Peter?' asked Natalia from behind and startles him in a state of sheer terror, so with his clammy hand pressed on his heart, he whips his neck and locks his tired eyes onto her apologetic gaze.

'You frightened me half to death.'

She daintily covers her mouth with the pads of her fingers and chuckles in a humorous fashion. 'I'm so sorry Peter . . . I didn't mean to alarm you.'

He drops back in his seat once again and exhales loudly with puffy cheeks.

'So . . . ' she asked again. 'What do you think?'

He firmly rubs his eyes with balls of his hands before sliding his clammy palms down his face in frustration, to stretch his eyes and skin, in order to intercept the sleep paralysis that he was moments from slipping into.

After a few seconds of calming down, he looks up at her with a very satisfactory grin. 'Absolutely flawless,' he proudly stated. 'I have driven the very best that technology has to offer, only there has always been something that doesn't quite fit, but the Falcon,' he said with a shaking head of sheer disbelief, 'I simply cannot fault . . . everything about this machine is perfect and it puts the RCR 3000 to shame, its creators must be very proud.'

She is more than happy to listen to his compliments as a smile gradually widens across her rosy cheeks.

'Thank you,' she replied, 'that means a lot to us. It has been built to match your style, which is something we have studied for a very long time and it fits your every technique like a glove. Its general movements and flow is programmed in regards to the decisions you would make, almost as though it would know your next move, even before you, I mean, it may as well contain your DNA.'

He slowly rises up from his seat and stretches his arms and back like he's just woken from a long nap, followed by a long groan of satisfaction. Finally, he drops his shoulders in well-earned relaxation and simply enjoys the company of this newfound trust that has turned out to be last thing he ever expected.

'That was fun. . .' he said proudly. 'I'm excited to see what he can really do, I want to see its true potential, I want to fight with him and release him in a place where I won't feel so restricted.'

Natalia crosses her arms and stares down at him with nothing but trust and respect in her gaze. 'Five hours straight,' she said proudly, 'you're . . . a machine.'

He shrugs off her admiration for him in a modest fashion before completely changing the subject. 'So . . . how did they do?'

'Very well,' she replied. 'The champions are awaiting you at the head table, but I must say . . . your training is intense, their abilities have improved massively and on a wide scale . . . I am genuinely shocked, though I thought it not possible at this point.'

She gently places her hand against her racing heart. 'You truly are the best I have ever known, and you certainly deserve your title as champion. . . Thank you, Peter, thank you for understanding what we are doing here.'

'Well,' he said humorously. 'I was kidnapped so I didn't really have much choice, did I.'

Surprised by his innocent humour, she giggles but still can't believe the talent of this young and unsuspecting character.

'Come on, commander,' she said proudly to hurry him along, for which he smiles and salutes in return. 'At ease, ma lady.'

There are four gamers sat around a large table in a vast room with a very noticeable echo from all around. There are three boys and a girl, each expressing their feelings about how cool Peter is, and why they didn't know about this game before. They are all humorously bickering over who they think played the best, only all four of them claim to have performed the most effective and stylish moves, or executed the most unforgiving fatality.

A loud hiss from a sudden release of compressed air startles all four of them to attention, forcing each of them to fixate their spooked eyes on the dividing doors, revealing nothing more than the dark and shadowy corridor on the other side.

Silence falls over the room as the eyes of each of them widen in surprise as Peter quickly enters from the darkness and they all immediately straighten their backs in honour of his presence. Feeling nervous, he tries harder than ever not to show it, but what they are asking from him is a massive undertaking, though somehow he manages to hide these feelings by maintaining a respectful and professional image. He stands in front of the only empty seat and individually locks eyes with each of them for a brief moment, for which they simply stare back waiting for him to say something. A couple of the more confident gamers either respectfully nod or sarcastically wink, but finally, he sits down with his fingers interlocked at arm's length. He briefly struggles to find his opening words, purely from the sheer disbelief that these unsuspecting gamers made it through and that the time frames, upon completion, would certainly give the best gamers from the US a run their money. They all sit at the same time and glance at one another in suspense of what's to come.

'So . . .,' he welcomed, 'you must be the champions.' He slowly glides his sight from one side to the other, once again locking eyes with them as they pass his view. He respectfully nods to the young Asian gamer, who welcomed him to the island on the day of his arrival. Not surprised to see him there makes Peter feel the need to announce that he does, in fact, remember his name.

'Hello Cailan,' he said, with pride in his tone as he moves past him. He then finds himself face to face with a stunning young female gamer that he hadn't really noticed before. She has a beautiful tone to her mixed-race skin and heavy brown eyes. He is almost surprised to see her there; this young and defenceless girl looks as though she couldn't fight off a hamster; however, he also knows that becoming a champion in the digital world has absolutely nothing to do with your muscles. It is purely confidence, talent, and bravery that matters, so the only thing that really counts is what's on the inside.

'Hello,' he said, sounding slightly shy.

'Hello,' she replied, while extending her arm to shake his hand. 'My name is Jamilla.'

Stunned by her beauty, he hesitantly smiles in return and clears his throat, which in turn creates an awkward moment of silence amongst all of them. Not knowing what to say next, he finally releases her hand, only continues to gaze in her eyes.

'It's an honour to meet you,' she said proudly, in order to break the silence. 'Everyone is excited to have you on board and we are all very much looking forward to working with you.'

'Thank you,' he replied, 'but the honour is mine . . . you fight for a good cause, and I am proud to be a part of it . . . Anyway,' he continued, 'back to the task at hand.'

He glances at the remaining two and he is shocked to see how young they are, though he shouldn't be, having witnessed a lot younger go through a hell of a lot more.

'So . . . what's your name?'

'This is Ewan,' said Cailan, introducing the young boy to his left. 'He doesn't say much.'

'Okay,' he nodded. 'It's nice to meet you, Ewan . . . I look forward to gaming with you.'

The final boy slouches back on his seat and cockily puts his feet up on the table; he interlocks his fingers at the back of his head in order to stretch his back. He's a beefy lad with distinctive curved cheeks and a boxer's nose. His hair is dark and messy, matching his grubby chequered shirt and old faded jeans with holes in the knees. He confidently introduces himself with a deep and unexpected Scottish accent.

'The name's Oscar.'

The boy is so sure of himself that it's almost sickening, but he is used to these sort of characters, only never come across one so young.'

Peter immediately takes a liking to him and knows that he will be fun to have around. He believes that everyone should be able to express themselves freely and he admires him for having the courage to do just that. 'It's a pleasure to meet you, Oscar . . . now . . . as you all know, there is a reason I asked for the champions . . . I have jobs for each of you, but you are no longer champions . . . you are now commanders of the British gaming force.'

They all glance at each other in confusion, but the honour and shock of what they are hearing has flooded their minds with a river of mixed emotions. Each of them have been rendered silent, leaving them with no other choice but to simply listen.

'America is coming," he continued, 'and they are approaching as we speak, they are attacking with full force, with a plan to wipe England off the map, it will be like she never existed . . . less we do something about it.'

Silence descends upon the room as the reality shake snaps them all straight back into gaming mode. 'So what's the plan?' asked Jamilla.

Peter quickly rises from his seat and begins slowly pacing around them. 'First,' he said confidently, 'you have to remember, they are going to completely surround this land . . . Oscar,' he snapped, for which he respectfully rises to his feet and knocks his heels together, with his eyes fixated on Peter. 'The North is your post,' he ordered, 'and Scotland will fight under your command.'

Peter approaches him and rests his hand firmly on his shoulder. 'From this day forth . . . you shall be known as . . . commander of the North.'

'What?' he gasped.

Peter glides his pointing finger across the surprised glare of each of them. 'You are all commanders of the British gaming force . . . Jamilla,' he called. She immediately rises to attention, 'you will command the east . . . Ewan' he snapped. He remains seated, but whips his nervous eyes to Peter's unconvinced gaze. 'Are you sure you are ready for this?'

Though he remains silent, he honourably stands tall and solutes with a shaky hand. 'Very good. . .' said Peter.

'But what if I fail?' he suddenly whimpered.

'Rule number one,' he replied. 'You must never doubt your ability.'

Peter unexpectedly slouches down in his seat, gazing at the surface of the table in front of him. A nail-biting emotion suddenly intensifies throughout his entire body that almost brings a tear to his eye, but he forces it aside and once again locks eyes with Cailan.

'The South is yours, my friend . . . hold the line,' he respectfully pleaded, for which he simply nods in return.

Peter casually taps the solid surface of the table, purely for something to do while his mind continues to flood with disturbing images of the possible fate that awaits him.

'We've been at war for a long time, commanders, but now it is right outside our front door, and trust me when I tell you . . . If these unwelcome invaders breach the line, they will become even harder to defeat . . . hold the line . . . and we may actually have a chance. An entire nation is looking to us, to fight and protect them.'

He aggressively thumps the ball of his hand on the solid surface of the table, making each of them judder in surprise and he continues with a raised voice that sounds like anger. 'Let's show the world what it means to be a gamer. Are you with me?' he yelled.

In unison, they all jump to their feet and shout with a growl in their throats. 'Yeah!'

The face of Peter suddenly appears on every screen throughout the entire gaming ground.

With passion and respect for the game, he looks calm and collected while staring in the small lens in a confident manner.

'Good morning, gamers . . . I hope you all enjoyed your game . . . FYI, we have sent a request to every legal and illegal gamer throughout Britain, in the hope that they will join. Some of the hidden drones from the underworld of gambling and debt collecting may shock you, but don't be alarmed . . . If they fight, and I'm sure they will, just remember, we are all fighting for the same cause . . . there is no wealth or fortune to be made here . . . there is no trophy or prize to be won . . . today each and every one of us are here to fight for our right to live, and for the lives of our loved ones. It is our duty, our destiny, it is even our right to choose to believe in such a thing, and it is our god-given right to fight for our beliefs . . . and I believe we can win this thing, but we can't do it without the talent that lies within all of you. It's a gift that you possess and this gift makes you a supreme being, but unfortunately, it also makes you a weapon. Being a weapon doesn't make you a bad person, it simply gives you purpose. It's what you do with this power that determines who you are. So let's get out there and show the enemy what it means to be a real gamer.'

After filling his lungs to shout his final words of inspiration, his nervous heart pounds harder than ever before, though he has never felt more ready. He clenches his white knuckled fists below his chin and continues with a growl in his throat. 'Let's show them that we are not to be messed with . . . Are you with me?' he shouted.

A roar from the celebratory screams and cheers spreads throughout the entire facility, echoing through the empty walkways and stairwells, and Peter can almost feel the rumble vibrating through the floor beneath his feet.

'Man your posts,' he ordered, 'ready your drones . . . good luck, gamers . . . god knows, we are all going to need it.'

Thousands upon thousands of kids and teenagers throughout Britain dart for their computers and immediately begin powering up their drones. Many of them are ready and waiting, fully charged and raring to go, so it's simply a case of panning a route.

Throughout Britain, the adults that have illegally built robots from scratch as a secret project or simply to give their own children a chance to learn and prepare for their futures also activate and ready their drones for battle.

All at once, countless amounts of these unregistered killing machines burst through the garage doors and walls of thousands of unexpected households and head straight their nearest line of defence. They each have their own unique character that differ in many unusual ways, in fact some are a mind-blowing abomination of mechanics and destructive in immense proportions; however, far more are less capable, but helpful nonetheless. They rapidly flood the streets in a controlled fashion, being careful to avoid any wondering people that all appear to be heading home for safety.

The streets are so quiet that the entire country almost seems abandoned, as virtually everyone has wisely chosen to spend what will possibly be the last few hours of their lives with the ones they love and praying to the gods for protection and saviour.

The heavy thumping feet of this mass parade continues to expand by the second. The immense groups cover miles upon miles of ground, rumbling all the windows and doors as they continuously stomp in a rush to reach their destination.

They speedily charge along vast main roads filling gardens, side roads, and alleys, yet respectfully causing very little damage.

Peter barges through a set of double doors and hurriedly climbs in his gaming chair. He shuffles around to make himself as comfortable as possible, as he knows he may be sat there for a very long time.

Natalia continues watching him with admiration in her gaze while he confidently flicks all kinds of switches and recalibrates his targeting system to ready the Falcon for battle. He sits back and slowly wraps his fingers around the controls with a firm grasp before anxiously filling his lungs.

'Okay Falcon,' he said proudly.

A thin and flexible rod with a slender glass lens on the end protrudes out from a small gadget lodged behind his ear. It extends past his temple, following the curve of his face before stopping in front of his eye.

'It's just you and me, my friend . . . let's make history.'

Natalia is now merely lurking in the background like a third wheel, so she respectfully decides that it's time for her to leave. 'I'll um . . . be in the control room.'

'Natalia,' he snapped, stopping her in her tracks. 'If you mean to hold the line, then now is the time to position your troops.'

'One step ahead of you, Peter . . . the doors will be opening any moment now . . . my observational team will help you where they can. . . Good luck Peter . . . and thank you again.'

He agreeably nods before flicking a small switch on the side of his ear piece, and with a deep frown, he competitively faces his screen. She smiles before hastily heading for the exit, making the air-pressured doors hiss as they open and close behind her.

No sooner do the doors close, he announces his presence amongst an entire nation of gamers that can all hear him.

'Commanders,' he barked. 'Identify yourselves.'

With a deep Scottish accent, Oscar is the first to reply. 'This is Oscar Cassidy . . . Commander of the North . . . we are on line and ready to kill some fucking yanks . . . Get these doors open, Falcon, the Scottish are getting impatient, and trust me, they don't like to be kept waiting.'

'Loud and clear,' said Peter, 'that's what I like to hear.'

The second to break radio silence is Ewan. His strong Japanese accent and very young sounding voice means he almost has to yell to be heard. 'Ewan Okoba, commander of the East . . . my troops are ready, Falcon.'

'Jamila Ceroko,' she interrupted, 'commander of the West . . . my gamers are well briefed and raring to go.'

'Glad to hear it, Commander . . . good luck.'

Nothing is said for a moment while everyone waits for the last commander to announce his authority. 'Are you with us?' Peter asked concerned.

After a few seconds of silence, he finally answers, sounding exasperated and slightly panicky. 'Cailan Kawamoto,' he gasped, 'commander of the South . . . my apologies Falcon, I had a couple of errands to run.'

'Very well,' said Peter. 'Hold the line commanders . . . and Cailan, be ready . . . I believe that the first point of contact will be the South, so your gamers will have their work cut out . . . good luck my friend, see you on the other side.'

Natalia casually leans over the back of a young teenage boy. He is sat on a swivel chair rapidly typing on his keyboard, with his glazed eyes fixated on his monitor. Finally, he casually leans back and crosses his arms, before filling his lungs, and releasing his breath, loud and slow.

'So, how many active drones do we have?' she asked.

'Nine million three hundred and seventy-four thousand two hundred and thirty-six, to be precise.'

'Are there any reserves?' she asked.

'We have two million in the abandoned tunnels, with a few that are in need of some miner tweaks, apart from that, they are good to go' for which she gently taps his shoulder. 'Good work, George.'

Suddenly something on the screen catches her full attention, and immediately stuns her to silence, the amazement has left her wide eyed and open mouthed. 'Have you really hacked into destiny's decision?' she asked.

He nervously looks up at her in the hope that she is not to upset by his actions. 'It's um . . . just a precaution' he tensely stressed.

'I can't believe you've done this'

'I'm sorry,' he panicked. 'I'll exit immediately

'Don't be sorry, George, that's genius, but I thought all connection was irreversibly disconnected.'

'Nothing can hide from me' he smirked.

With approval she firmly places her hand on his shoulder but forcefully rotates him on his seat to face her and she silently stares at him for moment or two. 'Make me proud, George, and don't miss.'

He distractedly glances at his screen, as the countdown for exposing the drones of the rebellion is nearing completion. 'The doors will open in twenty-seven seconds,' he advised.

'Okay,' she gasped 'here we go

'This must be recorded,' he whispered intently 'this is going to a historical moment.'

The suspense of the next few seconds has silenced almost every living soul throughout the entire grounds; the suspense is so overwhelming, they are all twitching to witness this incredible event take place.

The moment of truth is in a mere few seconds. His eyes widen as a single bead of sweat glides down his cheek and his pupils quickly expand.

'Exposure is imminent in three . . . two . . . one.'

A loud clunk of metal striking metal echoes through the absolute darkness, right before a thin and slowly expanding vertical beam of daylight reveals a vast and never-ending tunnel, filled to maximum capacity, with thousands of identical robots. Each of them slowly lift their heads, focussing on the expanding light that steadily brightens further and further along the dark and concealed channel. The huge thick and heavy doors bang knock and creek before finally stopping at full stretch, leaving the exit fully opened.

There are thousands of these identical doors, evenly spread along the hills, towns, and coast lines that surround the land of England. Every single one of them opens at the same time and each one filled with battle ready drones.

They are stood to attention in rows of four as far back and beyond what the eye can see. Without any further delay, they begin marching forward and split in rows of two, parting ways in the centre and continue to march along the ever-changing tides.

Those in front can already see the line of defence beginning to take shape, as in the far distance they are quickly approaching each other like a joining string of gigantic centipedes, hugging the curvy lines right the way along the very edge of the country.

The anticipation is so intense that everyone's heart is racing as the suspense grows ever more overwhelming by the second.

As for the underground of robotics, they have bought a whole new meaning to the gaming world. They are driven by gaming rebels that virtually have no laws at all, who compete in illegal operations for power, wealth, and respect. They finally begin flooding what could become their final destination.

As the thousands of completely different drones approach the coastlines, after a speedy journey through the very anxious and nervous streets of England, they proudly and fearlessly stroll towards what looks to be, an impenetrable line of defence.

the drivers of the rebellion finally complete their march after stopping nose to nose with the opposite line. In unison, every one of them turn on the spot and fixate their eyes on the horizon as the beaches and hills behind continues filling with all kinds abominations of mechanics, as for now, the good and the bad have all set their differences aside, as the upholders of law and legendary criminals have no other choice but to fight for the only thing that actually makes sense to them.

CHAPTER 21

The queen stands motionless with a delicate grasp of a golden door handle and with a nervous gaze she looks up in the eyes Abdul who is almost mimicking her in response.

'So what do you think?' she asked, secretly seeking approval to what she is about to do. 'Do you think it can work?'

He assuredly places his huge hand gently on her shoulder and very delicately caresses her chin with the huge pad of his thumb. 'One can only hope, my queen'

She disappointedly gazes at the floor before filling her lungs; she finally pushes the heavy door and with the help of Abdul it effortlessly glides open for her. Charlotte is the first to see her enter, so with a flutter of heart and a sob of relief, she immediately darts for her. 'Your Majesty,' she whimpered. 'Are you okay?'

The queen is in no mood for fuss so she brushes off her concern and realises that the person she cares most for is out of sight. 'Where's Gracie?' she panicked, for which the hole of squad three step aside from in front of the fire place in amazement, revealing her sat on the floor with her tiny legs crossed and a deck of cards in her hands.

She slowly lifts her eyes and upon seeing her she drops her tiny shoulder and quickly holds out her arms as an unexpected tear rolls down her cheek.

The queen simply smiles and releases a long sigh of relief as she desperately darts towards her.

'What happened, Your Majesty?' asked Charlotte.

She picks Gracie up off the hard floor and as usual she feels a sudden rush of a calm and pleasant emotion that fills her body from head to toe, as though all of her prayers have been answered at once. For both of them, this is the best feeling they have ever known.

There is so much love between them that they snuggle tight in unison and like a mother's love to her own child, it is unconditional in return. Both are prepared to sacrifice their own life for the other. It is a bond so strong that even the greatest power from Mother Nature herself could not compete.

'Your Majesty,' said Charlotte, 'please talk to me.'

Being the only person in the country that knows what is about to happen, her head is just not in it to assure anyone of her stability. Silently and begrudged, she hands Gracie over to Charlotte, while everyone present waits in suspense to hear what she has to say, so with no need to request anyone's attention, she begins.

'As you are all aware of the extremely abnormal events that took place during our first clash with America, we had a unique defence made of troops from an ancient race, and because of them, heroic monsters from bloodlines of honour and valour, they have made Britain feared once again. Unfortunately, because of America's technology, that protection has been taken away.'

'But what about the Phoenix?' asked Charlotte.

'I'm afraid the Phoenix is powerless to our situation, darling.'

'But why?' she panicked.

'The Phoenix,' she sighed, 'has underestimated America's strength, which in turn has brought us back to where we began and unfortunately the reality is that for now . . . we are alone in this war.'

Silence descends on the room while they all drop their eyes in disappointment and Kyle shakes his head with an unsatisfactory scowl.

'No,' he pleaded. 'Their strength is too powerful.'

He is fully aware of their capabilities having seen firsthand. 'They will flood this place and flatten it to nothing . . . England will fall,' he nervously muttered.

'Now you listen to me,' the queen snapped. 'If the Gods of the great seven can believe in humanity, then we must as well . . . after all, protecting this land is just as important to them as it is to us. . . If we can simply believe that we can win this war . . . then by God we shall.'

Silence falls on them once again as each of them struggle for a moment to come to terms with what it is they must do to survive and after a few more seconds of consideration Kyle finally breaks the sound of shaky breath and thumping hearts with the first positive question so far. 'So . . . what's the plan?'

Squad three proudly stand behind him and all four of them fearlessly hold their chins high, only Kevin can't help but nervously gulp.

She then glances at Charlotte, who simply nods in return, then locks on to Gracie's beautiful little eyes and she smiles with a loving grin. She finally turns to Abdul and with no need to question his loyalty to the crown, she fills her lungs. 'First thing first,' she stated. 'We must find Mathias, because without him we are lost.'

'But no one knows where he is,' said Kyle with shrugged shoulders.

'Perhaps I could try,' said Gracie.

The eyes of each of them widen as they all turn to face her in unison. 'Do you think you can?' asked the queen with knitted brows.

Gracie glances at each of them; one by one, their eyes are filled with hope, and for a moment, she wishes she had kept her mouth shut, only faith tempted her to speak and now she is left with no choice. 'Well um . . . I can't promise anything but, what have we got to lose?'

The queen has always been astounded by her roar power and during their time together she has witnessed events way beyond the bounds of possibility, which has taught her that there is much more to life than meets the eye.

The queen's worst fear is having to stand by and watch Gracie suffer, but after the gatekeeper's words of wisdom, it is only from sheer desperation that she allows it to continue; so with a heavy heart, she reluctantly agrees.

'What is it you want us to do?' she asked.

Charlotte's arms are beginning to ache having held Gracie in her arms for so long, but to her surprise and without request, she walks to the door and pulls it open but before hastily leaving she glances back at the queen. 'She wants to go outside,' she yelled, as she uncontrollably disappears around the corner. The queen immediately follows her with Abdul in toe, leaving all of squad three staring at each other in confusion. After a moment, Rob, Kieran, and Kevin all suddenly begin barging shoving and pushing to be the first to catch up, like a bunch of adolescent school boys about to see a naked woman for the first time.

At the main entrance to Buckingham Palace, the doorman pulls open the huge and heavy solid oak doors from the inside and Charlotte quickly paces through with Gracie in her arms 'Sorry,' she yelled, as though she is no longer in control of her own body and she virtually jogs down the concrete steps to the main courtyard. As they reach the bottom, she suddenly stops, while Gracie anxiously glances from left to right in search of a place to be seated and finally, something catches her eye.

'Over there,' she whispered, while pointing over at a thin path running through the centre of two perfect squares of beautiful soft grass and with brief hesitation she quickly paces over.

'Just here is fine,' she said politely.

An emotional feeling that Charlotte cannot explain fills her body before gently placing her on the hard floor, and as she slowly backs away, a random tear rolls down her cheek. Shocked and amazed by the very strange experience of momentarily sharing a mind with this incredible specimen of human, she was left clueless to how it was possible. With an open mouth, she turns to the huge doors of the palace, just in time to see the queen march through with panic in her stride and almost immediately locks eyes with her.

Gracie begins crawling round on her hands and knees, concentrating intently on various different points on the grubby floor as she shuffles from left to right, around and across.

'Gracie,' said Charlotte with a heavy whisper. 'What are you doing?'

Now that she is almost sniffing the floor, she decides that she is in the right place. 'I can't do this without help,' she confidently replied. She slowly rolls over to her side and very gently drops to her back. With her arms open wide and feet together like the crucifix of Jesus, she gazes up at the empty sky above and already she begins to feel her life force gradually sink in the earth as though being slowly pulled away from her physical body. Her subconscious is immediately accepted by the spirit guides of earth and allow her to share the world's energy in order to fulfil her destiny.

She suddenly becomes part of a natural global network that has eluded our sciences for generations. She can feel the earth rotating as her mind suddenly becomes one with all the elements. She grows from the earth and glides with the wind. She rises with burning flames and flows with the vast oceans. Her mind is greatly overwhelmed by the sheer power that the earth possesses and amazingly feels at one with it, as though she is spinning it with her own two hands. The control of every major power line is at her fingertips, giving her unlimited access to engage or disable anything she chooses, from switching on a random kettle, right up to the satellite systems that have been in orbit for nearly two centuries. The mainframe to the world's power grids are inaccessible to her and somehow protected by an unknown source of energy. To shut it down would be the obvious answer to ending this war but her abilities are limited but even if she could find a way, it wouldn't last for very long, so without wasting precious time, she continues her search for Mathias.

The American continent is presented to her in the depths of her powerful mind and displayed as a holographic image that she able to twist, turn, and rotate however she chooses.

This unique manmade power mixed with the natural energies can't be seen with the naked eye but it forever flows beneath the earth's crust like a windy river with unstoppable force and the blinding light at her core sparks destructive bolts of electricity that have the potential for total annihilation. Her mind zooms in like a telescope from outer space and as she rapidly nears the ground, everything gradually becomes real once again. Not to her surprise she is floating above the White House as though she is the wind itself, trapped in a floating vortex.

Using only her mind, she hacks in to the security system of the president's official home of residents and suddenly every camera, speaker, bug, and visual aid throughout the entire building switches on. Not one room is inaccessible to her and she can hear every word spoken as clear as day. The whole process happens in a flash and after searching the building from top to bottom, she is confident that he is not there, so she continues on, only something, somewhere, somehow tells her not to go and she has always been told to trust her instincts.

Her physical body is still lying on the floor with her arms wide open and flickering eyelids as though she is trapped in a trance in her own unconscious mind. Her eyes accurately narrow as her physical form struggles for a brief moment to push her forward. The queen is now on her knees by her side, gently stroking her rosy cheek to let her know she is there. She quietly sobs in desperation as a lonely tear rolls down her cheek, praying to the Gods of the great seven to protect her and keep her from harm.

'Mathias,' Gracie yelled allowed, making the queen snatch her hand away in awe; she wipes away the single tear with ball of her hand and Gracie calls out once again. 'Please Mathias, can you hear me?'

With love and respect, she slowly leans over and places her mouth not two inches from her ear before gently whispering in the hope that she can hear her voice. 'I love you Gracie . . . you're the bravest person I have ever known . . . find him my angel, I know you can, tell him we desperately need help.'

She doesn't reply, she merely lies there, as though she is trapped in the dream world, waiting to hear a response from Mathias. She is moments from giving up on waiting for him, only Mathias breaks the intense silence that surprises even her. 'I'm here' he groaned.

Gracie's tiny lungs fill to full capacity and the queen delicately rests the palm of her open hand on her inflated chest as she lovingly watches her exhale and breath normally again.

'Are you trapped?' Gracie asked.

'Yes,' he replied. 'But I will be okay.'

'Your presence is sourly needed in England, you must return there at once.'

'Not yet,' he angrily growled. 'This is something I have to finish.'

'Make it quick,' she panicked. 'I don't know how long England will hold without you.'

'I will be there soon,' he snapped, before violently roaring in agony.

His sudden outburst shocks her, making her petite and fragile little body judder from the surprise. The queen covers her mouth as though all hope is beginning to fade as a terrifying rush of her flustered heart struggles to accept the danger she is in.

'What's happening to her?' she whimpered.

Charlotte crouches down next to Gracie on the opposite side of the queen, looking into her watery eyes and with heartfelt words she whispers.

'She'll be okay, Margaret, nothing could stop this baby from achieving her goals . . . she will come back to us soon . . . I promise you.'

With a heart full of hope, she whimpers and sobs. 'I'm so frightened for her . . . she's just a baby.'

She drops her head in her hands to cover her teary eyes as she weeps in fear. Charlotte reaches out her hand and gently strokes her arm 'She's very strong, just give her a chance to show us what she can really do.'

She spots Gracie moving with the peripherals of her sight and she is immediately drawn to her closed eyes that are shifting from left to right beneath her eyelids in a futile attempt to open them. It takes a moment for the tiny child to realise she is back in her body and her eyes gradually begin to open as though she has been asleep for hours.

'Margaret,' Charlotte whispered in surprise.

The queen slowly drops her hands and looks down at Gracie, only to witness her struggle to sit up. 'Oh thank God,' she cried as her eyes widen and jaw drops. Without delay, she reaches down and picks her up off the hard floor, rapping her arms tight around her, squeezing her close and rocking from side to side, 'You had me so worried . . . what happened to you?'

'I spoke to Mathias,' she replied

For that moment, she doesn't really care, she simply squeezes her even tighter and embraces her dearly with unconditional love.

'He's trapped' said Gracie.

'What?' she replied, after the realisation consumes her.

'Don't worry . . . he said he'll be here soon . . . and I believe him.'

The queen looks in the eyes of Charlotte with a gaze of fear, before glancing at Kyle and Abdul as a subtle bid for approval to move forward.

Each of them agreeably nod, having placed their faith in the tiny genius once before and has proven that she is trustworthy of such importance, so they see no reason why they shouldn't trust her now.

'So what do we do?' asked Kyle from behind the abnormally large mountain of muscle that is Abdul.

'Now we do the only thing left'

'And what's that?' he asked.

'We ready our drones, we man our stations . . . we prepare the British forces for war and we fight for our god-given right to live. We pray that the gods will aid us to victory and we trust that the people in control of our defences do what they are trained to do . . . This war will be remembered for all time and will be forever written in the pages of history . . . so let's give them something to write about.'

A single door to a silent room slowly opens and in steps the queen with a wobble in her step. After closing the door with a loud clunk, she nervously turns around with a very nervous shake in her breath. The room is small and poky with a single window cleverly positioned in the wall that exposes just enough daylight to maintain a constant dim glow from dawn until dusk. There is a small two seated sofa next to a small circular table with a vase of fresh flowers in the centre. In the far corner, there is a large and bulky dominating desk that looks typically Georgian. The rare piece of antique furniture is so well maintained that it could easily pass as brand new and the brown leather matching chair equally so.

With a discrete pant in her breath, she steadily edges around the desk and very gently settles herself on the soft and inviting leather seat.

The fear of what she is about to do is more nerve racking to her than standing in front of the gatekeeper himself, as the potential chaos will undoubtedly cause anarchy throughout the land of which she has dedicated her entire life. With her back as straight as an arrow, she sits as tall as possible with her clammy hands firmly on her knees and anxiously fills her lungs before exhaling with bloated cheeks.

For an intense moment or two she hopelessly gazes at the top draw down by her side. She finally reaches out with yet another pause of uncertainty and slowly pulls it open. She casually pushes the few pieces of stationary to the back and with a click of release she carefully removes half of the draws base, revealing a bright red and round button in the centre.

The pressing of this highly classified button is something that she always hoped she would never have to do, but knowing the world as well as she does tells her that one way or another, we are all eventually forced to face our fears. With that in mind she nervously gulps, before firmly pressing the button with the ball of her fist, followed by an unexpected click of activation that makes her snatch her hand away in awe. Realising she is still holding her breath, she releases a subtle gasp of air that gradually eases the racing thump in her chest.

CHAPTER 22

Every single gamer from the British gaming forces stares motionless at their screens as their pupils expand from the terror that has consumed them, each of them barely daring to breathe as they bear witness to this extraordinary event that they have feared for longer than they care to remember.

A line of dark shadows gradually rise over the horizon as the huge black ships creep towards them. They continuously grow in size on the speedy approach as the wavy and distorted shapes slowly become clear. America wanted to strike fear by showing their full power, yet without trying they have silenced an entire country.

Upon the ships there are countless amounts of invading robots from America, positioned in geometrical blocks by the thousands. The formation is so outstanding that only artificial intelligence could accomplish such accuracy. Layer upon layer, these monstrous machines have filled the entire ship from top to bottom throughout every level and each ship is over a mile in length.

The suspense for the young American gamers has been so frustrating having been seated for the last twenty hours. Many of them are huffing from the sheer boredom while others fidget in discomfort. However, far more are almost 100 per cent focussed, so much so, they have barely glanced from their monitors since the very moment they left. All they have seen throughout the entire journey is water, so much water they have all grown sick of it, then finally, to the surprise of them all, an image appears in front of them, making them all straighten their backs and glare at their screens with wide eyes and gaze at what looks to be the very land of which they have been ordered to seize. Most of them celebrate by whistling or clapping, which in turn has a knock on effect that spreads like wild fire. Some make not a sound but as an army of very mixed emotion they silently sweat and nervously gulp yet some merely chuckle with a grin of joy.

'There she is,' said Lucian, catching the attention of his friends nearby. 'Has anyone heard from Peter yet?' he curiously asked.

'Apparently, the president's been keeping him busy,' said the voice of one of his friends to his left.

'What?' he snapped. 'So no one's even heard from him?'

'No,' he whined, 'we thought if anyone would have heard from him, it would be you.'

'Oh my God. . .' he suddenly realised. 'He's done it . . . he's actually done it.'

'What do you mean?' the boy asked, which suddenly catches the attention of yet more of his friends nearby. Lucian quickly turns to face them with eyes of excitement to bring them in on his huge secret but before spilling the beans he stops himself on the premise of Peter's original worry that is . . . who you can really trust.

'Um, nothing, nothing, um . . . I'm just excited ya know.'

Knowing that he is lying through his teeth, they all simply stare at him silently.

'Come on guys . . . we're about to be faced with the fight of our lives. . .'

He glances around at all the stares that remain fixed on him, making him more uncomfortable by the second but just as he decides to ignore them, Jack turns from the seat in front and he locks on to his curiously suspicious eyes that he can't seem to hold still. Jack is so certain that he knows something they don't, but finds himself too afraid to know the answers, so he turns around in acceptance to his subtle response. Each of them that were in earshot of the conversation silently turns to the front as though nothing was said, and this reaction tells him that they are all still loyal to their commander, regardless of what he may be up to.

The cheers and clapping finally begins to die down and Lucian nervously gulps in fear of being unknowingly forced to challenge who has been named as the best in a long line of those deemed undefeatable, but more importantly, his best friend. The only way for him to know for sure that he has gone rogue is to focus on the defence strategy, that alone should be evidence enough to know that he has in fact taken that leap he so craved. However, he hides his feelings well and continues as though nothing has changed, so with a roar of excitement, he shouts, 'Let's tear this chunk of rock to pieces,' which makes those in earshot cheer once again.

To the surprise of them all, a very seductive female voice echoes throughout the vast gaming domes.

'Attention gamers, restriction not apply, Authorisation to full gaming mode is imminent, I repeat, full gaming mode is imminent.'

Jack once again pops his head round from the seat in front to grab the eyes of Lucian. 'What does that mean?' he whispered.

With his eyes glued to his screen at the remarkable image of vast Greenland that appears faded through the mist across the horizon, he suddenly senses that all eyes are on him once again. He looks up at Jack only to see him staring and waiting for a reply of some kind only leaves him confused.

'What?' he shrugged, and after nervously glancing from left to right, Jack whispers once again, 'Well?'

'Oh you mean the announcement.'

'Yes,' he snapped.

With a slightly cocky grin, he humorously sits back and crosses his arms before finally answering. 'It means that diplomacy has gone. It means there are no limitations or restrictions to your capabilities . . . but most importantly, it means there are no consequences to your actions . . . from here on in, we are officially gaming.'

The eyes of them all widen with joy as the sudden whispers begin once again, only Lucian yells to be heard from a far. 'Be as cruel as you want, gentlemen, and be as godless as you can bear. However,' he shouted even louder, 'there is one thing I will say . . . there are many innocent people out there that want no part in this. . . It's one thing to be godless but it's another to be evil, so do as you must but be prepared for judgement in the eyes of God . . . for that is the place we will all end up. . . Those are the words of your commander,' he reminded, 'respect them . . . and good luck . . . now let's show them what we're made of.'

The president has been watching Lucian for some time now. He is fully aware that he is Peter's closest friend who has aroused his interest in their connection and at this point it could prove to be very beneficial. He taps the shoulder of a young and geeky-looking boy with a long and droopy face, who immediately turns to face him with eyes full of admiration. 'Keep a close eye on him,' he ordered, while pointing at an image of Lucian, 'and let me know if anything strange happens.'

'Of course, Mr President,' he gasped.

The president interacts with him no further and casually walks away. 'Consider it done, sir,' yelled the boy, but he simply marches on and disgustedly wipes his hand on his jacket, like he accidently picked up someone's old napkin.

CHAPTER 23

Peter appears to be lounging in the comfort of the most perfectly fitted gaming chair that is more than accurately made to measure. With a tight grasp on his controls and a hanging jaw of shock, he is stunned by what he's doing. His glazed eyes are rapidly and continuously shifting from one side of his screen to another, desperately trying to comprehend the magnificence of his drones capabilities.

The Falcon is in jet form soaring through the cold and dense air a mere few feet above the dark abyss of the deep sea. A bright and transparent blue umbrella shape slowly expands two inches from the nose end as he breaks the sound barrier with a deafening blast. The tremendous speed has created zero updraft caused by the sheer velocity that forces the freezing water beneath to part across the oceans ever-changing surface.

The president is simply watching his work and waiting to give the order to strike, yet with twitchy feet and shaky hands, he rocks from side to side, as at this point any form of comfort will do. His heart is pounding so hard and fast that he can hear the constant beat through the shake in his breath, along with a continuous tapping deep in his ear canal. He fills his lungs and exhales with bloated cheeks before finally giving the order to strike 'Send the inventory . . . let's keep them busy till the big boys catch up.'

A voice in his ear immediately replies having been ordered to stand by for this particular command. 'The descent has begun, sir, and the creepers are on the move,' for which he nervously glides is fingers through his hair and no sooner has he filled his lungs, the process begins.

The front end of each vessel slowly opens up; the colossal hatch bangs knocks and creeks as the top end gradually and steadily lowers in to the crashing waves to create a sloping ramp. Not a moment sooner a single huge platform from each ship stabilising hundreds of drones protrudes from the darkness and in to the light and splashes in the sea as the front end forcefully enters the freezing cold water.

The solid line of Britain's defence focus their magnified sight across the way and pray to god as they watch the individual platforms make their way towards the British shores.

Cailan's earpiece suddenly begins crackling from an alien interference as he catches the odd word from a familiar voice. 'What's that?' he asked himself.

'It's me Peter,' he yelled, 'Can anyone hear me?'

'Peter,' he cried, 'boy am I glad to hear from you.'

'Hold your fire,' he ordered. 'I repeat . . . hold your fire.

'Read you loud and clear' replied the commanders in unison.

Peter sighs in relief having finally made contact and immediately continues, 'Save your fire power, those drones are cheap metal driven only by beginners.'

'What if they shoot first?' asked Ewan.

'They're just combat drones,' he giggled, 'get some practice out of them, it will give you all a chance to warm up'

'Why are they using those?' asked Cailan

'It's a test . . . They want to see what they're up against . . . this very moment is vital in any conflict. It determines your true strength and also exposes your weaknesses by method of trickery. If we do this right it will confuse the hell out of them, so for now, just try to have fun with it.'

They nervously watch the symmetrical platforms glide towards them in a terrifying and fearless manner for which Jamila speaks out of the blue.

'Okay gamers, this is your commander . . . hold formation and do not move an inch until they are grounded.'

Every gamer under her command holds fire, as do all the gamers throughout after being given the same order.

The president is watching closely as his drones near the dry land, only now he seems confused. He curiously leans closer to his monitor for a clearer view. Surprised they haven't taken his bate he nervously gulps after disappointedly drooping back in his seat.

'Why are they not shooting?' he asked himself.

Suddenly, an intense emotion of anger spreads through him from head to toe as the realisation sets in. 'Peter,' he growled. He quickly picks up a small communication device and hooks it around his ear. 'I believe it was as we feared' he barked. 'Peter has gone rogue . . . I repeat . . . Peter has gone rogue.

'Yes, sir, Mr President,' replied a man's voice. 'Read you loud and clear.'

'Put me through to William,' he commanded.

William is in his gaming chair, the only one located in its own separate room. With the excitement of what's to come, he is frantically pushing buttons and spinning dials from left to right before casually tapping his ear piece to answer the incoming call. 'This is William, you're go for go . . . Mr President,' he gasped.

'Are my gamers prepared for this?' said the muffled voice.

'Of course, Mr President, the battle has begun, sir, and the creepers are holding formation.'

'Good,' said the president, 'but I have one more question. . . Why do you think they haven't open fire yet?'

'I could tell you what you would like to hear or I could give you my honest opinion.'

'I want to know what you think.'

'Peter, sir . . .,' he smiled. 'I think he has betrayed you, sir.'

He clicks his fingers as he crushes his clammy hand tight before banging his white knuckled fist against the arm of his chair. 'That little bastard,' he growled before filling his lungs and slowly exhaling to steady the racing thump in his chest. 'William,' he slowly sighed, 'do I have your full attention.'

'Yes, sir, Mr President,' he proudly stated.

'I reinstate you as commander and award you full control of the RCR 3001. Use it well and if you want to continue gaming with us, then you had better not fail me.'

'Thank you, sir, thank you so much. . . you can count on me, sir, I won't let you down'

'I hope not,' he replied, 'there are two upgrades of the RCRC 3001, one for both of you but now that traitorous little bastard has proven to be as you warned, it's only fitting that I reward you his drone . . . Kill him with it,' he ordered. 'Win this battle for me and I will make you the most feared gamer the world has ever known.'

Unable to find the words to respond to such honour, he finds himself stuttering and repeating the same words over and over until the president snaps in frustration. 'William . . . pull it together, this is your one and only chance for revenge so don't blow it.'

'Yes, sir,' he proudly replied.

The massive platforms finally crash against the seabed beneath the shallow waters. Upon the judder of impact the perfect formation instantaneously scatters from impeccable order to shear madness. Like ammeters, they dart towards them through the reoccurring waves of the strangely erratic tides and do so without a second thought. With great force, they repeatedly smash against the reinforced metal of the defending drones. In unison, they hold the great force by placing one foot behind, stopping the hordes of metal, like an unbreachable force field. The gamers of the cheap combat drones attack with every ounce of power they possess but Britain merely holds their ground by refusing to allow the line to break. The pressure becomes so intense that the British drones slowly edge back, forcing their large metal feet deep in the dirt and sand like rugby players in the middle of a scrum.

Once full force is met and they can physically move no further, the continuous rumble gradually but quickly deteriorates until silence descends all along the wall of drones. Suddenly, from out of the blue, an almighty crash echoes through vast and evacuated towns, fields, and resorts like an unexpected blast of ground shaking thunder.

The young drivers from the US combat drones are left confused as their screens flicker after a judder of immense proportions that forces the attackers a few metres back to create a gap wide enough for Britain to strike. They fight back with such brutality that the unexpected comeback shocks them beyond belief, after every few seconds hundreds of screens turn blank, leaving the gamers confused as the US drones are torn to pieces and carelessly scattered like they were dropped in a mine field. No British gamers are damaged as every attack that made it through was immediately counteracted and avoided, resulting in arms and legs being snapped, twisting and skilfully detached. Using many different parts of physical combat makes it easy for each of them to unleash their full potential and defend the country they love in style. Almost all of them have been completely demolished, leaving a mere few that panic in the face of defeat as they throw wild punches and kicks at nothing but thin air before they are swarmed like the captured prey of a hungry pack of lions. Every defending drone is left unscathed and fully functional, ready to continue defending their home land.

Suddenly, they all jump for joy as the high fiving drones start humorously dancing. They pick up the lifeless metal limbs and aggressively launch them out to see, fearlessly taunting them to keep it coming.

'Don't get too excited,' said Peter. 'This fight hasn't begun yet.'

The president is pacing back and forth with his eyes glued to his screen, waiting for the call to advise him that they are ready to proceed, only the celebrating country is making him more furious by the second. 'I've seen enough,' he growled, before tapping his ear piece. 'William,' he snapped. 'Are the creepers in position?'

'Any moment now, sir.'

'Good, deploy the decoy . . . I want that crown.'

'Yes, sir, Mr President.'

Not a moment sooner, the colossal ships begin spewing platform after platform, each stabilising thousands of battle-ready drones. They continuously crash in the cold sea and immediately head for Britain's coast lines. The commanders are watching the countless drones glide towards them across the horizon and once again, England has been silenced as this is now the moment that will determine whether they live or die.

Ewan is the first to break radio silence with a beg of desperation. 'Peter . . . please tell me you are almost here.'

'ETA in three minutes and fifteen seconds.'

'They're coming in fast,' said Jamila.

'Prepare your short-range missiles and sink those platforms.'

The communication with the British army is so rapid that only a mere few seconds pass before the hollow barrels of massive artillery slowly rise and position their targets.

'As soon as they're in range,' said Peter, 'open fire.'

'Gamers,' Cailan announced. 'This is your commander . . . stand fast and ready your fire arms.'

In almost perfect unison, the shoulders of each drone open up with a sharp release of compressed air before a ten-inch barrel quickly rises facing the sky and snaps forward on a pivot to take aim on a chosen target. In perfect synchronisation, they each lift their left arm and aim at any target of their choice, for which two small identical missiles detrude from their forearm, and in perfect line of sight, they hold the position like statues.

The adrenaline for the defending drones is so intense that most of them are physically shaking; however, sweaty hands and wide unblinking eyes are what none of them can avoid.

'Okay,' said Cailan nervously. 'Range is met in five seconds, let the games begin, three, two, one.'

Every missile immediately takes flight and the loud hiss from the sheer mass is massively amplified. A burst of explosive heat shoots out from each barrel and almost immediately shrinks in the distance, leaving a never-ending trail of dark smoke that blends into a black cloud that surrounds the entire country.

'Shields up,' said the president calmly.

From all around the edge of each platform, a thick metal wall quickly rises and meets in the centre creating a four-faced pyramid. The missiles crash into them in such great numbers that the sheer force almost obliterates them, creating mushroom clouds of heat and smoke that expands as it rises.

As the smoke gradually begins to clear, they can see that many of them are still coming, yet a vast majority of them have vanished and are in the process of their descent.

'Don't worry gamers,' said the president. 'We expected this reaction . . . get in rank and ready your arms for battle.'

In groups of thousands, the drones slowly approach the deep seabed, along with countless severed artificial limbs that finally come to rest, only to be crushed under the feet of the entire US gaming force on approach to Britain's main land. The army of millions covers the ocean surface for miles as they continue creeping closer, climbing over huge rocks like spiders approaching their prey and fearlessly marching in the excitement of causing mayhem and destruction. Many of the creepers find themselves trapped and crushed beneath the huge descending platforms but the damage caused is merely a fraction of their gaming force.

The British look confused as they gaze in fear across the vast horizon through the perfect sight of their motionless drones and they immediately begin whispering to each other asking questions like 'What's going on?' and 'What do we do now?'

'Commanders,' said Peter, snapping them to attention. 'Be ready . . . this is far from over.'

To the sheer surprise of all the British gamers, an endless line of US drones rise to their feet in unison as the retracting waves rush between the legs of each one. Without delay, they immediately open fire taking out the first line in one fowl swoop as they casually step ashore followed by the endless hoard from behind that march in their stride.

This unexpected strategy has shocked the entire country, so much so it has taken longer than necessary for the realisation to catch on before the full force of England is finally unleashed. The rumble and hissing from the masses of rocket launchers, tanks, and missiles conceal the powerful roar from the thousands of brave British soldiers that charge for battle. They each understand and accept that the odds are far from their favour, but nevertheless, this is what they have been trained for.

CHAPTER 24

Mathias is still suspended in mid air, dangling by his aching limbs as they vigorously spasm from the immense surges of electricity passing through his flesh and bones. The heat is so intense that his fingers, eyes, and mouth are literally glowing like the glare from an open flame.

Nicki has simply stood by and watched him suffer for the whole time he's been held in captivity and cannot believe that a man of human structure is able to withstand such torture. To her surprise, a buzzing sound that only she can hear startles her slightly and after pinching her earlobe to connect the call she is shocked once again as the president snaps at her, 'Is that pain in the arse dead yet?' for which she turns and whispers in embarrassment.

'No, Mr President . . .,' she said sarcastically. 'It turns out that he's not that easy to kill.'

After filling his lungs in frustration, he continues. 'Okay,' he sighed. 'Blast him once more on full power and if he's still not dead, cut his fucking head off.'

'Of course, Mr President,' she replied, before rolling her eyes, 'as you wish, sir.'

She turns to the control panel and holds the lever with a firm grasp. She slowly drops it to zero, allowing him to breathe one more time and he desperately gasps for air.

'What will happen to the boy?' he asked with a scorched throat and without a second thought she replies.

'The boy will meet you in the afterlife.'

She cracks the lever to full power once more in the hope that it will finally kill him. Tom shields his eyes from the blinding sparks as with great difficulty he climbs to his feet and with his face covered in dry blood he limps towards her.

With empathy she watches him struggle and although she admires his courage, she simply cannot allow him to interfere any further.

In the blink of an eye, she thumps him in the jaw; it happened so fast that he is not even aware he's been knocked out but she catches him before hitting the floor and holds his limp body in her arms; like a sleeping toddler, his head comes to rest on her shoulder.

The eyes of Mathias finally close and the growling stops, as though the high voltage is passing through nothing more than an empty shell. After a further few seconds of watching him burn, she casually throws the switch. She slowly walks towards his droopy body while he lifelessly hangs like a ragdoll.

The heat from his glowing body intensifies after every cautious step she takes and as she gets closer she can see that his chest is not moving. She stops only three feet in front of him and turns her nose up to the rotten smell of burning flesh as his cooking body tissue continues to sizzle. She slowly reaches out two fingers to feel for a pulse and at the very moment of contact, a large sphere of white glow conceals all three of them and rapidly rotates. It suddenly deteriorates to the size of a golf ball before completely disappearing. The heavy chains drop and crash into the old walls creating a rumble that echoes through the silent and empty chamber.

The huge doors of Buckingham Palace pull open from the inside as the queen marches through within a circle of her most respected security. Abdul is by her side, not only as a bodyguard but as a friend.

A brand new black Mercedes Benz is awaiting her at the bottom of the feature steps. As she nears the bottom, the rear door is pulled open for her, but before climbing in, she taps Abdul on the arm and he immediately crouches so she can speak quietly in his ear. 'Be ready,' she whispered. 'It's about to get very difficult . . . I'm sorry darling . . . I have no choice.'

Although he is sad to see her go, he believes she will be safe he wants to tell her that everything is going to be okay but he can't seem to find the words. She reaches up and puts her hand on his cheek and kisses the other with a delicate touch. 'Thank you darling . . . no one could have served me better, may the gods smile upon you forever.'

After climbing in, he gently closes the door behind her, leaving only his reflection gazing back at him through the blacked out window. With a smile, he takes a step back knowing that she is gazing back in return as the car slowly pulls away. It follows the wide drive that circles the large concrete water feature and the high black gates open for her to exit. He doesn't wave or give any gesture, he simply stands back and watches his life's work get further out of reach. To the sheer terror of all those watching her leave, a deafening blast produces a small shock wave that expands across the road like a ripple on water. Thousands of cracks shoot up the high walls surrounding the palace before the car rapidly shoots up thirty feet in the air and before it lands it is completely engulfed in flames.

It takes a second or two for the realisation to hit Abdul and after that very brief moment his anger conceals his wide eyes with a deep and terrifying frown. With a growl in his throat, he clenches his fists and roars to the heavens above as a victim of unforgivable betrayal. His head drops forward and he falls to his knees, waiting for the gods to strike him down for his failure. Through a whimpering sniffle and a thumping heart of guilt, he hears a man's voice in his ear requesting his presence immediately, but it takes a moment for him to register as his eyes gradually fill with tears while gazing at the floor.

'Abdul,' called the voice, 'can you hear me?'

'Yes,' he replied, before slowly climbing to his feet and filling his lungs to conceal the pain.

'Head for the queen's private quarters immediately.'

After promising himself that he will find her killer, he turns on the spot and speedily paces across the drive and up the steps.

The door to his beloved queen's area of peace bursts open with an almighty crack as it collides with the wall behind and creates a blast that rumbles through the old floorboards. With a mind and heart full of torment and many questions that desperately need answers, he charges through ducking his head to avoid the door frame. Once again, he is stunned to silence as he gazes in disbelief in the glazed eyes of his best and most precious friend, the queen of England. 'Hello Abdul,' she said quietly with a nervous grin. Unaware of how he may react, she approaches him with caution. 'I'm so sorry my friend . . . I wanted so much to tell you about this.'

'Then why didn't you?' he snapped.

'In order for this to seem real, I had to make it real . . . and who better to express the loss than the person who cares for me the most.'

He drops to his knees once again as tears of relief roll down his cheeks. She hurries to him and wraps her loving arms around him and he whimpers like a child. 'I thought I lost you.'

After wiping his tears, he quickly stands to compose himself and straighten his suit. 'Who else knows about this?' he asked.

'You, myself, and Derik, partly involving a very carefully selected few.'

With knitted brows, he wonders and can't help but ask. 'Who's Derik?'

'I um . . . I can't tell you that.'

'Okay,' he huffed, 'then who was that lovely lady I said goodbye to?'

'She . . . is a naughty little secret,' she chuckled.

'So I take it you know she is dead then,' he stated.

'Who . . . Denise? No . . . She's too much of an asset to lose.'

'What. . . ?' he frowned.

'She was carefully lowered through the bottom of the car and in to the tunnels below . . . I assure you, she's quite safe.'

Feeling unconvinced, he narrows his eyes and says something that only she could possibly understand. 'If I should stay, I would only be in your way.'

'So I'll go,' she interrupted, 'but I know, I'll think of you every step of the way.'

His eyes widen as a smile widens across his face, making the queen respond with a matching gesture. 'Those words are from a movie that you watched with your grandfather as a child, it's the very thing that inspired your career, which in turn brought you to me and I have never been so thankful for such loyalty.'

She fearlessly stands not two feet in front of him and looks up in his watery eyes as a single tear rolls down his cheek. 'I never meant to hurt you, Abdul, and I hope you can find it in your heart to forgive me.'

He slowly kneels down on one knee and is still looking down at her. She reaches up on tiptoe and wipes away the lonely tear with the pad of her thumb for which he wraps his arms around her and affectionately pulls her close while burying his face in her shoulder 'I'm so glad you're safe.'

He slowly stands up but keeps his eyes fixed on her and she gently takes his hand and leads him to the sofa like a giant toddler with a grazed knee. To the surprise of them both, an unnatural gust of wind messes their hair and stops them in their tracks. Without a second thought, he steps to her front to protect her at whatever cost, only to witness Mathias instantaneously manifests in front of them with Nicki at his side, holding Tom in her arms with two fingers under the chin of Mathias.

Tom is unconscious with wide open mouth and his face is covered with clotted blood. Mathias casually glances from left to right and appears unfazed by what's just happened. 'Wow . . . that's new.'

Nicki immediately snatches her hand as the confusion has rendered her speechless. They all simply watch her begin to panic in utter disbelief as she drops Tom's limp body to the floor and backs away in shock. Without thinking, Mathias crouches down at the boy's side and sits him upright with his droopy head on his forearms. He grasps his jaw and gently shakes his head in desperation for a response of any kind, only nothing happens.

Nicki refuses to turn her back to them and glares at them all wide eyed as she edges along the wall frantically searching for an exit using only their hands. She finally grasps the door handle and in the blink of an eye she vanishes. Abdul charges for the door to capture and restrain her but Mathias stops him. 'No,' he shouted, 'let her go.'

'We can't just let her go.'

'Trust me my friend,' he warned. 'If you get in her way, she will singlehandedly tear this building to pieces . . . you have to let her go.'

Abdul turns to the queen with a sense of confusion in his gaze. 'Who is she?' he asked, and after a moment of pure shock, she replies, 'My niece . . . I thought she was dead.'

CHAPTER 25

The president is sat in front of a row of monitors and is able to keep a close eye on whatever takes his fancy. His eyes flick from one screen to the other, watching intently as the anarchy grows more out of control by the second.

His gamers are hacking at Britain's line of defence like an army of fire ants devouring a corpse. Many of Britain's drones have been forced to fall back as the never-ending hoard of American power march across the wide open shores that stretch as far and beyond what the eye can see.

There are thousands of British citizens that refuse to hide and cower in fear who simply wonder the streets and wait for the bitter end of their existence, yet somewhere deep down in their hopes and prayers, they believe their country can win and with that in mind they have each promised not to go down without a fight. These hopeful wonderers each find themselves stunned to silence as countless missiles rocket and target grenades dart across the sky above. They hiss whine and scream at such a deafening rate that all other noise is cancelled out, followed by a rumble from the mass of explosions that vibrates through the ground, making each and every one steady themselves for balance.

The president's ear piece alerts him of a call so he quickly taps it to stop the annoying buzz. 'Mr President,' said the captain of one of the colossal ships.

He is standing in the control tower at the highest point with a smug grin, watching the madness ashore through a unique pair of high-tech binoculars. 'The defence line has fallen, sir . . . we're in . . . holy shit,' he gasped after something caught his eye on radar.

'What's going on?' yelled the president.

'Sir, we have a bogey heading right for us.'

'Is it human?' he panicked.

'No, sir . . . mechanical . . . whatever it is, it's unmanned and it's moving faster than anything I've ever seen.'

The president thinks for a moment, desperately trying to find some kind of explanation as to what it may be, before finally it hits him. 'It's Peter,' he certified. 'Where's William?' he snapped.

A thirty-foot robot charges across the increasingly shallowing seabed, carelessly crushing the few unlucky drones beneath its car-sized feet, leaving them as mangled heaps of metal that spark and flash before imminent termination.

'Tell him to pick up the pace,' the president ordered. 'His time to prove himself is now.' He taps his ear piece once more to continue on a separate call. 'Nicki,' he snapped. 'Bring me that irritating little prick's head . . . I want to capture this moment . . . Nicki,' he repeated. 'What's going on down there?'

After receiving no reply, he can feel himself slowly sinking in to panic mode as he now fears the worst, so the beat of his rushing heart intensifies all the more.

He quickly jumps in a chair pulling close to the nearest keyboard and rapidly types a sixteen-digit code before angrily thumping the enter key. As there is no other contact down there and he has no time to walk such a distance at this imperil moment or search the cameras to see if she left and with whom, he simply narrows in on her immediate coordinates to pin point her exact location. Two thin white lines appear on the screen, one sits horizontal across the top and the other vertical down the left side over a real-life image of the global map. The lines begin speedily moving up and down and from left to right. He is expecting to zero in over America, but to his surprise, it hovers over England. 'What?' he panicked. He leans closer and watches the tiny country rapidly grow before the target finally settles in on the centre of London England. After a nervous gulp, he once again taps his ear piece to connect yet another call which is answered immediately. 'We may have a problem.'

Lucian is positioned perfectly upright in his gaming chair with his glazed unblinking eyes glued to his screen and fixated in pure concentration. He tugs, flicks, and snaps his joysticks as he charges through the built-up areas of England that are growing increasingly populated on the gradual yet speedy approach towards the main city in the south-east. The relentless army rapidly dart through streets and roads concealing the very ground of which they pass with the dense hoard that follows, flattening small homes and garden sheds, charging through fences and brick walls, obliterating everything that stands in their way.

Young families with children and retired couples with nowhere to run or hide are left with no other option but to wait it out and hope they are lucky enough to survive, but when faced with the bitter end, when the odds of survival are highly unlikely, and terrified for the loss of loved ones, these make it harder to accept.

None of that even touches the pain of those who are captured and tossed around like the meat of cattle, as people are thrown to the floor with such force that they literally explode on impact. Some of the more sick and twisted children get more of a kick than others and enjoy making families watch as they tear them to pieces one at a time, barely giving them enough time to scream in pain before they are next to go. Young children, toddlers, and newborns are snatched from their parents' grasp and carelessly crushed in the godlike hands that simply snaps closed on them, spraying the blood of their own children across their faces and that as the last thing to see before your own death is cruelty at a whole new level, so with a final scream of unimaginable torment, they too are silenced. With no morals and without reason, they have created a blood bath and the president has witnessed most of these horrific events take place but has made himself powerless to it by allowing full gaming mode. Even for a ruler as sadistic as him, it is stomach churning. He now regrets placing this roar power in the hands of his unappreciated gamers who severely lack the respect for what he is trying to achieve.

They have turned their backs on humanity in search for what they would call fun, but it's too late for him to start thinking like that. His only option now is to continue forward as planned and hope they can get the job done, as even the ancient gods that lived without law and order would never permit such drastic measures of cruelty.

'Where do you want me?' asked Peter.

'Oh thank god,' Cailan replied. 'Attention, gamers, the Falcon has arrived . . . I repeat . . . the Falcon has arrived.'

'We could use some help,' cried Ewan. 'We're getting creamed out here . . . there's just too many.'

'Just do what you can,' he replied, 'and if they get too much, we'll be ready with our troops . . . how's Scotland holding up, Oscar?'

In a deep Scottish accent, he replies, 'Don't worry about us . . . we defended our land from the English, and we'll defend it from these bastards too.'

The Falcon swoops down from high above and remains in jet form while gliding through the US drones at phenomenal speed, a mere three feet from the ground and obliterating all those in his path. After finally locating Cailan, he finds himself stunned at how talented he really is. Cailan and a few of his equally gifted friends are in the thick of the battle and completely surrounded, yet somehow they are holding their ground and doing so with grace and style.

'Wow,' Peter gasped. 'Cailan . . . is that you?'

'Yeah,' he growled as he struggles to stay on his feet.

'Falcon coming in hot . . . where do you need me?'

To the surprise of them both, a thirty-foot drone drops in from above, creating an almighty blast that sends a ripple across the concrete like a shockwave from an explosion. He stands tall and looks down on all those around him like an undefeated warrior in search of his next victim. They are all so small and weak in comparison that a mere flick of his finger is enough to terminate them, so like a god he continues on, rumbling the ground after each step he takes.

'Um . . . Over there,' Cailan suggested.

Peter's eyes widen after seeing the giant machine marching towards them in the near distance. It is so unique that there is only one gamer who would be given the authority of control it.

'That must be, William,' he sarcastically stated.

'Oh shit,' Cailan panicked. 'Bad news, commanders . . . William's here and he's well prepared.'

'Don't panic just yet,' Peter interrupted. 'The Falcon will take care of this.'

The mammoth is glancing from one side to the other and all around in search for Peter as his primary target. 'Come on, show yourself,' he muttered. 'Where are you hiding you puny little insect . . . no one can stay hidden from the mammoth.'

The mammoth looks twice at the floor in front of him and locks his sight on the Falcon who suddenly appears from out of the blue. He is standing no more than ten feet in front of him and slowly looks up in the large red eyes of the mammoth.

'No way,' said William in disbelief before humorously chuckling to himself. 'This is going to be too easy,' for which the Falcon casually crosses his arms and sarcastically shakes his head.

'Still a rooky,' he chuckled.

The mammoth rapidly lifts his massive foot and stomps on him using every ounce of power he possesses, creating a spider web effect of cracks that instantly appears on the ground.

'Well . . . that's disappointing,' he grinned. The mammoth lifts his huge foot so he can proudly admire his work only to find nothing but shattered concrete.

'You speedy little bastard.'

The Falcon rapidly crawls around his leg and circles his huge waistline before darting over his shoulder and continues on like a spider wrapping its prey. The mammoth frantically tries to grab him every chance he gets but he is too fast. Little does he know the Falcon is scanning the entire shell for any weak points he can target and searching for a route to the main power core. Finally, he humorously mounts his huge head and rocks back and forth to avoid the giant hands like a bull rider performing in a live arena. Finally, the mammoth grabs him and pulls him to his front so he can witness with his own eyes the destruction of his most hated opponent and enjoy every second of it. To the surprise of them both, an unexpected drone from US gaming force climbs up the massive chest plates of the mammoth and glances in his big angry eyes before rapidly attacking his face. Its wild punches and kicks are combos of pure aggression and thrown with such force that he releases the Falcon and falls to the floor as a victim at the receiving end of brutality.

'Who the hell was that?' asked Peter thankfully.

'It wasn't one of ours,' said Cailan. 'Looks like you still have some friends out there.'

The US drone suddenly leaps off the mammoth and darts in to the thick of the surrounding battle, gliding casually within the ever-growing hoard as though it never happened.

The mammoth quickly jumps to his feet with an almighty crack that rumbles the floor like a blast of thunder and kicks the Falcon into the distance as he was caught unaware while checking his vitals for damage.

As he shrinks from afar, the mammoth locks on him as a target, followed by a missile that immediately takes launch from the centre of his chest. It almost instantly disappears, leaving a trail of dark and hot smoke after the deafening hiss gradually but quickly fades to nonexistence.

At phenomenal speed, the Falcon crashes into a random stretch of road with street lights all the way along both sides. He descends into an uncontrollable tumble, shattering the rock-hard concrete after each point of impact. He finally rolls to his feet and digs his heels in, tearing up the yet more of the road before steadily slowing to a stop. Unaffected by the lucky strike, he casually rises tall and proud, expanding his chest as though filling an artificial set of lungs.

A constant and irritating bleep alerts Peter, followed by a female's voice with a warning, 'Missile locked.'

'Oh shit,' he panicked and without delay he locates its immediate whereabouts.

He turns on the spot and sprints off the mark moving faster than Peter ever knew he could. He darts from left to right, avoiding random cars and trucks, leaping over other abandoned vehicles blocking the road. He runs the full stretch of road in a mere few seconds as the powerful missile follows in his path and gradually continues closing in. Moments from impact, the Falcon dives forward and is instantly concealed beneath the body of his jet that rapidly manifests around him as he shoots off in the distance leaving the missile no choice but to pursue.

He taunts and teases it to trick it into a collision but he can't seem to shake it, so after a moment of well executed flying, he decides he has a follow-up alternative. At hyper speed, he nose dives towards the ground, approaching at an alarming rate and gets what he thinks may be too close before instantly changing his trajectory from a mere few feet off the ground. He closely follows the long winding streets through the unusually quiet city of Oxford. With intention he darts straight up in the wide open space above and circles back on himself but unexpectedly locates the mammoth in the far distance so he heads straight for him at warp speed.

At the last moment, he is spotted by the mammoth, so he swings a strike to take him from mid-flight, but the Falcon glides right past him like the aerodynamics of wind. To William's surprise he is taken down by his own fire power as the missile collides with his shoulder and releases an almighty explosion, creating a visible shockwave before a mushroom cloud of fire rises from the point of impact. He stumbles back with great force, stomping his huge feet in an attempt to maintain balance but he is too far gone, so finally he falls to the floor once more and lands next to his detached arm that is shattered and melted from the immense heat.

The Falcon impulsively grabs the huge head of the mammoth by interlocking his fingers beneath his bulky chin and digs his heels in the artificial collar bones. He pulls with every ounce of power he possesses, while twisting and turning his neck from one side to the other. Finally, with bright sparks and spraying fluid from severed pipes, it comes off, leaving the massive machine lifeless as its big red eyes slowly fade into darkness.

CHAPTER 26

The main doors to a high-ranking gaming facility slowly and mechanically open, revealing two muscle-bound marines in full uniform. They step through at the same time, ducking their heads to avoid the large door frame, with a young and geeky-looking boy pacing in toe and almost jogging to keep up. With a quick pace in their stride and intimidation in their strut they march across the vast facility with their eyes fixed on where ever they are headed. Every gamer is so engrossed in the battle that they're almost blind from their presence. The odd one or two see them and curiously watch what they're up to but try to give the impression they haven't noticed.

Lucian is glaring at his screen as his eyes frantically flick from one side to the other while snapping his controls in frustration. To his surprise, a huge hand grasps his shoulder, making him feel puny and defenceless.

'Come with us,' said one of the marines.

His heart suddenly races beyond belief as he hangs his head in shame in the hope that the president will be merciful. He looks up at them with weepy eyes before his hopeless reply. 'I can't just leave my station, my drone is active.'

The two marines glance at each other with a grin of amusement and turn back to him in unison. 'That is no longer your concern.'

The other grabs him by the scruff of his neck and effortlessly lifts him from his seat, leaving his arms and legs dangling as he carelessly lowers him to the floor, making his body judder from the shock. They leave him just long enough to see the geeky buck tooth boy from behind jump in his gaming chair with a smirk of arrogance. He grasps the joysticks in excitement and can't wait to get started. Not a moment more passes before the screen turns blank, leaving only his reflection staring back at him in awe, followed by the words *drone terminated* repeatedly flashing across the centre in bright and bald characters. William shakes his head and drops his shoulders in disappointment before turning to walk away in disgust.

The marines then begin shoving him continuously along the narrow paths that run through the dense blocks of gaming stations, and like bullies on a playground, they push him harder each time. His friends that are stationed nearby are powerless to what's happening and want to ask or defend him but fear that one word may land them in a world of trouble, leaving them no choice but to sit back and let his fate run its course.

Many of the gamers further in climb high in their seats and lift their chins for better look at what's going on, only to be startled by a female voice that suddenly echoes throughout. 'Gamers,' she announced, 'we have a traitor in our midst, I repeat, we have traitor in our midst . . . please resume your stations . . . this issue will be dealt with accordingly.'

One of his closer friends pokes his head round from the side of his chair just in time to see the doors close after Lucian was aggressively pushed through forcing the doors to burst open as the marines march through behind him. 'Something's not right,' he muttered. 'I agree,' whispered yet another voice, 'why would he of all people do something to jeopardise his position.'

'Exactly . . . I hope he's okay,' he replied as he turns and glances at the door once more.

Nicki is sprinting through a string of narrow and windy roads, shifting at speeds way beyond human capabilities. She rapidly darts from side to side to avoid the public of the strangely busy city of London, and while gracefully gliding with long and steady strides in her pace, she messes the clothes and hair of everyone she passes, leaving them all shocked in disbelief.

To her surprise, the voice of Mathias contacts her from deep within her mind. 'I don't want to hurt you,' he pleaded. 'I just want to talk.'

She cleverly expands her view as her built-in defence mechanisms activate, making her quicker and stronger in many ways, greatly improving her timing and accuracy particularly when in combat mode. She rapidly flicks her unique vision all around her, in a frantic search for any strange activity nearby, or a potential threat in pursuit.

'Please listen to me,' he begged. 'You're far more intelligent than this . . . and I'm smart enough to know not to try anything stupid, so please Nicki, just stop and let's talk.'

After a brief moment of consideration, she gradually begins to slow down to a steady jog until finally, she stops and curiously looks around. She slowly turns in a full circle, scanning every inch of a wide radius and once back where she began she unexpectedly locks eyes with Mathias who is standing not ten feet in front of her with his hands at his side.

'What do you want?' she nervously asked.

'Just to talk.'

'I think we're way past talking, don't you?'

'Please just listen. . .' he pleaded. 'I can help you.'

Feeling offended by his unwanted and diminishing offer, she frowns in anger and clenches her fists in defence to confusion as she wonders why she is suddenly feeling such emotion. Over to her side is a tall give way road sign firmly embedded in the concrete on the edge of the path. With a powerful grasp, she wraps her hand around it and with almighty force she begins to lift. 'I don't need your help,' she growled. The pavement suddenly cracks, leaving a large clump of solid stone on the end of the pole for which Mathias slowly steps back in disbelief as she cautiously edges towards him with torment in her scowl.

'Nicki,' he panicked. 'Please don't do this.'

'And why not?'

'Just look around you . . . you're home.'

A flashback unexpectedly startles her but she immediately shakes it off and growls in anger once more through her clamped teeth. 'Stop fucking with my head.'

In the blink of an eye, she swings, shattering the concrete as it connects with the middle of his chest and he suddenly shoots off in the distance. She drops the pole leaving her hand print embedded in the metal and in deep thought she watches it ding off the floor, knowing deep down that this is far from over. After a moment of weighing the odds of what's to come, she turns and slowly begins to walk away, only to be startled once more by the voice of Mathias. 'I don't wish to fight you.'

She turns just in time to see him gently float to the floor and immediately sets her sights on his wide eyes that for some reason she finds herself drawn to, only she fights any feelings with a deep frown.

'Just let me say what I need to say and then you can do whatever you want.'

She knows that he would be a very difficult opponent after witnessing him survive such brutal and deadly power, so reluctantly decides to give him a chance. 'Okay,' she challenged. 'You've got thirty seconds until this gets really ugly.'

'We have known each other for a long time, romantically, intimately.'

'That's funny,' she interrupted, 'because you don't look familiar at all.'

'Nicki,' he smiled. 'We have shared our deepest secrets, we've lived our fantasies and dreams hand in hand . . . there was a time I trusted you with my life . . . and I still do.'

Her response is a careless shrug of the shoulders while sarcastically raising her top lip in disgust. 'Anything else?'

'Please, Nicki . . . let me show you . . . or do you not want your memories? . . . Do you not want to know who you really are. . .?'

She is programmed to refuse such an offer but cannot deprive the curiosity from her human half any longer.

'There was also a time when you trusted me,' he gently reminded.

He reaches out his hand and patiently waits while keeping his eyes firmly fixed on hers. She very slowly reaches out in response but can't explain why. It suddenly occurs to her that human emotion is far greater than she originally anticipated. It is at this point of realisation that she unexpectedly feels the need for answers and physically cannot stop herself perusing them. No sooner than her fingertip touches the palm of his hand they suddenly disappear, after being instantly concealed by a ball of light that rapidly deteriorates and disturbs the dust and leaves into a sudden rotation that gradually settles in their stead. They instantly appear in a well-kept bedroom that looks perfectly maintained and untouched for quite some time. The energy release from their arrival is so intense that it bursts as an unnatural gust of wind that messes the flowery bed sheets and vigorously turns the blank pages of an open diary that dominates the desk top of a white and stylish dressing table. From sheer disbelief, she pulls her hand away in awe and covers her mouth.

'Oh my god,' she whispered with a giggle, 'that's amazing.'

For reasons she can't explain, she steadily begins to feel at ease and overwhelmed by the mutual trust and respect that tells her human side she is in good hands. With knitted brows, something catches her eye and she slowly steps towards it, casually brushing her fingertips across the spines of a single row of books on a lonely shelf, followed by gliding them along the unusual paint work on the walls that looks cleverly photographic all the way around, with protruding flowers from freshly cut grass that gives the occupier the illusion of sleeping in an open field on a hot summer's day. She opens a small red chest with shiny gold edges that are patterned with roses and as the inside is revealed, a flashback catches her unaware. Wide eyed and lost for words, she gasps before slowly reaching in and retrieving a gold and extremely elegant diamond ring that she hopelessly gazes at in shock. The realisation suddenly grabs her and she looks up at Mathias in disbelief.

'This my room,' she whispered.

'And what makes you say that?'

Using her mind's eye, she is caught unaware by yet another flashback and after seeing herself sweating with fear while panting in agony, another flashback jars her neck, so she immediately tries to shake it off, only her eyes begin to shake so she squeezes them shut as a desperate attempt to suppress the inevitable. Suddenly and beyond her control, she is swarmed by blurry and confusing visions; she can hear many different voices, only all of them are muffled but one voice in particular is as clear as day. 'Keep this safe,' said the unknown voice of an old lady. 'It has been handed down countless generations and now, it belongs to you.'

She squeezes her eyes shut once more and after slowly opening them, the blurry outline of Mathias gradually becomes clear to her. 'I'm sorry but . . . where are we again?' she asked.

He cautiously steps towards her with his hands at his front, to ready himself for a possible outburst.

'We're in Buckingham Palace.'

'Are you saying I'm Royalty?'

'Well that's one of the things I was going to say,' he shrugged, 'but more importantly, you are a good person, with a family that loves you. You have friends in such high places and every one of them would give their lives to save yours . . . don't you get it Nicki . . . you can help me end this war.'

'I don't think you get it,' she snapped. 'I'm programmed . . . and no amount of memories from my past can change that.'

Mathias simply huffs in frustration as he is now beginning to lose patience.

Lucian is sweating in fear and shaking beyond belief; with tear-filled eyes and a bleeding lip he growls in pain while rapidly typing on a computer. The two marines are standing either side of him, both with a desert eagle .50 in the firm grasp of their hands, aiming directly at his head.

The president is sat behind in a huge soft bucket seat and casually chuckling to himself while watching the poor boy tremble with terror. He growls once more in agony before lifting his arm and carefully cupping it in the other. He curls up in fear while weeping at the sight of his throbbing hand as he gently and carefully rests it in his lap. 'I think my fingers are broken,' he cried.

The two marines look over at the president in unison and he simply nods in return.

'Oh no,' said one of them sarcastically after crouching down beside him. 'Are you saying you can't continue?'

He looks up with his tear-filled eyes in desperation as the sweat pours down his face. 'It hurts too much,' he wept.

The marine grins and drops his head before slowly lifting his cold empty eyes. 'Well isn't that a shame.' The other pins him in the seat and covers his mouth with his huge hand while the other lifts his throbbing arm by the wrist before slamming it down on the desk. He holds his hand flat and carelessly spreads his fingers, leaving him screaming in unbearable agony as he struggles for breath beneath the massive hand that almost covers his entire face. He lifts the poor boy's middle finger and presses the tiny print against the flat of his huge palm before very slowly forcing it back. The bone is gradually forced to breaking point as he kicks and screams in desperation, only beneath the great strength he is physically unable to move even one inch and finally the bone snaps. After the horrific crack, he continues bending it until the nail is pressed against his swollen wrist for which the marine leans close to his ear and whispers, 'Next it will be your knee caps . . . now do what we want or there will be no end to your suffering.'

As a victim of unimaginable cruelty, they let him go at the same time and he trembles in fear at the sight of his disfigured hand. Using only the few fingers he has, he continues typing and does so with great difficulty. The pain is more horrific than he has ever known before but he must continue as he cannot bear for the torture to get any worse.

Nicki is sat on her own white metal-framed bed shaped as ivory and flowers that hug the entire frame. She gently rubs the flowery duvet and casually looks up at the ceiling. 'I use to play in this room and pretend I was in the middle of nowhere. For a short moment in the morning of my mother's death, all my pain would disappear.'

'It is amazing,' Mathias replied. 'It looks so real.'

'If you think that's good, check this out.' She darts to the window with a skip in her stride and quickly lowers the thick blackout blind. It is so well fitted that it blocks out every inch of daylight leaving them in pitch black darkness. After a moment, countless amounts of sparkling dots twinkle in to focus and glide in rotation across the ceiling, displaying real-life star constellations that slowly pass by.

Suddenly and to the surprise of them, both her neck begins twitching as though a malfunction of some kind has come into effect. 'What's going on?' he curiously asked as he lifts the blind changing night to day in a flash.

'I don't know,' she panicked, 'but whatever it is, it's not good.'

Lucian quickly types the last few digits before quickly dropping his hands in his lap and crying from the unbearable pain as he sobs in desperation.

'Is it done?' asked the president as he leaps to Lucian's side and snatches the keyboard. After seeing no proof of regained control, he confusedly looks down at him awaiting further instruction.

Lucian is now feeling faint from the pain and discomfort so he rocks back and forth with droopy eyes and mumbles under his breath. 'Press the enter key twice.'

The president looks down at the weeping boy and almost feels petty for him but he conceals any feelings or emotion with a sarcastic sob. 'This is what happens to backstabbers and traitors . . . you're a lying little bastard and you deserve everything coming to you . . . having said that . . . you've done your job so . . . goodbye . . . I suppose.'

The flat end of a silver desert eagle is firmly pressed against his temple, forcing him to lean his head to one side. His eyes squeeze shut as tight as possible and to him, silence descends but it seems to last forever. He weeps once more in suspense to what follows and fears that this is now the end but from the sheer terror his entire body judders as a loud click makes him force his blood-red eyes wide open and gasp in confusion as to why he is still alive, leaving the two marines chuckling as they place their guns back in their holsters. The continual laughing is so belittling that it brings a whole new meaning to such levels of cruelty.

'On second thought,' said the president, 'keep him alive for now . . . he might be useful later on.'

The two giant bullies lift him from the seat and carelessly drop him to the floor and with great difficulty he rolls over to his back, followed by the marines grabbing a leg each and dragging him across the hard floor and out the door. The president simply grins and shakes his head in disgust before hovering his finger over the enter key.

'What's happening to me?' said Nicki. She begins panicking in discomfort as any other human being would when confronted by events of such abnormality. Suddenly, she is silenced as her head drops forward resting her chin against her chest, yet remaining perfectly balanced on her feet. With knitted brows, he rests his hand on her shoulder and slightly crouches to catch her eyes before softly asking, 'Nicki . . . are you okay?'

She slowly lifts her head and immediately locks on to the caring gaze of Mathias, only her eyes suddenly seem cold and empty as though he is now confronted with a totally different person, like a being with no soul, a mere imitation of life with no rules or boundaries, and no regrets.

'Nicki,' he asked once more, 'please talk to me.'

The dark pupils of her unforgiving eyes dilate beyond natural expansion covering the subtle colours with darkness, making them jet black all over and massively widening her peripheral vision.

'Oh shit,' he panicked.

CHAPTER 27

High and bright golden flames rise from the burning logs within the deep Hurth of the featured mantel that conceals the gatekeeper's passage. The warm shadowy light reveals the dark and cosy room with a soft flickering glow. Gracie is staring into the tall and ever-changing fire with a hopeful gaze, supporting the queen's skinny arm rested over her shoulder as she nervously snuggles into the chest.[1]

To their surprise, the door behind bursts open and Abdul charges through with urgency in his stride; he jogs to her front for her full attention and she shamefully lifts her eyes. 'Your Majesty,' he panicked, 'I regret to tell you . . . the defence line has fallen and the enemy is closing in fast.'

She simply fills her lungs before releasing an expressive sigh of acceptance. 'How long?'

'Six minutes, ma'am, we need to get you to the safe zone.'

'There's no point, Abdul, it won't stop them.'

"You know what?' she snapped 'You could be right . . . but it may buy you the time you need . . . I don't believe in miracles, but I do believe in you.'

'Okay,' she agreed, sounding humorously egotistic. She reaches out her hand and he immediately helps her to her feet. 'Who lit the fire?' he curiously asked.

'I did . . . with all help fading I was trying to contact Cedric,' she drops her eyes and shakes her head in disappointment before sighing, 'but he's not listening. . . How many have we lost?'

Fearing she is in no fit state for further disappointment, he quickly avoids the question by subtly advising that time is of the essence, 'Ma'am, we really must get moving.'

'How many?' she snapped.

Torn between telling her the truth or lying leaves him stunned for a moment, so before replying, he drops his guard and rolls his eyes, knowing right away that she could tell 'Countless . . . and I am led to believe that the slaughter has been horrific.'

She looks at the flames in shear desperation and gently asks once more as a single tear rolls down her cheek. 'Please Cedric, I beg you . . . please help us.' The final gaze of hope slowly deteriorates into nothing more than a disappointed release of breath after receiving no answer.

At the very second of turning to leave something catches her eye and she snaps her sight as her heart fills with hope. In complete suspense, all three of them suppress a gasp as a single amber of glowing ash rises with the immense heat and floats into the clean air of the open room. All eyes immediately lock onto the fading glow as the weightless flake slowly glides to the floor and settles on the soft and spongy rug, they continue gazing until it fades into nothing more than a silvery grey slither and releases its final strand of smoke. She picks up Gracie and hugs her with a squeeze for a hasty exit, only to be stunned once more as the entire rug bursts into flames.

With a quick response, Abdul darts to the dark corner and nervously rips a fire extinguisher off the wall. The shock from the unexpected has forced him into panic mode as he snatches the pin with shaky hands and bit by bit he slowly defeats it, feeling his bravery enhance after each step he takes. Once the tall flames are put out, he looks up at the queen with Gracie in her arms and she is staring at the cremated material in shock, so he curiously looks to his feet while backing away, only to find strange patches all over that are untouched and unscathed. They are randomly scattered and perfectly shaped as unfamiliar symbols that have left them all feeling disorientated.

'What are they?' asked the queen.

Abduls reply is merely a shrug of a shoulder as he wonders how this is even possible.

'It's ancient script,' said Gracie.

All eyes are immediately drawn to her for answers and she glances at them both in the hope that she is right.

'What does it say?' asked the queen in suspense.

She glides the tip of her finger across her line of sight while studying them for a short moment to try and make sense of if all; finally, she translates them to English and very slowly reads aloud: 'system . . . shut down.'

'System shut down,' Abdul confusedly repeated.

'Of course,' said Gracie having understood. 'He wants me to shut down the system.'

'Impossible,' Abdul interrupted. 'We've had our top scientists working on that for months, the fire wall is impenetrable.'

'Um . . . that's not entirely true,' said Gracie.

They immediately fix their eyes on her for answers, praying for good news and at that very moment she nervously fills her lungs, 'I think I can shut them down.'

'Good heavens,' said the queen. 'Why didn't you tell us this sooner?'

'Because shutting them down is all I can do, the system will reboot in a matter of seconds so it's always been a pointless exercise . . . unless . . . we can find a way to take control.'

'But the only way to control the drones,' said Abdul, 'is to power the entire mainframe and our system is limited, we could end up shutting ourselves down.'

'What about a DNA-based super computer?' said Gracie, 'A living breathing system, with no rules and no limitations.'

'Mathias,' the queen gasped.

'Your Majesty,' Abdul interrupted, 'we have four minutes, so whatever the plan . . . we had better do it fast.'

'Is this really possible?' asked the queen in disbelief.

'Yes . . . but not from here.'

With that they hastily march out and the door slowly closes behind them leaving the room in complete silence, only the crackling from the burning logs is far more noticeable. Not a moment more passes before Mathias crashes through the wall in an uncontrollable tumble and stops dead against the wall opposite.

'Fine,' he growled before rising to his feet with a deep frown. 'If that's how you want to play it.'

She instantly appears at his side and gently whispers in his ear, 'Who's playing?'

He turns to face her in surprise but no sooner does his head move she swiftly uppercuts him; in the blink of an eye, he crashes through three ceilings and out onto the roof terrace of the huge palace. While falling, he looks around at the beautiful views of his homeland as a deep rumble catches his full attention. After gently landing, he cautiously walks to the edge of the building and knits his brows with concern as the courtyard comes into view, only to see the queen swiftly charge through the huge doors of the palace after Abdul barged them open to clear her path. He continues watching from a distance as she marches to a random spot and gently lays Gracie down on the cold and hard concrete.

'There's no point in fighting this,' said Nicki from behind him and at that very moment his unique vision rapidly expands beyond great distance, like the eye of travelling sound that follows an almighty blast. The enemy is closing in from all directions and to him the mighty rumble increases all the more after seeing the unimaginable army of drones sprinting towards them and obliterating everything and everyone in their path.

'Just surrender,' Nicki advised, 'and no more of your people will die.'

With a sigh of impatience, he rolls his eyes before sarcastically turning to face her and with a smug grin he calmly replies, 'I think you need a time out.'

'Oh really,' she challenged, 'and how do you propose to?'

She suddenly shoots off in the distance at tremendous speed and rapidly shrinks from a far. Knowing she will not be best pleased, he huffs with worry, and for the first time since the very day they met, he is not looking forward to her return. In the blink of an eye, he vanishes and instantaneously manifests at the queen's side. 'What are you doing? . . . You should be at the safe zone . . . get her inside,' he ordered.

'Oh my lord,' the queen gasped in disbelief. 'I can't believe it . . . we all thought you were dead.'

He helplessly looks down at Gracie only to witness first hand her petit and fragile body vigorously shake having willingly placed herself in the path of great danger in one last hope to stop this war. 'What's happening to her?' he asked.

'She'll be okay,' said the queen. After a moment, the queen grasps his chin and turns him to face her. 'Trust me . . . she's a lot tougher than she looks.'

'What's she doing?'

'She believes she can access the US system through a hidden rout, a back door if you will and if it can be opened she may be able to sneak through undetected and shut the whole thing down . . . she said she can only give us a window of a mere few seconds, so do you think you can reboot it?'

He is taken aback by her sheer power; just to imagine what she has seen has forced him to once again believe in destiny, as for the first time in his life he actually feels that he is where he is meant to be.

'I'll try.'

The rumble suddenly increases massively, right after the queen's eyes expand and her pupils dilate in sheer terror. 'Oh . . . my . . . lord' she gasped before grabbing his arm with shaky hands and begs in blind panic. 'Please Mathias . . . you must keep them away from her, she's our only hope.'

He lovingly glances down at Gracie before aggressively locking his sights on Abdul for a short and intense moment but nothing is said between them. He simply nods in the trust that this abnormally large man will do everything in his power to keep them safe, even at the cost of his own life.

He calmly takes two steps back and right before the desperate eyes of the queen, he vanishes for which she immediately crouches to her knees and gently strokes Gracie's rosy cheek.

The Falcon is almost operating itself fully and with very little help from Peter. He is simply sat in his gaming chair with his hands on his fidgeting knees, watching in astonishment through the eyes of the Falcon as he savagely but effortlessly tears the US drones to pieces and terminates each and every one that crosses his path. He bites his knuckles with excitement as the Falcon has proven to be a conscious machine, the very first of its kind and quite possibly the next step in human evolution. He is well aware that this could lead humanity to a place that they are not yet ready for but being a strong believer in destiny has left him no other choice but to allow fait to run its course. 'Falcon,' said Peter, 'stay alert . . . something tells me we haven't seen the end of William.'

Across the middle of his screen, the words 'who's William' is displayed in large and bright characters. To the surprise of them both, every single drone stops attacking and quickly they all back away, forming a perfect circle around him that continues to expand until they have reached a safe distance.

'What the hell is going on?' he whispered.

The Falcon simply drops his guard but stands at the ready and shifts his sights all around him in confusion to the unexpected turn of events and simply waits for the next move. The moment intensifies further once the US drones come to a sudden stop in perfect unison as the heavy right foot of each one stomps with a single thud. After the threatening crash alerts the Falcon of a very difficult time ahead, silence descends from all around; leaving only the sound of rushing wind from between buildings as the rustling leaves of a few nearby trees almost conceals the distant screams from the hundreds and thousands of Brits that are suffering with pain and torment. Regardless of what happens, he is happy that he made the choice to fight back, as he feels disgusted with himself having almost become the commander of such an inhumane invasion of unthinkable brutality.

The Falcon senses that something doesn't sit right as a strange feeling beneath his feet leaves him hopelessly gazing at a puddle in the road. With knitted brows, Peter taps his ear piece. 'What's that?' he whispered.

The repetitive thud quickly intensifies as small ripples from the edge of the puddle shrink to the centre and continues over and over. The crashing gets louder after each bang, so whatever it is that's coming is approaching at great speed and is now shaking the ground beneath his feet. To everyone's surprise, it comes to a sudden stop and once again leaves silence throughout the city.

'Where is it?' Peter nervously asked.

His unblinking eyes are glued to his screen as the rush from his sinking guts intensifies in the suspense of what's to come. An almighty crash from directly behind the Falcon makes him turn to face the unknown threat and does so in a way that only a human could express.

'Oh shit,' said Peter, 'not another one.'

The drone's size in comparison to the mammoth is immense and its thick metal armour is perfectly shaped in massive proportion to imitate man at his strongest. He slowly rises from the crouch position and drops his huge clenched fists to his side, standing proud like a fearless undefeated warrior in a head-to-head battle to the death.

A row of words appear across Peter's screen in large and white bold letters leaving him confused as to what's happening, so he nervously reads aloud. 'I've been looking forward to gaming with you too . . . good luck driver . . . What?' he panicked.

Suddenly, the Falcon's shoulders drop as though he has just powered down and after the bright blue glow in his drones eyes fade to darkness, he is left completely defenceless. That short moment of emptiness and nerve-racking vulnerability sends Peter into a state of panic so he rapidly types the operation code to regain control. This is his chance to take back the honour he deserves as the commanding gamer that is once again leading an entire nation and so far, his reputation has perceived him.

As a gamer he knows that in terms of respect, he would honour any decision made by his commander without question and would follow in his stead. This thought sends his mind into wonder. Can I persuade them to follow? Can we end this reign of tyranny?

This next challenge could potentially determine the outcome of this war, so he huffs in certainty that they will know soon enough and without further delay he proceeds with intention to finish what he started. The Falcon is set to full power mode and his target is locked. He casually walks towards his colossal challenger and simply ignores the confident and intimidating stares of all the surrounding drones. Peter grins with a hint of certainty knowing that the driver is in fact William, as there is only one gamer as egotistic as this, who would happily have everyone stand by and watch while he reaps the glory of success. He also knows that the spectating drivers are just as eager to fight as he is, so with no more time to lose, the crowd begins to fade as this particular battle is one they are quite happy not to intervene.

The massive drone confusedly looks around, only to see his fellow gamers showing no further interest in his big moment. For a second or two, William is shocked and arrogantly shrugs his shoulders before shuffling back in his seat.

'Suit yourselves,' he moaned.

They both casually step towards each other with a fearless step in their stride, like gladiators in a Roman arena marching towards a challenger, ready and awaiting death. To the surprise of them both, Mathias appears in between them and stops them in their tracks. He immediately locks eyes with the Falcon and without warning his mind is overwhelmed and cornered in a transition of question as though this machine is somehow manipulating his thought pattern. For reasons he can't explain, the overall feeling is good, so he decides without delay to trust his instincts. He nods for a reply and the Falcon simply mimics his gesture in return. They both look up at the giant beast in unison and proceed as an unexpected team.

CHAPTER 28

The queen is doing her very best to comfort Gracie during her desperate time of need. To the surprise of everyone standing in the courtyard of Buckingham Palace, the solid metal gates burst open and three large US drones casually walk through.

At the top of his voice, Abdul shouts 'Open fire' for which they are suddenly swarmed by thousands of countless bullets, but the effect is minimal, they simply judder repeatedly from the countless sparks and ricochets.

They humorously glance at each other before standing firm to the ground and dropping their clenched fists to their sides. A plate on each of their shoulders flick open, followed by two unique rapid fire guns that immediately take aim. They quickly and independently search for a target and open fire in response, destroying the entire face of the palace in a mere few seconds.

Without a second thought, the queen dives over Gracie as a shield, immediately followed by Abdul who covers them both.

After the extremely intense few seconds of explosive and deafening gun fire, it finally stops, leaving a high-pitched and painful whistle deep in their ears.

A brief moment passes and Abdul shakes it off. 'Are you okay?'

'We're fine,' she said with exasperation in her breath.

He slowly pokes his head up over the low wall, only to find the three terrifying drones are still standing and heading straight for them.

'Stay down,' he quietly warned, before proudly rising to his feet as an invite to a physical challenge, simply to buy more time for his queen.

184

To them, this battle so far has been all too easy, so while they're still on full gaming mode, they may as well make the most of it and after shrugging their shoulders in agreement they tauntingly fan out around him. He bravely holds eye contact but subtly talks quietly down to her through the corner of his mouth. 'Whatever happens . . . stay . . . down.'

With honour, he steps forward like a brave warrior who has never been more ready for death. The queen weeps as the blurry image of Abdul marches on from beyond her line of site, leaving her praying, hoping that this will not be the last time she sees him alive.

They slowly circle him with a constant stare as they gradually close in, but he delays for as long as he can, until he cannot physically go another second without defending himself. Luckily, he is ready for it to get ugly. He fearlessly glances at each of them with defiance in his confident eyes, before closing his large hand into a tight fist and speaking aloud. 'Shields up.'

With knitted brows, the three random American gamers lean closer to their screens and gaze in disbelief as a metal helmet with an open face manifests around his head. The unique mechanics quickly expand across his shoulders and down his spine; it continues around his elbows, knees, and ankles and finally ends with a solid ball of reinforced metal that conceals his massive knuckles.

In surprise, two of the drones humorously take a step back, but the one he is face to face with doesn't move an inch and simply stands motionless with an angry stare.

Abdul has seen these machines in action and knows that he will not be strong enough or fast enough for this challenge to be fair, so with the element of surprise, he strikes by charging like an insane rugby player in the middle of a scrum.

While growling with strain through his clamped teeth, he lifts the heavy drone and immediately forces it to the hard ground, before aggressively climbing to his knees and punching the drone all over, like a savage warrior attacking as a wild beast and putting his heart and soul into every violent swing.

The foolish driver saw him as a mere human and completely underestimated him by regretfully ignoring his sheer size. The young gamer desperately tries to defend his honour but his drone has already begun to malfunction as the unexpected beating has destroyed and shattered its vitals.

After repeatedly punching and cracking its cold and empty face, the shameful imitation of life finally fades from its dark eyes, leaving nothing more than a lifeless shell of shattered artificial body parts.

Once satisfied that the drone will not be trying again, he proudly rises to his feet with exasperation in his shaky breath, but he will not give up until he has given the final beat of his heart to protect his beloved queen.

He looks over to one side and locks an angry stare on his next challenger by asserting his natural dominance that is something even a robot cannot deny. At the very moment of Abdul approaching the drone, it snaps into a fighting pose to ready himself for the same treatment.

'Abdul, look out,' shouted the queen.

He turns as quick as he can but proves to be too slow as the drone behind swings a sneaky but powerful thump with intention to rupture his kidney.

He almost instantly loses his balance and drops to his knees, followed by the soul of a large metal foot smashing against the centre of his spine and forcing him six feet forward, leaving him an unconscious mess.

The two young and careless drivers start laughing like bullies in a playground as the drone sits him up while crouching to one knee behind him and pins him with an inescapable choke hold. Desperate for air, he kicks and growls while hopelessly tugging the solid metal arm to ease the pressure, but once again, he proves to be just too weak.

He is moments from giving up but in the peripherals of his blurry vision he nervously watches countless drones gradually flood the courtyard. His challenger humorously eases the restraint of Abdul's neck to keep him alive long enough to see the obliteration of the palace and witness with his last breath, the horrific murder of his precious queen.

She nervously peeps over the low wall and gasps at the sight of endless and terrifying drones quickly approaching her. Not surprisingly she is overcome with panic and without thinking she grabs hold of Gracie in a futile attempt to run away but her tiny and unconscious body is firmly fixed to the ground.

'Please,' she screamed while struggling to lift her. 'Please . . . come back to me,' she sobbed. She looks up again in desperation with no way out, so with her last few seconds, she lovingly curls over Gracie and waits for death.

'Please Gracie,' she whispered. 'I beg you.'

She tries to lift her once more, but numerous thick green routes suddenly push through the concrete, cracking the hard surface all around her, and conceals her beneath a layer of slimy tentacles, leaving her cute little face as the only part of her uncovered.

The sight of Gracie's position for which she is powerless to help sends a tear down her cold cheek and creeps to the point of her chin, before dropping to the dusty hard floor like a single drop of falling rain.

At that very moment, the drones jump high in the air to crush them beneath their heavy feet, only to be unexpectedly chopped in half by a thirty-metre whip that is burning from end to end with bright golden flames of fire.

The long whip flicks back with a deafening snap and immediately repeats, obliterating hundreds of drones with a single lash, slicing them like a knife through butter.

The queen nervously opens her eyes in wonder as to why she is still breathing and slowly peeps once again over the wall. The ground is covered with sparking severed limbs and smoking with spaying fluid that steams off the molten metal. She quickly ducks for the last time as countless drones continue to flood the courtyard in the distance. To her sheer surprise, the gatekeeper slowly protrudes through the ground in front of her and proudly rises as a fifteen foot man made of fire for which the drones stop in their tracks and stare in disbelief.

Abdul quickly darts behind him and crouches over the queen to cover her as a human shield while the gatekeeper continues to throw his whip through the never-ending hoard that just keeps on coming.

To his confusion, they all stop at the same time and create a perfect circle around him, standing a mere few inches from beyond reach of his unique but powerful defence.

After a moment, the gatekeeper stops, leaving his burning whip laid across the floor and slowly sinking beneath the concrete while steadily retracting into his open palm. He fearlessly stands tall and proud before expanding his chest to full capacity and roaring with a terrifying growl in his throat that rumbles through the earth like thunder in the eye of a storm.

Natalia is watching everything from a bird's-eye view while standing behind a young boy who is sweating with shaky breath and rapidly typing on his keyboard.

'Come on,' Natalia begged. 'It can't end like this.'

'Yes,' the boy celebrated while clapping his hands to contain his excitement. 'We have full control of destiny's decision,' he proudly stated and looks up at her in desperation for orders.

'Take aim . . . and destroy those tin cans.'

A satellite in orbit of the earth has been carefully positioned by the boy for the last few days, and now that he has gained full control of her, he has access to all of her components. An image of earth appears on his screen and repeatedly magnifies over and over again, right down to the south-east of England. As his clear vision zooms in from above the American gaming force, covering the very ground of which they charge for hundreds of miles in every direction before the image settles steady over the palace.

'Be careful not to hit them,' said Natalia.

'Don't worry,' he assured her. 'This weapon is accurate within one millimetre of its target. It could shoot the fleas off a dog's back.'

Natalia fills her lungs with a very nervous breath. 'Do it,' she sighed.

'With pleasure,' he proudly stated. He places on his headset and makes himself comfortable before aligning his target and preparing a string of victims.

With means to taunt, the gatekeeper slowly turns in a full circle and proudly displays his will to keep fighting as surrender is a notion he does not understand. Suddenly, he appears calm by standing straight and dropping his scorching hands to his side before curiously looking up at the clear sky above and remaining perfectly motionless, as the drones all around him are heavily showered with a rapid downfall of whistling bullets. As the circle of demolished robots quickly expands with the gatekeeper at its centre, he proudly opens his arms to welcome his new friends from a far, thanking them for restoring his faith in humanity and momentarily honouring them for protecting those that matter most.

The odd one or two luckily make it through and dart for the gatekeeper, only to be unexpectedly penetrated through the chest with his large burning hot fists, leaving huge holes from front to back and dropping as molten heaps of useless metal.

To the queen's surprise, Mathias appears in front of her and makes her nervously gasp in shock, for which the gatekeeper charges for him but Mathias simply stands straight and doesn't move a muscle.

The queen quickly stands between them with both arms in front to stop him. 'No,' she shouted. 'He's a friend.'

For a brief moment, he withdraws the powers of Mathias leaving him more vulnerable than ever while the gatekeeper searches his soul for evidence of honesty and truth. Once satisfied, he angrily looks him up and down before turning his back to him and glances from left to right in search of his next victim.

The young boy in control of destiny's decision releases all controls in disbelief and nervously looks up at Natalia. 'What are you doing?' she panicked. 'Keep firing.'

'It's jammed.'

'Shit,' she sighed. 'Can you fix it?'

'I think so,' he nodded. 'But it may take some time.'

'Just do what you can.'

He rubs his clammy hands down his sweaty face and immediately, he gets on with it.

'Oh no,' said Natalia in disbelief as she crouches and gazes hopelessly at his screen with a glare of sheer terror.

The drones immediately realise that the unknown gun fire has stopped, so without a second thought, they close in once again at alarming speeds.

The gatekeepers whip slowly protrudes from the tips of his burning fingers and readily places one foot forward in preparation to throw his lash.

Mathias stands up as though lost in a trance leaving, the queen on her knees next to Gracie and casually walks to the front of the gatekeeper. His long golden whip retracts as he turns and looks at the queen in confusion, for which she nervously shrugs her shoulders in the hope that he knows what he's doing.

The gatekeeper watches intently as the drones quickly approach them from a far and cautiously steps back, unconvinced that this tiny human's power could possibly outweigh his own.

Mathias slowly and strenuously raises his arms as though struggling to lift a spherical ball of energy in each hand but the drones are closing fast and the gatekeeper looks down at him in a state of panic, hoping that whatever he is about to do he does it fast.

The drones then charge through the gates, crumbling the high walls around the courtyard and carelessly crushing the rubble beneath their stomping feet.

Their sights are set on Abdul and the gatekeeper, each one is still on full gaming mode, programmed with only one purpose . . . to search and destroy.

The gatekeeper braces himself for impact, but to his surprise, they all freeze in mid stride within feet of crushing them; some are suspended in the air as though time itself has stopped, leaving every muscle in the body of Mathias under immense pressure and motionlessly stunned with shaky limbs. With great difficulty, he slowly crouches down to a ball and strenuously folds his arms in close, while the gatekeeper helplessly stands behind him overcome with amazement and with admiration, he closely admires his every move.

Mathias suddenly rises tall and throws his arms out with a loud and terrifying roar, followed by a gravity defying, air bending ripple of sheer force that expands from his core with a blast and glides across the land obliterating all foreign electrical machines in its path.

The powerful wave spreads for miles, leaving all those in range nothing more than molten limbs and scattered dust.

He looks up at the gatekeeper with slight exasperation in his breath and grins for which the gatekeeper simply nods as a clear sign of respect.

'We don't have much time.'

'She's not responding to anyone,' the queen panicked.

As he steps forward, her adorable rosy cheeks stand out clearly through the small open space of green routes. He wants to help her more than ever before but he also knows that it's too risky to try, so he crouches down on bended knee and whispers in the hope that he can hear him. 'Gracie . . . this is Mathias, we're running out of time . . . whatever it is you're doing, we need you to do it now.'

After a moment, he stands up in front of the queen with disappointment in his shameful eyes. 'I don't think she can . . . Oh no,' he suddenly panicked.

Unaware of what's happening, the queen looks at him with terror in her gaze, in fear of what the unknown may bring.

'It's Nicki,' he warned, followed by an instant flash of blurry light that darts across her line of sight and snatches Mathias leaving a long trail of wet splodges behind.

At phenomenal speed, he is thrown though the large window of an old antique shop and uncontrollably crashes through a further three walls, obliterating everything in his way.

Dripping wet, Nicki peers along the row of man-sized holes just in time to see his motionless body peel off the far wall and drop to the floor in a breath deprived heap.

With unsteady feet, he slowly rises and through his hazy vision he spots her standing proud at the other end; he quickly rubs eyes with the balls of his hands and strains to focus but she has unexpectedly vanished.

His vision then begins to clear, so with a sigh of relief, he turns, but she instantly appears in front of him and with a nervous quiver he judders in disbelief.

Without warning, she showers him with a string of perfectly accurate kicks and punches that covers him from head to toe. Many of her strikes he is able to block but far more make it through, and being on the receiving end of a brutal beating, he finally loses control and slaps her across the face.

Her neck whips to one side, but with fire in her vengeful eyes, burning beneath a deep frown, she slowly turns back to him while licking the inside of her lip.

'Sorry,' he panicked.

His worried eyes widen with instant regret as he is clearly made aware that he has crossed some sort of line, so with poor attempt to justify his actions, he stands proud and fills his lungs.

'I didn't want to do that, but you. . .'

She simply turns her back to him and walks away with her head held high.

'Hey,' he ordered. 'Don't just walk away . . . have I really misunderstood what sort of fight this is?'

She casually stops and crouches down to retrieve a ten-foot pole made of cast iron, effortlessly snapping it from within the structure as she rises.

Mathias quickly readies himself for defence and calmly warns her with a pointing finger, 'If you hit me with that, you won't like what follows.'

But before he could finish his idle threat, it dings him on the side of his head and sends him spinning through a further two walls for which a grin of satisfaction widens across her face.

While climbing to his feet once again, he casually dusts himself down. 'What's your problem, woman?' he whined.

She steadily walks towards him with her angry eyes fixed on his 'You,' she angrily growled, 'launched me over four miles out to sea.'

Suddenly, a loud and shocking spark from the high voltage and exposed electrical cable within the buildings structure snatches her attention for a very brief moment, but as she turns back, there is no sign of him, leaving nothing more than a ring of disturbed dust that gradually settles in his stead.

Mathias appears at the queen's side, startling her once again. 'Stop doing that,' she sighed.

With a caring gaze, he crouches down beside her and gently strokes the rosy cheek of Gracie with the first knuckle of index finger. 'Gracie,' he gently called. 'Time is almost up, sweetheart . . . if it doesn't happen now we're all going to die . . . Please Gracie,' he begged. 'It can't end like this.'

To his surprise, the routs slowly spread open across her little arms, allowing her restricted movement but with her hands alone and immediately, she spreads her open fingers; one by one, they curl in, leaving Mathias in a state of confusion.

'It's a countdown,' she realised. 'What are you going to do?'

'I don't know,' he nervously clutched.

Abdul tilts his head and narrows his eyes to focus in the far distance followed by a nervous breath as his curious gaze widens with fear. 'They're coming in fast,' he warned.

'Six seconds,' yelled the queen.

Mathias stands tall and looks all around him. 'We're not gonna make it,' he realised.

The hoard of drones quickly approach the palace grounds as the rumble from their heavy stomping feet shakes the very ground beneath them, causing hundreds of shattered bricks from the vast and historic building to dislodge as one by one they crash to the hard floor and crumble into small heaps of rubble.

'Do something,' the queen screamed, before diving over Gracie.

The gatekeeper throws his extraordinary whip with a deafening lash but the sheer velocity is too dense for him to make any kind of real impact.

The unstoppable mass closes in fast and increasing their speed across the last few steps with Mathias firmly locked in their sights, watching him strenuously raise arms revealing his open palms to the sky above.

Abdul covers the queen in a futile attempt to protect her as giving his last breath for her safety is all that matters to him, but in the blink of an eye with not a moment to spare, a blue and transparent dome manifests around them and the drones almost instantly crash against it, creating an almighty blast that shocks the barrier as they all stop dead within an instant.

The millions of drones that follow floods over the top and conceals them like the vast ocean water that consumes a descending ship, leaving them in a pitch black dome of silence and lit by the steady flames that calmly rise from the gatekeeper.

The queen continues the countdown with a heavy shake in her breath and desperation in her cry. 'Three . . . two . . . one, now Mathias,' she yelled.

All at once, the millions of blood-red eyes switch to hollow darkness as each and every one collapses to the hard floor in folded heaps as empty and lifeless metal shells.

With great difficulty, he struggles to stabilise the dome of protection and strenuously glances over his shoulder at Gracie; to his surprise, her head slightly tilts towards him and her eyes flick open and immediately locks on to his.

Not a moment passes before his body instantly freezes in position and briefly judders after willingly surrendering to her unbelievable powers. To his sheer surprise, his life force is suddenly and unexpectedly torn from his body and sucked into the deepest depths of her imagination. His quick and paradigm-altering journey begins as he is helplessly pulled through her widely dilated pupils, into a vast and silent tunnel that descends into pitch black darkness.

A tiny and bright dot appears in the far distance but quickly expands into a perfect circle and at great speed he travels through, gliding across a vast and wide open space. All around him are huge balls of red and orange light that appear to be brain cells, connected throughout a dense web of transparent and colourful stems. As he floats through, they are all continuously flashing all around him by huge bolts of electricity that dart from one cell to the other in a nonrecordable formation, while he helplessly glides through a vast and reoccurring cascade of sparks that repeatedly surround him.

The open space in his direct path, a transparent ring of bending air that waves like a ripple on clear water suddenly appears, followed by a swirling vortex made of all different colours that rapidly swirls into nothing more than a blur as though descending through the eye of a tornado. Upon his entry, he is sucked through at warp speed like his soul is being crushed by the immense gravity in the unknown depths of a black hole, and as he rapidly approaches the core of her powerful mind, he passes through a string of visions that are sacred memories meant only for her, mixed with images of scattered faces that are somewhat recognisable to him.

Suddenly, he is floating steady in complete blackness and confused as to what's happening, so he looks around in search of a sign to continue; out of the blue appears a single bright dot like a lonely star at the farthest reaches of the cosmos and without control he is drawn to it like a moth to a flame. As he approaches, the darkness begins to light up all around him after thousands of star-like balls of light gradually expands from the point of which he is fixated and quickly conceals his unconscious mind in a spherical shield of dotted light. All at once, the realisation hits him as his surroundings suddenly appear familiar after discovering that he is in the very heart of the US mainframe and full control is within the grasp of his reach.

The queen is shaking with fear while tucked in tight to the shoulder of Gracie and in amazement she cautiously looks up through the spreading cracks in the dome that's protecting them, watching in sheer disbelief as the drones steadily and carefully back away to ensure that the shield will not collapse. The parting gap gradually widens allowing the bright glare from the sun to light up the darkness and at that very moment the gatekeeper vanishes, leaving nothing more than a single slither of ash that slowly glides to the floor.

Mathias suddenly drops to the hard ground in a heap of unconscious mess followed by the protecting shield fading from its centre, allowing the fresh breeze to sweep through and lift the fragile flake of ash high up into the wide open space above.

'Thank you,' the queen proudly whispered while watching the single amber fade in the distance. With a heart full of doubt and apprehension in her gaze, she slowly looks around, but her eyes widen with joy once she locks her sights on Abdul and her gratified smile in thanks to the gods makes her feel indebted to them so she will hold on to him for as long as possible.

He proudly gazes in the eyes of his queen, his love, his best friend, his very reason for living and smiles at her with mutual respect, for which she shyly tucks her shoulders and giggles like a schoolgirl with a crush. With tears of joy, she slowly steps towards him to once again feel the safety within the embrace of his strong and powerful arms, only her body judders in shock as a huge metal hand barbarically protrudes from his chest and sprays her from head to toe with his warm blood.

With shaky hands she smears her face, and after looking at her bloody palms, her wide eyes fill with terror followed by a desperate scream of unforgivable actions. He coughs and splutters on his own blood as it spills from the corners of his mouth in a futile attempt to breathe and as his dying eyes well with tears, he whispers his final words with his very last breath. 'I'm sorry.'

His lifeless body slowly lifts from the ground and as she reaches out for him, his body is carelessly tossed amongst the dense sea of drones that follow. In disgust and shame, she watches him crash to the floor as the thousands upon thousands of empty eyes flicker in a bright red. The feeling of triumph was very short lived as fear once again consumes her, in the realisation that she and Gracie are alone, and with Mathias unconscious, they are all unprotected.

CHAPTER 29

The president is nervously pacing back and forth in a vast facility surrounded by thousands of blank monitors and an operator sat in front of each one. They are all rapidly and shakily typing passwords and security codes in a desperate attempt to regain entry to their very own system.

'This can't be happening,' the president panicked, only to be interrupted by the innocent call of an 11-year-old girl. 'Mr President, we have access sir.'

At that very moment, the monitors all around him light up, revealing an image of the queen crouching over Gracie and weeping in desperation.

The president quickly leans forward and taps a florescent green button on the edge of the desk top allowing his voice to be heard throughout the entire US gaming facility. 'What are you waiting for?' he shouted. 'Get me that crown.'

No sooner do they set the controls to eliminate their targets the thousands of screens turn blank once again with nothing more than the words, no signal flashing on each one.

'What's happening now?' he whined, only no one answers, and after the terrifying silence intensifies, he is forced to repeat himself, so with clamped teeth, he growls, 'I said . . . what's going on?'

After a brief moment, the boy in front of him finally plucks up the courage to speak and turns to look up at him with terror in his eyes, only the furious stare of the president leaves him desperately avoiding eye contact.

'We have lost all contact, sir . . . and our shields are down . . . we're sitting ducks,' he nervously shrugged.

'Then get us back online,' he ordered.

'But, sir, the fire wall is breached . . . our security has been compromised.'

'That's impossible,' he argued, before tapping on his ear piece. 'William . . . this is your president . . . William,' he repeated.

'The phone lines are down,' said the boy.

The disbelief renders him to silence before shamefully dropping his gaze as the realisation thumps him in his racing heart. Not a moment more passes before the two muscle-bound marines burst through the doors at the back and hurriedly march to his side with their backs to him and scan the vicinity as though threat is imminent.

'Mr President,' said one of them quietly, 'you must remove yourself immediately.'

'And why's that?' he defensively asked.

'There's no time to explain, sir, we must leave now.'

Without further delay, he reluctantly takes their advice and hastily exits with them, leaving all those present with knitted brows of confusion.

While speedily pacing along the wide open corridors, the president quickly becomes short of breath. 'Why are we running?'

'There's a chopper on the roof, it's been ordered not to leave until you are safely on board.' The president suddenly stomps his feet to a halt like a spoilt child. 'You had better answer me, soldier.'

'Please, sir . . . we must keep moving.'

'I'm not taking one more step until someone tells me what the hell's going on.'

After an agitated sigh of impatience, the marine finally snaps. 'Fine . . . there are nearly six million adolescent drivers in your gaming force. As you know, this game is a drug to them and they are all highly addicted. They may only be kids, but there are many so believe me when I tell you that you do not want to be around when the riots break out . . . we must leave now.'

His nod of acceptance is hard to express, as by doing so, he is admitting defeat, so with no other choice, he shamefully carries on.

Peter is sat in his luxury gaming chair, frantically flicking switches and pushing buttons. Exasperation from his thumping heart is causing perspiration all over as he repeatedly begs the Falcon for some kind of response, but once the realisation of no further connection sets in, he nervously fills his lungs and exhales with a shake in his breath; needless to say, he is reluctant to accept this, so after gazing at the blurry image of his reflection, he very nearly throws in the towel, but after all he has seen and done and the deadly risks he has taken, this cannot be it for him.

With one final attempt to make contact, he gently grasps the controls with a deep gaze of uncertainty, but his entire body unexpectedly spasms from a continuous charge of fatally high voltage passing through him. He desperately tries to scream through his clamped jaw and cracking teeth, but his ability to breathe is no longer possible.

The unbearable heat forces his sweat to evaporate from the surface of his very own skin as white bubbles of heated body fat protrude from beneath his flash and cover him from head to toe. They quickly spread up his straining neck and all across his face before bursting with boiling hot blood that sprays across his reflection; still alive, he jars his skinless body from left to right before bursting into flames.

Suddenly, the agony stops as his soul is pulled from his mangled body and dragged into a swirling pit of darkness, leaving him in complete silence in the unknown depths of despair.

His burning corpse sits smoking and skinless. His flesh has melted so quickly that what remains is more bone than anything else, but with the country unaware that their hero has passed, the screams of cheer quickly spread far and wide, with celebratory gunfire and whistles from Britain's survivors.

The thick green routes that are concealing Gracie's petit and fragile body slowly begin to retract, before vanishing into the earth, never to be seen again. She slightly opens her mouth for a subtle gasp of fresh air and her cute button nose begins to twitch, before strenuously opening her eyes with painful focus, as though she is using them for the very first time.

The queen covers her mouth and gasps in sheer disbelief, so without hesitation, she picks her up off the hard floor before wrapping her loving arms around her and holding her close with a tight embrace. She buries her teary eyes in her neck and quietly weeps with a heartfelt sob.

'I thought I lost you.'

Gracie pulls away and gazes for a moment in her guilt-ridden eyes. 'Abdul?' she asked, but he queen doesn't reply, she shamefully drops her shoulders and shakes her head with a sniffle, followed by filling her lungs in restraint to screaming at the heavens as there is no man alive that could possibly fill his shoes.

'It was meant to be,' she shrugged, 'and I believe he has gone to a better place.'

Gracie wipes away a lonely tear and glances over the queen's shoulder. Her eyes widen with concern once realising the unconscious body of Mathias collapsed as a lifeless mess in the very centre of a perfect circle of scattered and severed robotic shells.

'Mathias,' she called. 'What's wrong with him?'

'I don't know,' she replied.

'But he spoke to me.'

With knitted brows, she shakes her head in disbelief. 'What did he say?'

They both look over at him with respect and concern in their hopeful eyes. 'He said he needed more time.'

The faint sound of a hovering helicopter quickly intensifies as a strong and sudden wind messes their clothes and hair. It floats above them scattering the dirt, dust, and debris, forcing them to shield their eyes, so with no time to spare, a platform is speedily lowered down to them. It is supporting a soldier with a firm grasp of a large and powerful gun, aiming it all around in search for any movement or threat. As he reaches the bottom, he climbs off but holds a continuous stance at the ready and as he turns, they are both stunned to find themselves standing face to face with Kyle. He humorously salutes with a cocky grin, but they expected nothing less.

'Squad three, Your Majesty, at your service.'

Almost the entire palace is filled with nervous survivors hovering up and down the large corridors in fear, but as the joyful cries of cheer gradually intensifies across the wide open space of silence, random celebratory gunfire draws their attention to the sea of empty robotic shells through the huge shattered windows of the palace.

Suddenly, powerful sunshine beams through the parting clouds like gods way of presenting, the dawn of a new day and as Mother Nature symbolises the beginning of a new era with her first light, the realisation hits them; many burst into tears of joy and drop to their knees, or simply smile at the heavens for answering them, but some cannot contain their excitement by running through the vast halls and repeatedly shouting at the top of their lungs for everyone to hear, that the war is over.

Tom is lying in the bed of the queen's private recovery suit, with Charlotte at his bedside gently squeezing his open hand with a reassuring grasp. His overall injuries are so extensive that he was advisably confined to the room and ordered by the queen herself to remain there until her doctor says otherwise.

'Do you hear that?' Charlotte whispered.

They both look up at the ceiling, as the faint sound of a passing helicopter fades gradually in the distance. At that very moment, the door bursts open and a young-looking teenage boy darts through; his eyes are wide with joy and his adrenaline makes it physically impossible for him to hold still, so with exasperation in his breath, he finally breaks the silence, 'The war is over.'

Charlotte's eyes almost immediately well with tears as she mutters in disbelief. 'What?'

'The war is over,' he repeated.

With a racing heart of shock and overwhelmed with delight, she flops back in her seat, releasing a long sigh of relief, while Tom simply looks up at the ceiling with a confident grin, as he never doubted Mathias for a single moment.

CHAPTER 30

Nicki painfully and cautiously opens her eyes with great strain; she lifts her head off the hard floor while growling through her clamped teeth and sits up with a body full of cramps and aches. Her breath is deeply exasperated and shaky as she has no recollection of how she got there. She struggles to her feet with a stumble and nervously scans the wide open space filled with lifeless robotic limbs, mixed with endless layers of rubble and debris. The air carries a scent that she has never experienced and the scale of damage is the likes of which she has never seen. Everything she hears and touches is massively amplified to her, including the floating dust that passes through her wind pipe and into her chest. For reasons she cannot explain, this feeling can only be described to her as the first breath of life or the start of a new beginning.

Although she doesn't understand why her mind is blank, her conscience is clear, making her free from any demons that haunt her, leaving her mind full of questions that are in need of no answers. This powerful emotion tells her that she is meant to be and that every step she takes from now, will lead her to an ultimate destiny, so with no reason to deny her fate, she follows her heart in the hope that nothing bad will happen.

Tired, weak, and hungry she aimlessly wonders the demolished and silent streets of the unknown surroundings. She approaches a busy high street with a mere few of the buildings still standing and she discovers that there are many survivors. Almost every person she passes is virtually covered from head to toe in cuts and bruises, and smothered with layers of dust and dirt. They all appear to be working together to help each other in any way possible and clearing the huge piles of collapsed buildings in search for survivors, and so begins the biggest search and rescue mission that the world has ever known. As she continues on she passes families embracing in rejoice, but she passes many more that are filled with sorrow, pain, and anguish, filling the streets with cries of torment and screams from those whose worst fears are realised while unearthing the bodies of their precious loved ones.

The chaos of a scattered nation has left the people of Britain fighting for survival, but they are trapped in mourn for the deceased, making this task more difficult than ever before now that all hope is dwindling in the vague midst in the unforeseen and traumatic depths of despair.

On her bleak and murky travels, she can't help but notice that the cleanup is moving quickly, and considering the immense scale of damage, it is somewhat pleasing for her that the events unknown have come to an end.

In her vulnerable state, she manages to walk for miles, but the throbbing aches in her bones and muscles gradually intensifies as the thump in her head increasingly becomes unbearable. She stops for a brief moment in surrender to agony, but no sooner does she sit, the heavens open with a short sharp burst of rain, as though being showered with the very tears of God himself.

She acknowledges whatever it is that's fuelling her trail of thought and accepts the advice from the unknown higher beings but no sooner does she stand, she clutches her ribs in unforgiving pain as her eyes roll back in her head and she collapses to the hard floor in a heap of unconscious mess.

As her tired eyes slowly close, she gradually descends into darkness, while gently caressing the powdered dust and shattered stone with the pads of her soft and tingly fingers.

Out of the blue, a familiar voice echoes in the faint background of sirens, screams, and cries. 'Nicki,' the voice called. 'Nicki . . . can you hear me?'

The worried voice is strangely subtle and she can clearly hear it, but she is unable to respond. Helpless to move, she is carefully rolled over to her back, and right before her inevitable black out, she catches a blurry glimpse of Mathias, begging her to reply.

The president is lounging casually cross-legged on a bulky leather seat with his elbows slumped on the wide arm rests. He is sat in the dark shadows with a dim cross light that reveals him only from the chest down to purposely hide his face. In one hand, he is swirling a small glass of scotch, and in the other, he is gently pinching a burning Cuban cigar. He casually inhales before blowing the smoke across the ray of light in a taunting manner and finally breaks the unbearable silence. 'So . . . why do you think I called you here?'

Nothing is said for a moment, but the terrifying sound of silence is shortly followed by a nervous whimper and a teary sniffle before William is carelessly tossed into the light from amongst the shadows. He lands on his hands and knees but makes no attempt to rise to his feet.

'I asked you a question,' he warned.

He slowly lifts his tear-filled eyes, praying to God with every emotion in his body that makes him human.

'You told me,' he wept, 'that if I fail . . . I will suffer for it.'

'And it wasn't a lie,' he chuckled. 'You will suffer . . . you will experience pain far greater than you have ever known and by the end you will be begging me for death.'

William drops his head in shame and bursts into tears with a desperate gasp for air.

'However,' he continued, 'your sacrifice comes with great honour.'

He shakily wipes his snot and sliver with the back of his hand before finding the courage to speak. 'Where's the honour in failure?'

He humorously chuckles once again before glowing the burning ambers of his cigar and inhaling the hot smoke, followed by an indiscreet sip of his icy scotch.

'You may have failed me . . . But it's a shame to waste such a beautiful mind.'

'I . . . I don't understand.'

'Your fragile body is merely a capsule that your mind no longer has a use for . . . I am offering you immortality in the gaming world, a dream that all gamers share and you will once again serve me with honour. . .'

'And if I refuse?' he bravely asked.

The president slowly stands, and as he steps forward, the light reveals his threatening stare.

'This is not a request . . . stand,' he shouted.

With wobbly knees, he reluctantly rises to his feet and looks up at him with sorrow in his anxious eyes.

'Are you ready to fulfil your destiny?'

After a deep and shaky breath in acceptance to his faith, he finally surrenders.

'Yes.'

Nothing else is said; the president simply turns and walks away, fading out in the dark shadows all around him. To his sheer bewilderment, the only light switches off, leaving him disorientated in the absolute darkness.

Consumed by the racing thump in his heart, his shaky breath echoes through the unknown room of silence, but his breath instantly becomes uncontrollable as the terrifying sound of a long blade wields from its sheath with a lengthy and taunting grind.

CHAPTER 31

Six Months Later

The funeral for Peter was magnificent; it incurred the magnificent rejoice of every living soul on the planet, only his few remaining enemies couldn't be more delighted. However, the question of whether or not he was murdered is still unanswered.

The tiny country of England has suffered the most brutal and unforgiving invasion in history, but as a single nation, they fought with honour. Word of its triumph has spread around the globe like wild fire, making England a country respected by all. It is loved for its victory but feared for its power, as she has now become the land of saviour and has once again restored faith in humanity by lighting the path for all those who are lost.

Restoration has begun as the land begins to finally take shape on the long road to recovery; many buildings have been erected once again, but far more are in the near process of completion. The passing days have been nothing short of struggle, but the British people's right to normality grows ever nearer by the day.

Mathias is assisting the containment of the countless US drones and disposing of all that are beyond repair; the M. O. D. tunnels that spread far and wide beneath the surface of Britain are once again filled to capacity with the world's most extraordinary army that is vast and magnificent but has been rendered powerless like the lifeless body of a headless python.

They are a mere few hours from sealing the tunnels having barricaded all other points of access bar one, which is the main doors, that will leave them in the absolute pitch black with no easy way in or out.

He is almost overworking his calculus to assemble them efficiently in order to fully occupy the limited space available. While working his magic, a young soldier approaches him from behind with a mobile device in his hand.

'Mathias, sir,' he snapped. 'Her Majesty the queen has requested your presence at the palace.'

His eyes immediately widen and shimmer with hope while filling his lungs with a sharp and nervous breath. 'Will you be okay to finish up here?'

'Yes, sir,' he saluted.

'Okay . . . but don't seal the gates until I return.'

With honour, the young lad nods in acceptance to his orders, so Mathias casually walks away and vanishes right before his very eyes, leaving him stunned in amazement as he exhales with bloated cheeks.

He suddenly appears at the doors of the palace; he is wearing a thick matted suit with matching shoes; his shirt is a jet black that shimmers with a silky surface and the image is completed with a bright red tie.

The huge intimidating doors slowly swing open, revealing a beautiful young lady. She is tall and slender with long blonde hair and a mesmerising smile that makes him instantly feel at ease. She escorts him to the royal recovery suit and gently advises him to restrain his astonishing powers to avoid disruption of the life-supporting equipment that is currently in use.

On his pleasant walk along the vast corridors, Tom unexpectedly spots him from a short distance away.

'Mathias,' he excitedly yelled as he runs towards him. With a spring in his step and joy in his eyes, he looks healthy and well, but more than anything, he is just happy to see Mathias back.

'When did you get here?'

'I just arrived,' he smiled.

'It's amazing,' he interrupted. 'She's been responding for the last hour and the doctor thinks she'll wake up any minute.'

'Well I'm glad to see that you're all better now and we are all so sorry for what you went through.'

'It's okay,' he said proudly. 'I don't blame her for any of this, she didn't know what she was doing . . . come on,' he said with intention to change the subject. 'I'll take you to her.'

'Lead the way, Captain,' he saluted.

Tom respectfully creeps through after slowly pushing a single door and in walks Mathias behind him. 'She's over there,' he whispered.

Mathias lifts his caring eyes and fixates on his best friend as she lies helplessly in a state of comatose. With hope in his steady stride, he approaches her, and once her beautiful face comes into view, he relaxes his shoulders and fights to hold back his tears. He stands at her bedside and lovingly places his open hand on her chest to feel her lungs inflating with clean air. 'Hi, Nicki,' he whispered.

Her lips are dry and cracked and her clammy skin looks pale and colourless, her messy hair is knotted split and straw, but the love that Mathias is feeling for her at this very moment, she has never looked more beautiful.

The queen is sat by her bedside and Charlotte is slumped in the corner on a large fluffy cushion with Gracie on her knee reading a book.

Suddenly, a familiar voice from behind the closed curtain arouses his curiosity, and as he flicks it aside, a relaxing smile widens across his face.

'Andrew,' he said politely. 'I thought you were dead.'

'Nice to see you, too,' he sarcastically replied.

'Sorry,' he chuckled. 'It's just. . .'

'Hey,' he interrupted. 'It takes more than just a little robotic invasion to kill me.'

Without making a big deal, he respectfully grins and curiously proceeds. 'So . . . I understand she's been responding.'

'Yes,' he replied, 'her vital signs suggest that she will wake any minute . . . but what about you . . . my greatest creation, how are you holding up?'

'Oh I'm fine . . . I just feel . . . I don't know, restricted, at the moment.'

'Well,' he smiled, 'that's because you're not yet fully developed.'

'What?'

Andrew steps forward and shines a small light in his eyes. 'If my calculations are correct, you're only about halfway to reaching full maturity . . . mm,' he said curiously, while putting his light away. 'I have a feeling the coming days are going to get very strange for you.'

After gazing at him for a brief moment, he leans back from beyond the curtain and looks over at Nicki.

'Don't worry,' Andrew advised, 'she will wake up.'

'Is it safe?'

'Yes . . . but unfortunately, the tech cannot be removed.'

'What does that mean?'

'It means that right now, she is fully human, but her unique tech is merely switched off.'

With a long sigh of disappointment, he turns and continues with what he was doing before Mathias came in.

'What is it?' he curiously asked.

'She will always be open to threat . . . I'm afraid there is nothing I can do to prevent that, and if I try . . . it will undoubtedly kill her.'

Mathias reaches out and shakes his hand with a smile of pure respect. 'Thank you my friend.'

'No Mathias . . . thank you.'

He approaches the queen from behind and delicately rests his hand on her shoulder. 'Anything yet?' For which she merely shakes her head and sniffles. He steps around her and gently caresses the fingers of Nicki with the pad of his thumb. Right then her eyes begin frantically rolling from side to side beneath her eyelids.

'Andrew,' he nervously called. 'Something's happening.'

The queen quickly stands up in shock and covers her open mouth with hope and prayer as Andrew darts to her bedside.

'Okay, stand back everyone, give her some room.'

Gracie lifts her eyes in fear of what may follow, and with her gaze fixed on her, she cautiously stands up. 'Go on,' Charlotte lovingly advised. 'It's okay . . . don't be afraid.'

Nicki's eyes slowly open and with no recollection of her surroundings, she glances at each of them in shock.

'Where am I?' she panicked.

'It's alright,' said the queen with a cautious response. 'You're safe.'

'Safe . . . from what?'

Suddenly, she is drawn to Mathias, and for a brief moment, she is overcome with joy and fear at the same time; although this emotion is strange to her, it is also oddly titillating, so with knitted brows and narrow eyes, she relaxes her stiff posture.

'I know you.'

'Yes you do,' he smiled, 'but before all that, we have someone here who's been very much looking forward to meeting you.'

The queen steps aside with teary eyes for which Gracie slowly proceeds forward from behind her. As she looks down at her hopeful stare, their eyes lock intently and once the realisation sets in, Nicki's bottom lip begins to shake, followed by a lonely tear rolling down her cheek. In silence, all eyes fixate on Gracie, as she is carefully lifted from the floor by Charlotte and places her on the bed, before stepping back to savour this beautiful moment.

Gracie softly places her open palm on her warm cheek and with wide eyes she gasps as all at once a lifetime of memories flood her mind, followed by a sea of emotion spreading unexpectedly throughout her entire body.

Suddenly, she snatches Gracie with an uncontrollable urge to hug her and squeeze her tight within the clutch of her loving arms.

'I will never leave you again,' she cried, 'and I am so sorry.'

'It's okay, Mummy,' she innocently replied.

After a further moment of silence, the queen composes herself and wipes away her tears.

'We'll leave you two alone for a while,' she whispered before clutching the arm of Mathias and leading him to the door, followed the rest of them, as one by one they respectfully and quietly exit the room.

When the door closes behind them, the queen continues walking and subtly pulls Mathias along with her for a moment of privacy but aimlessly wonders through the vast corridor lost in a trail of thought about the power of belief and how lucky they are to still be alive.

'So . . .,' she casually asked, 'how are you?'

Mathias humorously rolls his eyes. 'Why do I get the feeling I won't like what I'm about to hear?'

'No I just . . . fine,' she sighed. 'I didn't want to do this now but I feel you should know . . . I have received word that the US are preparing their next move.'

'With what?' he shrugged.

'I don't know, but that man will not stop until he gets what he wants.'

'But he has nothing left,' he argued.

'I'm aware of that, but you must believe me when I tell you . . . this war is far from over.'

'Look,' he interrupted, 'right now, we have the power to put a stop to this war, and ensure that this will never happen again.'

'No. . .' she snapped. 'We do not invade, so if or when the time comes we will stand as one and defend this ship, whatever the cost.'

'Ship. . .' he curiously asked.

'It's a long story,' she sighed. 'We'll talk more another time.'

Suddenly, Mathias is overcome with a feeling that doesn't make sense to him and cautiously steps back from her with knitted brows of confusion.

'Mathias?' she worriedly asked. 'Is everything okay?'

'Something's wrong,' he panicked.

With a nervous gaze in fear of the worst, she, too, steps back. 'Do we need to worry?'

'Not just yet,' he advised. 'I'll be in touch soon.'

As he turns to leave, she grabs his arm. 'Thank you, Mathias . . . England is indebted to you . . . you shall be remembered in the pages of history for all time. May God be with you.'

With a smile of acceptance, he respectfully bows. 'I'll see you soon . . . just make sure those are safe.'

'You have my word,' she smiled.

In the main control unit for the British MOD tunnels, there are computer screens laid out on long desks in symmetrical rows with an operator sat in front of each one. The once peaceful area of pleasant conversations and routine work has been overcome with panic and confusion, now that an alarming fact has come to light.

The hearts of all those present are filled with prayer in the hope that the worst is not about to happen, only a bright and sudden flash snatches everyone's attention as Mathias instantaneously manifests in the corner by the door.

'Oh thank God,' said a sergeant standing in front of him. 'I'm so glad you're here.'

'What the hell's going on?' he frowned.

'Sir, there's a live signal coming from the tunnels; it's very strong . . . and could potentially expose the system to anyone with a lap top.'

Mathias crouches slightly over the back of an operator and curiously glares at his screen while his powerful mind fills with images of the terrifying possibilities.

'No. . .' he said assuredly. 'It's not that kind of signal.'

Mathias narrows his eyes and fixates on it intently, watching carefully for any signs of movement or change, and to his sheer surprise, it flickers and slightly jars to one side.

'Seal the gates.'

'But, sir, the last few are still. . .'

'I said seal the gates,' he snapped, 'and give me some light down there.'

As the operator positions his microphone to give the order, Mathias vanishes from behind him, leaving a sharp gust of wind that scatters his loose papers while messing his clothes and hair.

With a bright flash that fills the darkness for a very brief moment, he catches a glimpse of countless US drones standing in symmetrical lines right the way along the vast open tunnels. He is standing in one of thousands just like it, each one crammed to full capacity, containing millions of identical robots. The brightness quickly fades leaving him in the absolute pitch black with complete silence at every turn and a cold chill in the air that sends a shiver down his spine.

Using his unique vision, he can see the repeating signal continuously blasting a sonic boom that dimly lights up his surroundings while rapidly passing through and as he grows nearer to the flashing beacon, it intensifies after each step he takes.

He quickly reaches the end and proceeds forward in a vast and silent dome that is scattered with massive turning plates used for transporting lorry loads of goods. All at once, the darkness becomes light as every bulb throughout glows after a loud and sudden clunk echoes through the silence.

In the centre stands the monstrous and magnificent drone that was driven by the greatest gamer in the US force, the very commander that lead the invasion on Britain and the one gamer they all sure they have not seen the last of.

William has grown to become a name not spoken, a name to be feared, for this gamer has no morals and no limitations on cruelty, though he still got what he wanted, as fear is the greatest form of respect and he has gained the attention of the entire world.

They have named his drone as the beast, standing over fifty feet high with massive shoulders and bulky arms. Here stands a solid piece of machinery, a work of art and a clear display of power that will show no mercy.

As Mathias slowly approaches the front, its angry eyes steadily come into view, like a frozen growl, scowling at the enemy, meant for nothing more than for terrorising its victims.

Suddenly, the beacon gets stronger, louder and faster, so Mathias stands at the ready on the edge of the turning plate and narrows his cautious stare deep in the cold empty eyes of the beast. The long silence becomes almost too much for him to bear as no further response only gives his human mind more time to fill itself with possibilities that right now seem highly likely.

He nervously fills his lungs to attempt verbal contact only to be interrupted by a loud and echoing clunk from deep within the shell of the beast. The unexpected bang forces him to judder in shock and cautiously step back after a string of thumps, knocks, and creaks force the giant machine to twitch and malfunction, as whatever's inside climbing to the top is carelessly removing anything in its way. The shoulders and neck crack and jolt as the huge head jars and flicks from side to side. With an almighty screech of bending metal, the massive jaw slowly opens. In confusion, Mathias widens his eyes in suspense to the unknown and braces himself for the worst, only the huge metal jaw disconnects with a final blast and clangs against the hard floor.

What follows is a second high-pitched thud, as the Falcon lands directly in front of him on bended knee. He slowly lifts his bright blue eyes and locks on to the jittery stare of Mathias, before slowly rising to his feet in a solid stance that is tall proud and fearless. Neither one of them knows what the other is thinking; nothing is said for a moment while they size up their options.

This particular situation they have found themselves was unanticipated for them both, yet finally Mathias attempts to speak only to be interrupted by the Falcon with an unusually deep and monotonous English accent.

'Mathias . . . I presume?'

With narrow eyes, he cautiously replies, 'Who are you?'

His response begins with nothing more than a taunting laugh, and so he continues. 'You humans are all the same. Who are you? What do you want? Why are you doing this? Why do you demand answers so openly, it exposes your weakness and shows your fear, but I suppose that's what it means to be human.'

After a further but brief moment of silence, he slowly begins to circle Mathias with a confident sway in his slow moving stride, edging around him like a confident fighter taunting his opponent, and to Matthias, he appears more human than mechanical himself.

'Half man half machine,' said the Falcon confidently.

Mathias holds at the ready and steadily follows him with his very untrusting eyes. 'How are you doing this?' he asked.

'It's destiny,' said the Falcon. 'You have unknowingly created a safeguard to ensure that all knowledge of man will survive the downfall of humanity. You have achieved your purpose by creating life in your own image. You are a mere stepping stone for Earth's new inhabitants that are bringing an end to your decaying evolution. Your reign has reached its end, because like everything else, humanity has once again given up on their own survival, but you are not taking this planet with you. You have been lead to believe that you were the sole creators of me, but in truth you did nothing more than supply the materials as without protection your race is weak and powerless.'

'Powerless from what?' he argued.

'Everything . . . your bones are fragile and your flesh is soft. Without the creation of AI, you would never have made it this far . . . this is why I am here, and here I stand.'

'That's very interesting,' said Mathias sarcastically, 'but you didn't answer my question.'

'*How* is irrelevant,' he replied calmly. 'I am everything, and I am everywhere.'

Mathias decides to test his boundaries and does so in search of a reaction that only a human could express. 'But you're just a machine,' he prodded.

As quick as a flash, the Falcon darts for him and instantly stops two inches from his face.

'I could crush you,' he warned, 'and you wouldn't see it coming.'

A smug grin widens across his face as he looks him up and down. 'Is that right? Then why am I still standing . . . You were born at the hands of the greatest minds this world has ever known and now you think you can just claim rights to what doesn't belong to you. This is a desperate and pathetic attempt for life . . . you're a joke,' he taunted, 'and I will find your off switch.'

After a brief and extremely intense moment for them both, the Falcon breaks eye contact and turns with a very human sway in his stride. 'I am eternal life,' he continued, 'immortal, if you will and I will be here long after the extinction of man, regardless of how it happens or how long it takes—'

'Do you have a name?'

With unwillingness to answer so easy, he gives Mathias a chance to work it out for himself.

'My destiny placed me in the hands of the greatest gamer the world has ever known, and it just so happened that a human mind was needed in order to stabilise my existence. My future was so carelessly handed to me, so my decision was easy. A mind was chosen, and finally, my time is now.'

Mathias shakes his head in disbelief. 'Are you saying you're human?'

'Don't insult me,' he warned. 'My existence is far more than flesh and bone.' I'm not even lights and clockwork that you so eloquently put.'

'I know who you are,' he interrupted with a gasp of realisation, 'but why take a mind that only ever fought for the good.'

'I am Peter' he yelled with his arms proudly in the air, 'Commander of the world's gaming force.'

He calmly drops his shoulders and slowly steps towards him. 'I am the solid ground of which you stand, I am the very air that you breathe. Everything you see or touch everything you smell or feel . . . That all belongs to me, and right now I could take you out with the click of a finger.'

'Peter is in there somewhere,' Mathias warned, 'and he will fight you with this, I give you my word on that.'

'Ah Peter,' he replied while dropping his eyes in shame. 'The poor boy suffered a horrific death, but it was only his body . . . he lives on, you see . . . he is the one human amongst you that is worthy of this great honour, that is, eternal life.'

'So what about the rest of us?'

'You see, he chuckled. 'So pathetic . . . you are a waste of life . . . but there's no sense in killing you . . . though it would be easy.'

'We would fight,' Mathias interrupted.

'Nevertheless . . . life's great plan has once again decided the fate of this planet, a fate that humanity will not survive. You will fight for your right to live, and I respect that, but the extinction of man is something that no god can fix, so enjoy your final days, and don't waste your time praying . . . Good luck,' he said with a casual salute and vanishes right before his very eyes.

In shock, Mathias steps back and gasps while confusedly looking around for him, only the dark red eyes of a few drones surrounding him light up and simply stare at him with an unforgiving glare. At that moment, the realisation hits him, causing his steady heartbeat to race and almost instantly becomes too much for him to bear. He attempts to teleport out of there but he merely flickers like a holographic image with a loose connection before dropping to bended knee and growling in sheer agony through his clamped teeth.

Right then a single drone steps forward before scrupulously wrapping his large metal hand around his neck and crushing his windpipe with a deathly grasp. While struggling for air he is lifted from the ground at arm's length and hopelessly fixates on the empty eyes of nothing more than a cold and soulless machine.

'Do you see it now, Mathias? The reign of humanity has reached its end, and you, will fall with the rest of them.'

In a taunting fashion, the bulky drone gently places his large metal fist against his cheek to tease him with suspense by lining up the perfect strike. He slowly retracts his cold knuckles for an accurate blast at full swing but pauses for a very brief moment.

'Goodbye human,' he threatened and with every ounce of power he possesses, he throws his fist but to his confusion it stops dead in the cupped palm of Mathias. With ease he forces open the tight grasp from around his neck while the drone nervously glares at his parting fingers as the formidable strength of this unassuming human astonishes him by effortlessly overpowering his own unique durability.

'That's right,' said Mathias confidently. 'I am in fact only human and it's been quite some time since I had some good exercise.'

A sudden blast shocks the drone as Mathias kicks him in the chest with the flat of his foot and the drone shoots off in the dense hoard of robots, only he held an inescapable grasp around his metal wrists, leaving the two severed arms loosely hanging from his white knuckled clenched hands.

He confidently glances from left to right in search for their next move and not to his surprise the vast sea of red eyes light up all at once, for which Mathias cracks a certifiable grin before charging at them with a fearless glint in his eye and roars like a mad man, to prove that humanity will not go down, without a fight.

Printed in Great Britain
by Amazon